HOME IMPROVEMENT

"It is dark. I dislike the dark," said Vincent, frowning.

Penelope went to the other windows and shoved back the heavy bundles, allowing in a bit more daylight. "There is too much overgrown shrubbery on this side of the house, which is part of the problem." She whirled around, glancing here and there as she did so. "The other is the dark wood and darker wallpaper. I wonder who chose that heavy red with what must, when it was new, have been a gold motif. Much too formal for a room this size."

"What would you do?" asked Vincent, curious.

"Strip off that paper to begin with. Paint everything a pale green. Order new hangings with a pale background and leaves or flowers or some other soft design. Re-cover the furniture in a slightly darker green, in a fabric that would wear well."

She put her finger to her lips, gazing around the room again and in a much more thoughtful manner. Vincent's eyes were drawn to her mouth. He felt an urge to feel its softness and took a step toward her before he caught himself. She had agreed to help him. She had trusted him enough to put herself in his power by coming here with him. He could not, *must* not, do anything that would frighten or anger her.

And kissing her as he wished to kiss her was sure to do one or the other or both . . .

Books by Jeanne Savery

Published by Zebra Books

The Christmas Matchmaker

Jeanne Savery

ZEBRA BOOKS
KENSINGTON PUBLISHING CORP.
http://www.kensingtonbooks.com

ZEBRA BOOKS are published by

Kensington Publishing Corp.
850 Third Avenue
New York, NY 10022

All Kensington titles, imprints and distributed lines are available at special quantity discounts for bulk purchases for sales promotion, premiums, fund-raising, educational or institutional use.

Special book excerpts or customized printings can also be created to fit specific needs. For details, write or phone the office of the Kensington Special Sales Manager: Kensington Publishing Corp., 850 Third Avenue, New York, NY 10022. Attn. Special Sales Department. Phone: 1-800-221-2647.

Zebra and the Z logo Reg. U.S. Pat. & TM Off.

First Printing: October 2004
10 9 8 7 6 5 4 3 2 1

Printed in the United States of America

CHAPTER 1

George Vincent Beverly ducked his head against the sleety snow. Cold. Wet. Nasty. It suited his mood.

"Why did I tell Georgi I'd spend Christmas with them?" he asked.

His gelding, Black Spot Flying, did not respond. The gelding's head was lowered against the weather and his ears laid back, expressing his annoyance with the situation. A gust of wind lifted heavy snow and cast it against Spot's withers. The animal flinched, sidling. He tossed his head, rattling the chain attached to the O-ring at the bit.

Vincent controlled the tired horse easily and then, when the gust was followed by a sudden moment of utter stillness, he pulled up. It was one of those lulls that occur in the worst of storms and, for a moment, neither man nor animal moved. They stood in the uncanny stillness, just breathing, readying themselves to face a new onslaught.

In the silence, faintly, Vincent heard a sound of distress. He listened intently, peering into the increasing dusk—but heard no more. Almost, he moved on, but something made him look again. This time he detected movement when a lumpy shape he'd thought a tree stump shifted its position. When he peered more closely the lump became a figure huddled against the bole of a large tree. He clucked and Spot crossed the shallow ditch, moving some paces nearer.

A woman?

Vincent was uncertain. Not with the light fading and the figure wrapped in what looked very much like a military cloak. The drab color made the individual difficult to see, but, huddled into the leeward side of the tree, the person's misery could be mistaken for nothing else.

"I'll regret it," he muttered and the gelding snorted. "Yes, well, I know what *you'd* say," Vincent retorted, his voice sour. "I'll regret it *more* if I don't."

The wind picked up, gusted, lifting a long strand of dark hair to flutter against snow-encrusted tree bark. Vincent walked the gelding still nearer and, when he could actually see something of the exhausted woman, muttered, "I knew I'd regret it."

More loudly, he said, "Madam . . ."

When she didn't move, he cleared his throat but she gave no indication of knowing he was there. Vincent dismounted from his horse. He held the reins tightly since Spot was not trained to stand to a dropped rein. In weather such as this, the *last* thing he needed was to be a mile or so from his destination with a half-frozen woman on his hands and no horse.

"Madam," he said, a trifle more loudly.

The woman's head jerked up, panic in her expression.

"I'll not harm you," said Vincent, quickly reassuring.

She cowered away, the whole of her being shouting disbelief.

"Tell me where you want to go and I will take you there," he said, trying to speak soothingly when all he wished was to turn tail and run—especially when a low harsh laugh, rapidly turning to something approaching hysteria, was her response. Vincent sighed. "Madam. It is cold. It is wet. I wish to help, but frankly . . ."

"No one can help."

Vincent leaned nearer, straining to hear the muttered words.

"My father . . ."

"Yes?" he encouraged.

She straightened, pushing herself against the tree, her head going back. "He denied us."

"Us?"

Vincent glanced down and, belatedly, noticed the woman clasped a goodly sized bundle wrapped in a fold of the cloak. He rolled his eyes. Georgi was holding her first house party as a married lady. She'd have planned it down to the last inch of space and the last minute of time. She'd have no room . . .

"There was no room at the inn!"

Again the low voice broke into that half hysterical laughter, but, decided Vincent, there was no madness in it. Not yet anyway.

"It is *Christmas,*" she said on a high note, "and there was no *room.*"

"You are at your wits end and—" Vincent tugged at the rough wool, uncovered a head. Huge blue eyes stared at him, a sweet child's face topped by dark curls. He dropped the edge of the cloak. "—you are worried about your child. You cannot remain here. I'll take you to Georgi."

The woman stiffened. "I am not a whore."

"I didn't think you were," he said mildly, nothing of his normal cynicism showing. "Unless whores have begun wearing wedding rings." Again he lifted the cloak. This time he pointed to the gold band gracing a long narrow finger of the hand cradling the child's head.

Her mouth slightly twisted, the stranger closed her eyes. She opened them and stared down at the hidden bundle. Her eyes fluttered shut and she leaned her head back against the trunk.

Tired, defeated, she said, "I've no choice, have I?"

"None," agreed Vincent. "Come."

"What did she mean, no room at the inn?" hissed Lady Everhart, nee Georgianna Thomasina Beverly.

Georgi had seen the stranger and child settled into the nursery and had summoned a young maid she could ill afford to release from assigned duties, but whom she nevertheless designated to care for the two. The woman slept, the child was warm and fed, and Georgi wanted answers to the questions swarming through her fertile imagination.

"Who is she?" she demanded, glaring.

Georgi and Vincent stood in a dimly lit hall beyond the closed door to the day nursery. She stared up at her favorite cousin who reached out and touched the frown pulling her brows down over greeny-brown eyes—more green than brown just now.

"You saw how it was with her, Georgi," said Vincent, a matching frown creasing his brow. "She held herself together until I mounted behind her and put my arms around her to guide Spot. Then she collapsed. It was all I could do to keep her and the child and myself on the horse. I don't know who she is. Should I have left her there to freeze to death?"

"No, no," said a harassed Georgi. "Of course not. No one suggests you should have done any such thing. But, Vincent . . ."

"Yes?"

"I looked through the things we took off her . . . there was a locket . . ."

"And?"

"Vincent, I think I know her. Well, knew her." The creases crossing Georgi's forehead deepened. "Maybe."

"So who do you think she is?"

But Georgi wasn't quite ready to open her mind—even to her favorite cousin. She might be wrong. In fact, very likely she was wrong. *Surely* she was wrong. *Oh, but what if it is . . . ?*

Georgi was horrified all over again by her suspicions. "Her father refused to acknowledge her? How could any father treat a daughter so? Oh, Vincent—" Georgi turned and threw herself against her cousin, her arms going around him, and tears running down her cheeks. "—surely it isn't possible we were *lucky* to be orphaned? To have had *Grandfather* rear us?" She stared up, her eyes wide. "Instead of parents, I mean?"

Vincent's arms tightened around her. They had been, despite their differing natures, two against the world for a long time. Now they were adults and things were different, but there was a time that, if it were not for their grandfather . . .

"Unhand my wife, varlet," said a new voice before Vincent could do more than tighten his arms around the sobbing bundle that was his cousin, holding her in a tender embrace.

Only half joking, Lord Everhart strode toward where the two stood in the dim hall of the topmost floor of the old house his lordship had inherited the preceding summer. While attempting to sort out the estate, Everhart had met, learned to love, and married Miss Georgianna Thomasina Beverly.

"I'll have your ears for breakfast, Vincent!" warned Everhart.

Vincent's arms held Georgi tightly for another half a moment. Then he released her and turned her. Gently, he pushed the woman with a tear-streaked face toward her husband.

"Here now," said his startled lordship. With a rueful glance at Vincent, he, in turn, embraced his wife. "What is this? What has happened?" He stiffened. "*Georgi*. Not Lord Tivington?"

"No. Oh no. Not grandfather. Nothing so bad as *that*," she said, turning lashes, wet and sticking together, along with emotion-blotched cheeks up to her beloved husband. "Nothing *could* be so bad," she said, the words a simple statement of her love for the old gentleman who had raised her and then loved her enough to help her to a marriage to this man with whom she'd fallen deeply in love.

"In that case . . . ?"

Georgi snuggled closer. "I don't know why I'm such a watering pot." For a moment she indulged in the comfort of her husband's arms before she straightened and turned within that embrace to stare at the closed door to the day nursery. "Surely it cannot be . . ."

"Cut line, Georgi," said Vincent, losing patience, never his strongest suit. "Out with it."

Still surrounded by one of her husband's arms, the small, deceptively fragile looking woman turned a frown his way. "Vincent, do you recall a story about Lord Tennytree? And his daughter? And my dearest Everhart's friend? Lord Wakefield, I mean?"

"No." Vincent spoke the word baldly before adding in a biting tone, "And, since I hear them all, I don't believe there was one. Not," he added more slowly, "that I knew Remington Wakefield before I moved into rooms in London, or that I know him well even now—" He frowned. "—and there was that year and more I saw neither hide nor hair of *any* tonnish boy or man—" He shook off those particular memories. "—but, Georgi, since I came down from my college and began living in London . . ."

Georgi's eyes brightened and she interrupted. "Vincent! Was Lord Wakefield one of the choice spirits who led you astray?"

"More likely, if any leading was done, Vincent led Remington down one or another primrose path," interrupted Lord Everhart, speaking of one of his oldest, but not one of his closest, friends.

Wakefield was younger than he, but they'd grown up neighbors and had known each other forever. As adults their habits and interests had diverged but they remained something more than acquaintances.

"Georgi," said her fond husband sternly, "you are allowing yourself to be distracted by irrelevancies. Tell me what is bothering you."

Georgi bit her lip. She opened her mouth, paused before speaking, and then closed it with just a bit of a snap. She shook her head, the stubborn look both men knew well appearing. "I do not see how my suspicions can be true, so very likely I am wrong. *Therefore* I will hold my tongue." She nodded firmly. Once.

With one of those quicksilver movements so much a part of her, Georgi escaped her husband's clasp, avoided his grasping hand as she slipped from his embrace, and was halfway to the stairs before either Vincent or Lord Everhart knew what had happened. When the sound of her footsteps faded the two, coming out of the bemused state Georgi's behavior so often induced, started for the stairs as well.

"Do *you* remember a tale about Wakefield?" asked Vincent.

"What? Oh yes. You should as well, although it is old gossip. He was virtually stood up at the altar and not at all happy about it—but it was *years* ago. What can that have to do with anything?"

Neither man could answer that, so, deciding time would solve the mystery, they took themselves off to the library. There a recently decanted bottle of burgundy, part of the latest shipment from his lordship's dealer in fine wines, awaited them. They enjoyed a glass, knowing it was their last peaceful drink together before the party began.

The next morning Vincent sighed as he turned from the sideboard, his plate heaped high. Georgi had not stopped ranting and raving since he'd entered the breakfast room.

". . . and furthermore, Vincent, my oldest friend—" Georgi had spent a sleepless hour, maybe two, worrying about her house party. "—what am I to do if she comes down with a coughing sickness and infects the household? It will ruin the party."

"I am never ill," said a soft voice from the doorway.

Vincent turned, stared. The half-frozen white-faced woman of the evening before, half soaked and exhausted, had been transformed into a straight-backed, Madonna-faced matron, the long hair, straggling about her face the evening before, now hidden, trapped in a sleek bun at the back of her head and covered with a simply trimmed cap tied in a small bow under her chin. She was dressed in a somewhat out-of-fashion black mourning gown that, despite a maid's efforts, showed signs of hard usage. Vincent swallowed, hard, wasn't sure why, and dropped his gaze before she could see him gaping like a rustic.

"I must thank you, Lady Everhart," continued the stranger, "for taking me and Tal in for the night. I fear I must ask some further aid of you in order to reach a post house, so that we may continue on our way. There is no reason we should be a bother to you. Especially at this season. Christmas should be a time for family and friends."

As she rose to her feet, Georgi cast a red-faced look toward Vincent. "I have embarrassed myself and you and for that I apologize," she told the stranger in her frank fashion, approaching the woman as she spoke and drawing her farther into the room. "First tell me what you prefer to drink with your breakfast so I may order it, then allow Vincent to fill your plate, and *then,* when you have eased your hunger, you may tell us who you are and how we may best serve you."

Even as the words flowed from her mouth, she motioned to Vincent to pull out a chair, snapped her fingers at the footman hovering in the hallway, and, never pausing for breath, added, "And you must also tell me if there is anything else needed for your child. Oh, such a *beautiful* boy—"

Vincent's head jerked up. He'd assumed the child a girl with those big pansy blue eyes, curly hair, the unformed but perfect little features . . .

"—he is," finished Georgi a trifle wistfully. She hadn't been married more than a few months, but she did so wish for a child. The depth of her love for Everhart demanded of her that she add to her new family, expanding that circle of love between herself and her wonderful Everhart.

"Tal is beautiful, is he not?" asked the woman softly, faint color rising into her face and her eyes smiling. "As to needs, your maid knows exactly what is required. We want for nothing."

A smile lit Georgi's face. "Matty Brownlee comes from a large family. As the second oldest daughter she has, from an early age, had the care of littler ones. Now, if you truly need nothing in the nursery, do tell what you prefer in the way of breakfast."

A pot of coffee was quickly produced and a plate full of eggs and ham set before the woman. Toast, dripping butter and preserves, was added to that and then, having taken a few quick neat bites, she looked up. "I believe I would have died last night if you, sir, had not found me. And Tal, too, which is worse. There is no way on earth I can thank you, but I will pray every day for you, for your health and happiness."

Vincent felt his ears heat. "It was nothing. That I happened to be there when you needed me, *that* is the miracle. Please do not refine upon it. And please finish eating before you tell us your story. You must be famished."

He knew, because Georgi had told him so, that the woman had not wakened when disrobed and put to bed the previous evening. She had been at the very end of her strength—but here she was, awake, alert, and, obviously, determined to get on with her life. He admired that.

"Do eat," he encouraged, pushing a small pitcher full of thick cream near her hand.

She poured cream into her coffee and then made no effort to hide the fact that she ate a great deal, something a tonnish woman would have felt unfeminine and shame-making. She ate so neatly, however, she avoided any accusation that she'd wolfed down her food—at least not more than the first bite or two. At last she sat back, holding a final cup of rich dark coffee into which she'd stirred another dollop of cream.

When it came, the story was a simple one.

"I fell deeply in love with a man my father felt unworthy. He had made his own choice for me, a gentleman I'd met only once or twice and barely knew. Without informing me, he and this gentleman came to an agreement. I was unaware of what was going forward until a mantua-maker arrived at the house to fit my wedding gown, fussing that it could not possibly be finished properly in the brief time she had been given."

"Do you mean the man did not even make a proper proposal to you?" asked Georgi, surprised into interrupting.

"Not a word. I objected as soon as I realized what was proposed, but my father was determined. He would not allow me to speak to or write to this particular gentleman, the one he'd chosen, and would not, himself, pass along my objections. My maid took a message to my beloved and . . . we eloped." She spoke the last words in a choked up, embarrassed fashion. She swallowed, hard, at the distressing confession but soon raised her head to a proud angle. "I was married from his family's home," she said, her voice firm. "Although we escaped to Scotland, we did *not* wed over the anvil."

Vincent looked at Georgi and found his softhearted cousin had tears in her eyes. His mouth twisted. It *was* an affecting story. The question remained, however, whether the stranger should be believed. Vincent cynically believed she should *not* be accepted at face value and was ready to urge caution on his cousin when his cousin called the stranger by a name that had not been mentioned.

"Lady Penelope," said Georgi softly, "you are welcome in my home for however long we find necessary in order to make things right for you."

Vincent cast an openmouthed look at his cousin. Belatedly, he thought to interfere—and was instantly glad he had not when, her head once again set at that proud angle, the woman responded.

"I am no longer Lady Penelope. I am Mrs. Lieutenant Kennet Garth and I do not need assistance. At least, it is not that I am penniless," she amended, remembering she would require a carriage to help her on her way. "Kennet's family, despite my father's stubborn insistence, is not a poverty stricken crofter family. I inherited a neat competence from Kennet and am well able to care for Tal and myself."

That rang true and quite obviously Georgi knew something he did not or she'd not have called the woman by name. Vincent, thinking of Georgi's tendency to aid every lame dog, every bird with a damaged wing, was immediately thankful Mrs. Garth did not fall into a class that Georgi would find impossible to ignore. Everhart might object to taking a penniless widow into his establishment on a permanent basis.

"My error," continued Mrs. Garth, interrupting his thoughts, "was that I assumed my father would wish to meet his grandson. I had paid off my post chaise before he was informed of our arrival. Once he did know, he sent me packing, refusing me even so much as a gig for transport." Again her innate pride was evident in the difficulty with which she added, "Although I am *not* destitute and am able to pay my way, I *will* beg your help in making the necessary arrangements for traveling onward."

Once he no longer feared his cousin's personal involvement in the woman's problem, Vincent relaxed, allowing Mrs. Garth's deep, rather husky voice to very nearly mesmerize him. There was something about it that surrounded him, sank into him, filled him—and made him long for more . . .

"Are you in such a great hurry to reach your destination?" asked Georgi softly.

Vincent, alerted by her tone, straightened. Perhaps he had assumed too much? Once again he debated interfering. He had seen that expression of innocence on his cousin's face far too often in the past. It was one that instantly roused wariness and suspicion concerning whatever plot she plotted. Not that he'd succeed in thwarting her, he thought, half in humor, half in despair. Once Georgi had the bit between her teeth, she'd not be gainsaid. Obviously, since she could not be stopped, he would once again find it necessary to bestir himself on her behalf and rescue her from the chaos she'd produce around her.

"I had meant," Mrs. Garth responded, once again interrupting Vincent's thoughts, "to spend Christmas quietly with my father. I think *you* mean to suggest I join your house party, but I am in half mourning and, frankly, such jollification does not appeal." She smiled a sad sweet smile. "No, it will be far better if I take myself elsewhere—to my husband's family, I think, until I can take up residence in the little house I've leased in Edinburgh but cannot occupy until the New Year."

"Edinburgh?" Georgi put her hands on the table and used them to raise herself to her feet. "That settles it," she said firmly. "Not only do you admit you cannot yet get into your new home, but the weather is far too unsettled at this time of year for further travel. *Especially* if one is traveling north. You will stay here."

Vincent knew there was no arguing with Georgi when she used that tone. He sighed in resignation as he glanced at Mrs. Garth. Although she frowned, it seemed she realized it as well.

"If you do not wish to mingle with the guests," continued

Georgi, kindly, "then you and your son may remain in the nursery, where, I fear, you will have to sleep in any case. Minnow Manor will be as full as it can hold—assuming everyone we've invited arrives. Ah!" she said, turning back from the door through which she'd been about to exit. "Surely, since you are not, as you say, destitute, you own more than the clothes in which you stand?"

"My father had everything thrown into the drive," said Penelope, rue and humor fighting for dominance in her expression. In the end, it was embarrassment she revealed as she said, "It was my intention to send from the inn and have them brought to me there . . ."

"But," interrupted Georgi, "there was no room at the village inn. It is a very small inn, is it not?" She nodded. "I will order that our coachman and a groom retrieve your boxes and trunks," she added and, in her usual whirlwind fashion, turned and disappeared.

"And I," said Vincent, rising as his cousin disappeared, "will go with them to Tennytree Hill to assure myself that nothing is forgotten, and that nothing was burned or otherwise destroyed."

Vincent felt a certain grim frustration. For her sake, he hoped they would find her possessions intact. For his, however, he rather hoped he'd have an excuse to confront Lord Tennytree and berate him for this, his most recent perfidy.

Mrs. Garth's story only added to his hearty dislike of the man, a dislike that had its roots in his youth. Years earlier, a mere boy out exploring, he had wandered in to the Tennytree Hill home wood. There, barely avoiding it himself, he had discovered a mantrap half hidden among fallen leaves. He'd sprung it before returning to his grandfather, Lord Tivington, where he'd ranted and raged that such devilish contraptions could exist in the modern world.

When his rant burned itself out, he demanded something be done to stop such atrocities. In particular, Vincent demanded that Lord Tennytree be stopped. It was a rather nasty shock to discover his omnipotent grandfather was *not* omnipotent and that, in this particular case, there was nothing Lord Tivington could do to alter things. The law was clear. Poaching was a crime and a landowner allowed any means he felt necessary to stop those who would, despite the law, poach.

That experience had been the basis of Vincent's dislike for Lord Tennytree, but there were more recent reasons to find Mrs. Garth's father despicable. In these latter years his lordship had turned to the courts, suing everyone and anyone—occasionally for cause, but far more often for no good reason. Even *Grandfather* had been forced to defend himself against the nuisance of false accusations. *Twice.* All this ran through Vincent's mind as he strode out to the stables.

Lord Tennytree, he concluded, *isn't playing with a full deck. He's half a loaf short of a meal. A peck short of a bushel . . .*

Vincent, even as he thought up half a dozen other ways of saying his lordship was not all there, laughed at himself.

He was halfway to Tennytree Hill before it occurred to him to ask himself why he was doing something so out of character as play the knight-errant to a distressed lady. It was no surprise when he found an answer to that riddle. Vincent understood himself pretty well. If Georgi could never pass by a living creature in need, Vincent could not bear to witness injustice. Tennytree and the concept of justice were total strangers. Ergo, Vincent felt required to see Mrs. Garth did not suffer—perhaps one should say, suffer *more*—from the man's viciousness.

Besides, he'd rescued Mrs. Garth from freezing to death. He was surprised to discover that was not the end of his role in her life. In fact—a far greater surprise—he discovered a sense of responsibility for the lady that, previously, he'd felt for no one but Georgi.

Vincent crossed his arms, braced a foot against the padding of the seat opposite, and scowled. "This is nonsense," he muttered. "She is a stranger. She is safe. She has admitted she needs no particular help, aid, or comfort. So why . . . ?"

His voice trailed off and the frown deepened. There was, he discovered, no easy answer to be found to *that* question—even if he *could* bring himself to finish framing it.

The trunks and all else lay where they'd been thrown. One crate had leaked a great deal of something into the badly raked gravel, leaving a frozen puddle of reddish hue. When Vincent sniffed it, he guessed it had been a case of port wine. He left it lying there, but a portmanteau had broken open as well and Vincent feared that much of its contents were strewn by the wind half across the county. They gathered together what could be found and then hefted Mrs. Garth's possessions to the carriage roof—or, in the case of the broken portmanteau and some other smaller items, inside the vehicle.

Vincent, climbing up beside Georgi's driver, took the reins. "No word of this needs find its way to the inn," he warned the man.

"Won't have to say nothing, will we then?" asked the driver laconically. "Will be all over the county already, that old Spindleshanks denied his daughter." After half a moment's pause, he added, "Again."

Vincent sighed softly. All too true. Someone among Lord Tennytree's servants would have told the tale. "Then I'll change that to *no more* need be said."

"Lady Everhart already had a word with us. Said the old man didn't need to know where his daughter's gotten to. Serve the silly old bugger right, to my way of thinking. Christmas! Tisn't the season for being nasty. For all one knows, the inhuman lobcock might even suffer a twinge or two in his conscience—" The coachman cast a sideways look toward Vincent.

"—a-wondering about her fate. Weather *frightful* cruel last night . . ."

The mumbling trailed off, but Vincent had no trouble reading meaning into the satisfied tone. Even servants who need have nothing to do with his lordship detested Lord Tennytree and hoped that just perhaps he'd suffer remorse for this, his latest ill-tempered idiocy.

CHAPTER 2

Vincent had preceded the footmen who toted Mrs. Garth's possessions up to the nursery. He paused in the doorway. Penelope—

Instantly, he changed that in his mind to the more proper "Mrs. Garth."

—was seated on the floor. On the braided carpet before her lay her child, kicking his feet. A silver teething ring was clutched in one hand and the tot, a serious expression on its young face, burbled as if telling a long and involved tale.

Vincent, enjoying the scene, heard a throat cleared behind him and realized he was in the way of the footmen. He rapped on the doorframe and moved on into the room.

"We've brought your things. What we could," he added apologetically.

"What you could?" Mrs. Garth first eyed the footmen and then counted under her breath. "Everything seems to be there," she said, turning back to Vincent. Her look was half a question.

"There was a crate that perhaps had wine in it?"

She nodded, comprehension putting a flush to her cheeks.

"Broken, of course." She drew in a deep breath. "I hope you left it."

"We did. I fear I didn't check to see if a bottle had survived. I am pretty certain nothing could have."

"It was," she said in a dry tone, "a Boxing Day present for my father. An excellent Portuguese port that he would have enjoyed. There is, if anyone bothers to check, a label with his name."

Vincent felt his lips twitch. He was pleased to observe that Mrs. Garth's eyes held a glint of amusement. "A peace offering?" he asked.

"A present," she said firmly.

"There was one other casualty," Vincent said, ignoring the challenge he heard in that, but pleased that she hadn't felt a need to bribe the old man. "A portmanteau broke open and I fear some of the contents is missing. We collected what we could find, but it wasn't much . . . ?"

She nodded. "I will check to see what is lost. Everything of any value is in that trunk." She pointed and then shrugged. "Most likely someone will be surprised to discover a well-worn shift plastered against their thatch." Realizing what she'd said, she raised startled eyes to meet his. Noting his arched eyebrow, she blushed. "I apologize," she said quickly. "I am too use to the less strict camaraderie in the army and must quickly re-accustom myself to society's ways . . ."

"You followed the drum?" asked Vincent quickly, wanting to divert her from her obvious embarrassment and unneeded apologies. "You didn't stay in Lisbon as I am told many wives do?"

"I wanted only to be with Kennet. Once or twice he sent me back—when they had a rough campaign ahead of them and the expectation of a great deal of moving about—but I could rarely stand it for more than a month or six weeks and would find a means of returning to as near the army as I could get."

"It must have been a difficult life."

"Difficult, yes, but fascinating. I was very young when we wed. I hadn't a notion what I faced and had all to learn. I am ashamed of how ignorant I was. But more important than the education I received, was being allowed to be part of the comradeship, the wonderful closeness that develops when one knows danger is near. Besides, there were good times as well as bad. When the army was in winter cantonments, for instance, we invented all sorts of make-do entertainments. Races and balls. Very odd dinners where each shared what he had. Picnics and hunts. Oh, I don't know what all. I will never regret marrying my Kennet." Her mouth drooped and she dropped her eyes to her son. "He never saw Tal . . ."

"The baby was born after his death?" asked Vincent softly.

"Months after Talavera. I hadn't known for certain that I carried a babe . . ." She straightened. "At first, after Kennet's death, I'd no desire to leave the area where he was buried. And then, when I was certain I carried his child . . . well, frankly it was not an easy time. I was too ill to travel for much of my pregnancy and then Tal was unwell his first months of life. I feared again and again that he'd die. I couldn't bear the thought I'd lose him as well as Kennet . . ." Her eyes held nothing but pain. "And he never knew . . ."

There was such anguish in that that Vincent longed to take the straight-backed, dry-eyed woman into his arms, longed to comfort her, ease the pain he saw coursing through her rigid body. "He knows," he said, his voice firm. "Your Kennet knows and is glad."

She stared at him. "You believe that? You truly believe it?"

He nodded. "My parents died when I was very young but—" He continued with some difficulty. "—I have felt my mother's touch when I most needed her. Oh, not for a long time now, but that last time, I was convinced I'd die. I wasn't so very old myself then and frankly—" Vincent felt blood rush up his neck and into his ears, the heat unmistakable, but what he'd begun he was determined to finish. "—I wanted my mother!"

She reached out, but drew her hand back instantly. "You . . . sensed her?"

"She spoke to me," he said, his voice firm. "She said it wasn't my time and that I was not to fear. That I would come safe through the battle but I must put aside my pride and write Grandfather, ask him to come for me. Her words, her voice, they were very clear to me."

"Battle?" Mrs. Garth tipped her head. "You were in the army?"

Vincent grimaced and trod heavily to the high windows. Putting his elbows on the sills and his chin on his fists, he looked out. He didn't turn to her as he told the story.

"I was a well-grown boy and a damned fool." He laughed but there was no humor in it. "I ran away. Enlisted. That particular battle, my last, was . . . bad. An officer and I were trapped together under his fallen horse. He was dying and knew it. I held him, spoke with him." Vincent felt his throat closing up at the memory. "It was . . . an impossible situation." He turned and stared. "I was in a funk after that and remembered my mother's words. I wrote and Grandfather rescued me. He could, you see, since I was, even then, underage." Red spots marked Vincent's high cheekbones. "When we reached Beverly Place, I found a white feather. I kept it in my pocketbook for a long time," he finished, his chin high, a muscle jumping in his cheek.

"The symbol of cowardliness? You thought yourself a coward?" she asked. When he grimaced, his expression admitting it, she scolded, "You were a *boy.* You'd not shown white when you were *not* trapped, when you *could* fight. Well? Did you?"

Vincent frowned slightly. "No—but the excitement. There

is something that draws you on. You keep doing what you have to do and don't think about it . . ."

"You were not a coward."

He drew in a breath. "I guess I accepted that. Finally. More or less." He grimaced again. "It wasn't easy."

"Accepted it? Have you? Or have you never been *quite* certain?"

The flush rose up again. *Why,* he wondered, *am I saying any of this? I never told even Georgi about that damn feather.*

"You don't wish to discuss it," she said quietly, recognizing he'd given her as much as he could, "but I am glad you told me. Your story of hearing your mother's voice has eased me, Mr. Beverly, and I thank you for sharing it."

Story! Lord, I forgot where this began, thought Vincent. He waved a hand, dismissively. "I had to tell it in order to explain why I believe your husband knows about his son." He shrugged, looked around, and then down at the child. "He is a beautiful boy," he said, once again startled by a beauty that spoke more of the feminine than the male. The child would have a rough time of it as he grew up—assuming he did not harden into a manly frame and countenance.

"I see you think him too beautiful," she said, smiling a rather rueful smile.

"You are perceptive," he said. "I cannot help but feel concerned," he added with only a touch of harshness, "about the sort of teasing he'll face when he goes to school. Boys can be cruel, you know."

She nodded. "I too have worried a trifle, but that is for the future and we will think about solutions when the time comes."

The "we" startled Vincent—until he realized she referred to herself and the babe and not to the two of them. A touch of regret feathered through him. Regret? He shook his head at the notion.

"We won't have to?" she asked, blinking.

"What?" He too blinked, then recalled her last words and said, "You must think about it, of course, and far sooner than you might wish." He drew in a breath. "May I suggest you find a tutor for him who can not only teach him his Latin, but also such things as wrestling and boxing, and that he begin such training at an early age? And be certain the tutor is the sort of man who will not forget to teach the rules, the ethics, that attend to proper fighting?"

"Rules?" she asked, looking confused.

Vincent nodded. "So your Tal doesn't turn into a bully, doesn't use his training for his *benefit* rather than for his *defense*."

She blinked again. "My goodness, you are concerned for him, are you not?"

Vincent laughed. "I wonder if, with those looks, he'll not have people worrying about him all his life. Perhaps that is another thing you'll need to do."

This time she merely raised a questioning brow, curious as to what this strangely sensitive man would say next.

Vincent shrugged off the embarrassment he was feeling and explained. "You must see that he doesn't come to rely on others to get him out of the fixes he gets himself into."

She laughed—but then sobered, a thoughtful look replacing the humor. "You mean I must see that he realizes there are consequences to his actions?"

Vincent nodded. Then, his discomfort increasing, he huffed a quick breath. "How have we come to discuss the rearing of children when I know nothing about raising them?"

She laughed. It was a low-in-the-throat sound, husky, a siren sound, and Vincent found himself taking a step toward her. He forced himself to stillness. "You've a lovely laugh," he said, and heard a wistful note he didn't recognize. "I wish I could remain to enjoy it," he added, speaking more harshly to cover the soft note, "but I promised Georgi I'd help with the decorating. She has had huge piles of greens brought in and ribbons of all widths are available. She says everything must be finished today since her first guests arrive tomorrow." He backed toward the doorway.

She stopped him as he was about to exit. "If I did not say thank you for retrieving my possessions, I do. Thank you, that is. Very much."

He waved that away. "Once you've unpacked and settled in, perhaps you'd care to come down and help," he said before he could stop himself. Not wishing, even in his own mind, for that to sound like a personal invitation for her company, he added, "There will be more than enough to do, I fear. Georgi tends to go quite beyond any reasonable person's notion of proper decorating when it comes to putting up greens." Then, with something approaching a salute, he ducked from the room and hurried away.

Penelope stopped at the top of the stairs, her hand on the railing, not convinced she was right to join those working below. For a long moment she watched Mr. Beverly deftly form long swags from the fresh pine-scented balsam, tying one limb to the next with wire and reaching for still another bough as he finished the last.

She swallowed. He'd been so kind when they'd talked upstairs. Previously there had been a hard side to him which she'd sensed even in those first moments when he found her, half frozen, frightened half to death, and fearing for Tal's survival far more than her own. Occasionally he'd revealed a cynicism that bothered her—but it had not been evident while they spoke up there in the nursery.

Was it that that drew her now? That glimpse into a side of him she guessed few saw?

If I'd any sense I'd go right back upstairs and stay there.

But, even before she'd finished the thought, Penelope set

her foot on the top step and kept right on moving down until she neared the bottom.

"You do that very well," she said, her hand on the banister.

Vincent looked up from where he knelt among the fir and holly. He grinned. "Georgi trained me well. In former years, of course, we decorated Beverly Place—" He stood, a faint scowl darkening his brow. "—but what is there in all this to make you look so . . . odd?"

"Beverly Place. Lady Everhart was Georgianna Beverly?"

"You did not know?"

"I should have, but I did not. She has . . . changed a great deal since I last saw her."

Vincent, doing some quick calculations, grinned. "She'd have been perhaps as much as thirteen? Fourteen, at the outside? Oh yes. A *great* deal."

Penelope chuckled. "I didn't know her well, but what I knew I liked. My father, however . . ." Her voice trailed off when, reluctant to voice an insult, she didn't know how to finish her sentence.

"Your father," said Vincent in an exceedingly dry voice, "very likely thought her a hoyden of the very worst sort." A devilish look entered his eyes and he grinned a quick flashing grin before adding, "What is more, he was nearly correct in thinking so. On the other hand, she has not grown up to be a missish pea hen with no thought in her head but that her gown be perfect and that every fop in town must sit at her feet, which I, at least, find a great advantage to the way she was reared."

Penelope came on down the stairs, chuckling. "I can see she is first oars with you, sir—" She repressed a sudden sadness that it was so, not understanding why she was bothered by the notion. "—but now you must tell me how I may help."

"Ribbons," he said promptly. "I cannot tie a bow to save me." He pointed to the long narrow table set against the wall nearer the front door. "There. All widths, you see, and scissors, and other things you may need. You can, can you not, tie a ribbon?" he asked, pretending anxiety.

"We will see. It has been some years since I last attempted it. Ribbons are not plentiful on battlefields. At least—" She sobered, a bleak look about her eyes. "—not the sort of ribbons we discuss here."

"Far more important ribbons," he said softly. "Ribbons attached to medals indicating valor under fire, for instance."

She nodded and, making an effort, put aside thoughts of war and a small case containing Tal's father's medals hidden deep in the largest trunk. Soon she and Vincent were both occupied, working silently but companionably. Footmen passed through the hall. A maid came down the stairs with a pile of linens that she should have taken down the backstairs, but no one scolded her. Georgi flitted in and, after praising them for their work, flitted out again.

Penelope's pile of fancy rosettes grew so high a few slipped to make red splotches on the polished floor. She was constructing the very last bow out of the last long strand of ribbon when, without ceremony, the door was thrust open, slamming against the wall. It startled her into allowing the curves of the rosette to burst into a tangle at which her hands scrabbled in an attempt to contain it.

"Ha! *Whore!*"

A rather short, paunchy gentleman with an exceedingly red face stood in the open doorway, a shaky finger pointing at Penelope.

"How dare you enter a decent house? Brazen bitch! Strumpet!"

Vincent, who had just finished the longest swag, the one meant for the stairway, rose to his feet and moved on light feet to the rescue.

"Fancy man!" The pointing finger swung toward Vincent. "Whoremonger!"

"Lord Tennytree, one must presume?" asked Vincent sarcastically.

"Ha! You can forget getting a penny out of me! Not a groat!" blustered the red-faced gentleman, his cane lifted although no one—

Everhart appeared at that moment from one side of the hall and Georgi from the other.

—knew if it was his lordship's intent to point, to defend himself, or to use it as a club.

"You nasty old man! How dare you insult guests in my home?" demanded Georgi, stalking near and putting an arm around Penelope's waist. She glanced at the white-faced woman and gave her a gentle squeeze.

"Lord Tennytree, I presume," said Everhart in icy tones, unknowingly echoing Vincent. "Sir, if you cannot behave as the gentleman you were purportedly born to be, you will remove yourself from my hall. At once!"

Tennytree reared back. He glared from Georgi to Everhart. "What is this? What sort of rig you running here?"

"Rig?" asked Everhart, his voice cold. "I know nothing of rigs. I merely prepare my home for the guests who are to arrive for our Christmas party. You, my lord—" His voice could not have been more chill. "—were not invited."

Vincent had to hide a grin at that. This was a side of Everhart he'd never seen and one he liked very much. Hearing it, Vincent knew his lordship would defend what was his, which was good, since it meant he'd defend Georgi. The poor dear very often found herself in need of defense, thanks to an impulsive nature that, all too often, had her running *on* where anyone of sense would know to run *away*. Georgi, dear little Georgi, was far too prone to jumping right into the middle of things with nary a thought of consequences—so knowing her husband would defend her was a relief.

Tennytree's voice pulled Vincent from such thoughts.

"Wouldn't want to be invited," growled his lordship. "Scurvy doings, house parties. Just the sort of thing that draggle—"

"*Be careful,*" inserted Vincent, his voice harsh.

Tennytree ignored the warning. "—tail would like!"

"*That's enough,*" Vincent roared.

"*More* than enough." Everhart's cold tones echoed Vincent's sentiment.

With nary a glance at each other, Vincent and Everhart moved forward.

"You were warned," said Everhart softly.

No plan was discussed, but Vincent took one of Tennytree's arms and Everhart the other. They backed his lordship, stumbling, out the door, swung him around between them just as if they'd practiced the maneuver, and then escorted him, far more quickly than befitted his lordship's dignity, to his carriage, into which they thrust him.

"Take the fellow home. He is not welcome here," Lord Everhart ordered the Tennytree coachman.

Vincent noted the twitch to the driver's lips and wondered if the man did not rejoice to see his master mortified. The coachman cracked his whip and the ancient horses leaned into their harness. Reluctantly, slowly, the over-large, over-heavy, old-fashioned carriage rolled off down the drive. Vincent felt pity for the pair of horses that pulled it, in place of the team of four that *should* have been harnessed to such a rig.

Vincent shook off his pity for the horses and brushed off his hands. "That," he said, "should settle *that.*" Quite happy with their victory, he walked quickly back into the house— to discover Penelope Garth had disappeared. "Where'd she go?" he asked a sad looking Georgi.

"Up to her room. She was badly hurt by his insults."

"Blast the bastard to . . ."

"Shush!" Georgi, frowning, put a hand over his mouth. "We've a child in the house and you are not to say such things!"

Vincent's brows climbed his forehead. "Getting into practice, Georgi?" he asked, sardonically. Then he too stalked off—but he went in the direction of the stables.

CHAPTER 3

Penelope Garth stared down at her sleeping son. After a long moment, she moved away from the bed, going to the window where she stared out over the leafless trees toward where she knew her father's home lay. She sighed, turned back, and again stared at her son. She could forgive her father his thoughts concerning herself. She could not forgive his attitude toward his grandson.

"Such an innocent," she murmured. A sweet innocent child, rejected by a bitter old man. "Why is he that way?" she asked the unresponsive room. She sighed again. Her father was the way he was. There was nothing she could do to change him.

Penelope seated herself in the softly padded chair she'd been surprised to find when she rushed upstairs away from the scene caused by her father. Her room, originally furnished for a governess, had been adequate if rather Spartan. Now, not only the chair was added for her comfort but also a small Queen Anne desk. A delicate straight-backed chair was pushed under it and writing materials set out on top. Against the wall was a half-length mirror to help with her dressing. And, finally, an oil lamp sat on a table near the chair in which she seated herself and, on it, a selection of books.

"Lady Everhart has been busy," mused Penelope, finding some distraction in itemizing the changes that had occurred after she went to help with the decorating. For a moment she wondered if she should return and ask what else she might do to prepare for the guests who would begin arriving the next day.

Embarrassment held her where she was. She could not bring herself to face those who had witnessed her father's insults. *How could he do that to me,* she silently wailed. "How could he do it?" she repeated aloud, and then glanced to see that her son had not roused at the sound of her voice.

Georgi, appearing in the open doorway just then, bit her lip. "He is an unhappy man who cannot bear those around him to experience the slightest bit of happiness when he does not," she said softly. She entered the room and looked down at the boy. "He is so beautiful."

Penelope smiled. "He is, is he not? Your Mr. Beverly thinks he'll suffer for it when he goes to school—or perhaps still sooner."

"*Vincent* said such a thing?" Georgi looked genuinely surprised. "I was unaware he'd even seen the child. I mean since you arrived here."

"He came up with my possessions and we talked." It occurred to her that perhaps that conversation had been private, so she hesitated before introducing a topic about which she'd wondered. But she *was* curious so, putting aside the thought she intruded where she should not, she said, "He must have suffered a great deal, joining the army when he was a mere boy."

Georgi's eyes widened still more. "He told you about *that?*"

Penelope tipped her head to the side. "Should he not have done so?"

"There is no *should* involved. It is merely that he does not. Speak of it, I mean."

Penelope nodded. It was what she'd thought. "I was honored, then, that he told me. But he spoke only to reassure me about—" Suddenly she was certain his words had been for her alone, that he had not even told his cousin about hearing his mother's voice. "—something. Is there," she asked quickly, "anything I can do for you?"

Georgi dithered for half a moment. She wanted to know why her cousin had revealed things about a time he did his best to forget, but, still more, she wanted to reassure Mrs. Garth that she was not to allow the scene with her father to overset her. Georgi wished to make certain that it did not lead her guest to avoid the household. That was the more important errand, so she said the piece she'd climbed the stairs to say.

Penelope, unraveling Georgi's rather confused explanations, exhortations, and reassurances, nodded. "I know I am not to blame for my father's raving, but I cannot help but be embarrassed that he feels the way he does. Soon after our marriage we received a letter from his attorney. He believes, or pretends to believe, our wedding was not legal, that we were not married, and that, since he'll not have a whore for a daughter, it follows that I am no daughter of his! Sometimes I wonder if he is quite sane," she added half to herself and then, once again feeling embarrassed, looked up, meeting Georgi's sympathetic gaze. "Please forget I said that."

"I don't know that it will make you feel better, but you may as well know that half the countryside wonders the same thing." Georgi's wry expression drew a bit of a chuckle from Penelope. "My grandfather says we must be patient with him, but frankly, his . . . his *antics* have stretched nearly everyone's patience to the snapping point."

This time there was a wry sound to Penelope's chuckle. The boy stirred and, quickly, she moved to put her hand on his shoulder. The child snuggled down and drifted back into the deep sleep of early childhood.

Georgi gestured, silently suggesting they go into the day nursery onto which the governess's room opened. "You did not have Matty put him down in his own bed?" asked Georgi, curious.

Penelope smiled. "I am used to doing all for him. Besides, I guessed there are things Matty should be doing downstairs. When I asked she hemmed and hawed, making me certain of it, so I sent her off to her real work. She can return later if she has time, but in the meantime she will do the things she was hired to do."

"We were going on very well without her. I'll tell her to come back up. What I really came to tell you is that we very much hope you mean to join us for dinner. If you are concerned about meeting strangers, no one is expected until tomorrow and then people will arrive throughout the coming week. The first thing I planned of a formal sort is a dinner that includes my family. From Beverly Place, you know? You *will* come down, will you not? At least this evening?" coaxed Georgi.

Penelope hesitated. "Very well," she reluctantly agreed. "I truly have no wish to celebrate the season. You understand, do you not?"

"Oh yes, but there are things you *will* wish to do. There are church services for which we will provide transportation. And I hope you will feel free to ride whenever the weather permits. I've two lovely mares in the stables and I'll not have time to ride either as often as I would wish, so please feel free to take one out whenever you wish. Then we mean to hold a children's party to which I hope you'll bring your son . . . What else?" she asked rhetorically. "Ah. There are many in the area who felt you were badly treated after your elopement and who will wish to welcome you home. I've a soiree planned for late next week to which many neighborhood families have been invited. There will be no dancing or anything of that nature. Please join us for that or I'll be accused of hiding you away!"

"Hiding me . . . ?"

"Surely you cannot think there is a soul in the whole of the Cotswolds who is unaware of your presence here?"

For a moment Penelope looked appalled. Then she looked enlightened. Then, finally, she looked resigned. "I've no choice, have I? Except to leave here as I meant to do," she threatened a trifle more than half seriously.

"Please. Do not attempt to travel north," said Georgi earnestly. "The weather . . ."

It was certainly true that the weather was not to be trusted at this time of year and also true that they had heard nothing good about the roads to the north, but that was not Georgi's real reason for urging every argument which came to mind in order to convince her unexpected guest she must remain at Minnow Manor.

Georgi could not bear knowing others were unhappy and do nothing to correct the situation. She was very nearly certain she'd come up with a scheme which would not only reconcile Lord Tennytree to his daughter, but would, if the widow would allow it, make Penelope happy as well— although she might not think so right at once.

". . . and furthermore," finished Georgi, still speaking in a firm tone she'd adopted from her least favorite governess, "you must think of your child. You should not take such a young one on such a difficult journey under these conditions. I know you should not."

Vincent, who had been listening from beyond the doorway, backed away. Georgi was up to something. What it was he could not guess, but that particular innocently solemn expression was part and parcel of her more outrageous notions. Vincent returned to his room, thinking furiously.

Unfortunately, his thoughts added up to three when they should have come to four.

* * *

"Where are you going, Vincent?" asked Lord Everhart some minutes after Vincent had changed to riding gear and made his way to the stables. Everhart put his hand on Black Spot Flying's neck.

Vincent looked around from where he tightened Spot's girth. "Hmm? Oh. I mean to ride over to Grandfather's. It has been well over a month since I last visited Beverly Place."

"Do you wish to go alone or would company appeal?" asked Everhart.

Vincent's brows arched. "Company, by all means."

Everhart motioned to a groom who fetched tack and saddled up his lordship's favorite hunter. The two men chatted until the horse was ready and then mounted, riding under the arched entrance to the brand new stabling. Everhart and Georgi had designed it together, each compromising their preferred style until they reached agreement.

"What," asked Vincent once they'd discussed half a dozen things of interest, "is your wife up to?"

Everhart blinked. "Georgi? Up to something?"

"I've an idea of what she's planning and, if I'm right, I don't approve. She should stay out of it."

Everhart thought for a moment and then his brows arched. "You think she'll attempt to arrange for Tennytree and Mrs. Garth to work out their differences?"

"It has to be that."

"Surely not. She'd be a fool to think it possible. Tennytree . . ."

"Lord Tennytree is a cods-head and beef-witted to boot," said Vincent, mincing no words when Everhart appeared to be searching for a polite way of saying much the same thing. "Georgi's no fool, but she is softhearted to the point she is likely to make things worse in her attempts to make them better."

"I'll have a word with her," said Everhart.

"Oh, that will do a great deal of good," said Vincent, his usual cynicism turned to outright sarcasm. "With Georgi a talking-to is more likely—" He spoke in the tones of someone offering polite advice. "—to result in a stubborn determination to prove herself in the right and you in the wrong. *I know.* I don't know how many times in the past I've done my best to steer her into more sensible paths." He winced as several such occasions raced through his mind. "Once she's put the yoke over her shoulders," he finished in a rather tired tone, "she will not be deterred from plowing a straight furrow—even when the ground is rocky and unproductive."

"My wife is not an ox!"

"A mule, then," said Vincent, obligingly—but with a touch of mischief as well.

Everhart very nearly responded still more angrily, but, with a glance at his companion's expression, closed his mouth.

Vincent chuckled. "You are learning, are you not?"

"Marriage to Georgi," said Everhart ruefully, "would teach the least perceptive of men to be wary of that overly innocent tone and I refuse to believe I'm particularly dense!"

"Not dense," responded Vincent quickly, "but still unconvinced that Georgi is so unlike other women that she will not be led by wiser heads. Ours, I mean."

"I think I begin to see why you wish to visit Lord Tivington. His is a wiser head to which she might pay attention?"

"I repeat. You are not dense," Vincent retorted in that quick way of his. He then changed the subject and they completed their ride discussing the war, each making ever more outrageous suggestions as to what Wellington should do in the coming campaign.

Lord Tivington was happy to welcome the men to his study. Georgi's marriage the preceding fall had left the old gentleman feeling very much alone—although his spinster daughters, the Ladies Georgia Marie and Georgina Anne, who lived with him, would have been surprised and insulted to learn of it. Georgi had been the child of his lordship's heart. He had raised her very much as he'd have raised a boy and the resulting woman had, to his mind, been a delight, a constant stimulant, making him stretch his own thinking, and keeping him young.

It had not been easy for Lord Tivington to accept that he could not keep her beside him forever. Once he had, he worried she'd not find a man who would understand that she was not particularly adept at womanly things such as stitching and watercolors, that she had a mind which needed stimulation, and, perhaps worst of all, that she had a creative side she expressed by writing novels.

Lord Everhart had appeared in their lives at just the right moment.

Vincent poured glasses of the light canary his grandfather had recently taken to drinking, serving the other men before taking up his own and taking a seat. Again the talk was general, the discussion lively—but, when one spoke of perceptive men, one immediately thought of Lord Tivington.

"What is it, Vincent?" asked his grandfather. "What has you working yourself into a dither?" added the old gentleman. And then, under his breath, he said, "As if I could not guess, of course."

Vincent grimaced. "Georgi is headed for disaster."

"Again?"

Everhart chuckled at Tivington's dry tone. "Vincent has it in his head she wishes to reconcile Tennytree to his daughter."

Lord Tivington instantly sobered, one brow arching in a characteristic manner. "Impossible."

"That's what we think. Will you talk sense into her?"

"You wish me to deter her from what she would do?"

"You are the only one likely to manage the trick," said Vincent.

"She is married." Tivington turned to Everhart. "Surely . . ."

"You would suggest she should listen to *me?*" asked Everhart quietly when the sentence trailed off to nothing.

Lord Tivington grinned and his eyes danced. "*Should* listen? Of course she *should.* It is the way of the world that a wife listens and obeys her husband, is it not?"

"But," said Vincent, not in the mood for levity, "we speak of *Georgi.* You must do something, Grandfather."

Lord Tivington's fingertips came together, tenting, his forefingers touching his chin. "Do something . . . Has it never occurred to you, Vincent—" His eyes rose suddenly, his keen gaze catching and holding his grandson's. "—that Georgi never *has* come to fiddlestick's end? That she *always* comes up smelling like a rose? That whatever outrageousness she plots, the seeds she plants *invariably* result in a successful crop come harvest time?" Unknowingly, he had, with this last image, completed Vincent's earlier figure of speech. "And," he added, grinning broadly, "if you think to say that was a mixed up mess of metaphors, a stewpot into which I threw anything and everything, then you are free to say so. But, however *you* would say it, you know what *I* say is true."

"You suggest she can manipulate Tennytree as she does the rest of the world?"

Lord Tivington grimaced. "No. What I suspect is that she has no intention of *manipulating* his lordship." His lordship's voice was exceptionally dry. "Georgi is not stupid. If you will stop and think you will admit she never attempts the impossible."

"You didn't see her, Grandfather," said Vincent, something one might call a touch of desperation in his voice. "She is *plotting.* She had that *look. You* know it. It is unmistakable."

"I do not believe I suggested that she does not plot," said Lord Tivington mildly. "I merely said that whatever it is she plots will harm no one and is very likely to do a great deal of good. Now, I believe your aunts would like to see you, Vincent. Lord Everhart? Will you come and make your bow to my daughters?"

Vincent knew he'd get no more from the old gentleman. *As usual,* he thought wryly, *it is up to me to see that Georgi doesn't fall into the briars*. It was with great surprise that Vincent realized he didn't mind. In fact, what he *felt* was something approaching *relief*. He searched his mind and heart for *why* he felt that way.

Half chagrinned, half rebellious, he found the answer. It seemed that after all, he hadn't lost Georgi to her marriage. *His cousin still needed him.*

CHAPTER 4

While checking the house to see that all was ready for her guests, most of Georgi's mind was occupied with her uninvited guest.

Guests, she reminded herself. *I must not forget the boy. Tal. Talavera. Such an odd name.* But the boy and his name were unimportant. *Except he is not,* she decided. *It is possible he is very important.*

It would not be difficult to bring Mrs. Garth and Lord Wakefield, an *invited* guest, together again. This time, they could meet in a manner that might lead to the desired result. Unlike the first time, Wakefield could woo his runaway bride properly. After all, men married widows all the time. Especially when the widow was endowed with a competence that stood as a dowry. It had required only a trifling bit of guile to determine that Penelope's *did,* that it was not tied to Lieutenant Garth's family, reverting to them at the widow's remarriage. So that was no problem.

But some men did not marry widows with children with *equal* alacrity. They wanted their own offspring and had such odd notions about those of other men. Especially *male* children.

Such thoughts had rampaged through her mind as Georgi spent a housewifely hour with her housekeeper. In the Tapestry Room, a third floor guest chamber, Georgi pointed out that the towels provided were a bit frayed, not at all in proper condition for a guest's use. The housekeeper immediately glared at the maid. The maid, her color high—because it had not been *her* fault—collected the towels and hurried off to find proper replacements.

Georgi moved on. In another room her eagle eye noted that one of the drapes was not properly tied back. She took care of the problem herself, much to the housekeeper's chagrin and, without a glance at the woman—which was still more worrisome—moved on again. This room was in perfect condition as was the next and the next.

A few more minor problems solved and the housekeeper breathed again as they returned to the ground floor. There Georgi bustled into the butler's pantry, dismissed the housekeeper with compliments on a job well done, and turned her mind to inspecting china and glassware. The silver was polished to a see-yourself-in-it shine and she complimented the butler. He, in stately fashion, offered to pass on her praise to the young footman who had accomplished the miracle. She nodded, changed a few orders as to which china service was to be used at which meal, and left him, thankful that her only remaining chore was a discussion with her cook. Cooks were always the touchiest of servants . . .

She entered the kitchen. Cook folded her arms in her apron and, stolid as stone, listened with equal disdain to Georgi's praise of her work and the few new orders for the first few company meals. It was, after all, her kitchen and she allowed no one to question her decisions—although she was quite willing, since it did not interfere to any great degree, to provide the particular menus prescribed by Lady Everhart.

Lady Everhart, after all, did not demand the impossible—turtle soup when there were no turtles to be had, for instance. Nor did she express a desire that fancy fairy cakes be provided for tea just when one was in the process of producing a complicated dinner for a dozen extra guests. Nor did she change her mind about a menu hours too late, long after it would be impossible to carry out the new orders.

Cook would never allow Lady Everhart to know it, but her ladyship was the easiest mistress with whom Cook had ever had to deal. However, it would not do to allow her ladyship to realize she had such an advantage. One never knew when one might need to put one's oversized foot down, setting it squarely onto some command, and insist one could not under any circumstances accomplish such a thing.

Besides, Cook had ambitions. She meant to replace the fancy French chef who presided over the Everharts' London kitchens—although she'd allow herself to be nibbled to death by ducks before she'd admit such a thing to anyone at all.

Georgi, unaware of either the esteem in which she was held or Cook's ambitions, was suitably humble in making her few changes and Cook was suitably gracious in accepting them. The two parted with mutual sighs of satisfaction, each aware it could have been far more difficult to achieve one's ends.

Leaving the kitchen for the hall, Georgi took a moment to consider whether there was anything left undone. She reviewed her list of things to check, discovered she'd completed it, nodded one firm little nod and, feeling free as a bird, headed for the stairs.

She would see if Mrs. Garth would care to take advantage of the exceptionally nice weather to go riding.

Penelope dithered. She owned a habit, old and well worn, and had, before her marriage, loved to ride. While in the Peninsula she had, far more then she cared to remember, ridden long miles through rough Portuguese terrain, climbing steep grades or, worse, going down the other side and often in weather that made it all rather worse than merely impossible. At other times she'd been forced to cross hot, dry, exceedingly dusty Spanish plains with an enemy army far too near one's heels for comfort. As Kennet's wife she had ridden because she had to and not because she wanted to and, as a result, had very nearly forgotten one might ride merely for the pleasure of it.

She glanced at her son who chortled at something the young maid did. Most likely the girl was making faces at him, an entertainment that kept Tal amused for as long as Matty would keep it up. Penelope's child did not need her and she felt a pang at the thought. She had known the day would come, but she had believed it to be far in the future. Not, perhaps, until she had to send him to school, or apprentice him to some trade, or, worst of all, allow his Scottish family to buy him a commission. *Not,* she prayed, the latter. She did not wish to lose her son to battle as she'd lost her husband, but if that were the boy's choice . . .

But this was not the time to be thinking of such things.

"Ride? I used to enjoy it," she said to Lady Everhart with that tiny stress in the phrasing that indicated uncertainty.

Georgi chuckled. "What you mean is that you've not had an opportunity to ride for no reason at all for so long you do not know if you would still enjoy it? Do come," she coaxed. "We will simply ramble about the estate and I will show you my favorite places. There is a river and a mill and a new bridge where the old one collapsed, nearly drowning me and . . ."

"Collapsed? Drowned?"

Georgi grinned. "It was a race. I lost. And nearly lost my life. I will tell you as we ride. Will it take you long to change?"

"Twenty minutes," said Penelope, giving in. With one last look toward her son, she moved to her room. In the doorway, she turned. "You will provide a gentle mount, will you not?

I've no desire to try riding for pleasure with a hardmouthed stubborn beast with whom I must fight for control."

Georgi laughed. "Everhart would not have such a creature in his stables," she said. "I promise we'll take no fences flying or indulge in any racing. Come down when you are ready. I'll have the mares at the front door."

It was nearer half an hour before the two rode off together. After complimenting Georgi on the horses, Penelope asked how long she and Everhart had been married. Talk of the wedding, at which the Prince Regent was a guest, took them down the lane, across the road, and through a gate opened for them by the groom who followed at a discreet distance. A meadow spread out before them and Georgi glanced at Penelope who bit her lip and looked slightly guilty.

Rueful, Penelope shook her head. "I did say I wanted a gentle ride, did I not?"

"Have you changed your mind?" asked Georgi, almost hiding a laugh.

"It's been so long . . ." Penelope bit her lip again. "I'll suffer for it tomorrow, but *yes.* Do let's."

They put heel to flank and, obligingly, the mares lengthened their stride. The women pulled up at the far end of the meadow and looked at each other. And grinned.

"You were right," said Penelope. "I do like riding. It is just that for so long riding meant long punishing days crossing difficult country and often with the enemy nipping at one's heels. I had forgotten what it is like to merely *ride.*"

"Now you have rediscovered the joy of it, do feel free to go out whenever you wish," Georgi repeated her earlier invitation. "The river is a boundary, but Beverly Place is on the other side and you may ride there as freely as here. There—" she pointed with her crop. "—is the new bridge. I have not yet found time to examine it. Shall we go on?"

The distant bridge was barely in view. Penelope judged it to be getting on for a mile. "I am already likely to wish I'd

merely ambled up and down the drive a few times, so riding
farther is unlikely to do more damage. Let us go."

She was off before Georgi realized what she meant to do,
and Georgi, pleased that Penelope was not a prissy dawdling
sort of rider, took off as well. They crossed the intervening
fields at an easy ground-covering lope and were soon reining
in near the river.

"How beautiful," exclaimed Penelope. "The design is not
one I've seen before."

Georgi looked surprised as well. "Aaron must have designed it. Aaron Sedgewycke," she added when Penelope cast
her a look of inquiry. "Late last summer he married Cassandra.
A cousin," she added, in case Penelope had forgotten the rami-
fications of the Beverly family. "He's an inventor and works
with engineers building things like bridges."

"He works?"

"By choice. His inventions have made him amazingly
wealthy. I hadn't a notion Aaron had a hand in this particular
bridge but I am sure he must have. I will ask Everhart." She
studied the intricate ironwork that decorated the arched under-
pinnings as well as the delicate railings. "Everhart indulged
him outrageously," she scolded. "This is far too fancy for a
country lane from nothing to nowhere."

There was a whoosh of sound and both women turned
their mounts. Water had been let into the spillway and, gradually, reluctantly, a mill wheel began a creaky turn.

"Not exactly to nowhere," said Penelope, tongue in cheek.

Georgi nodded. "That was another thing poor Everhart
had to do. His elderly relative from whom he inherited Minnow
Manor had allowed all to go to rack and ruin. Among other
things, the mill had fallen into disuse which put a hardship
on the local people who were forced to take their grain many
extra miles to get it ground. I don't know where he found the
new miller, but I have heard nothing but good about him and
his wife . . ."

"I don't recall that I have ever been this near a working mill," said Penelope, shifting in her saddle.

Georgi brightened. "We will visit it. Mrs. Berring is certain to ask if we'd like tea and perhaps she'll have a scone. I find our ride has made me thirsty and I can always eat . . ."

"And besides, you wish to check on your husband's new tenants?"

"There is that," admitted Georgi, her eyes sparkling with humor. "I am so glad you do not need things explained to you. My cousin Cassandra would, quite seriously, have insisted we go directly home, if I were hungry, since one could not possibly submit one's clothing to the dust one is bound to find in even the best kept mill."

"She worries about her appearance?"

"Very nearly to the exclusion of everything else! She and Sedgie will be visiting my grandfather over the holidays. My uncle and his wife will also come and another cousin and his wife." Georgi bit her lip. "I hope," she said a trifle diffidently, "you will not be shocked when you meet George Elliot's wife. She is Sedgie's sister and of good birth, but she is quite frankly something of a miser. She is quite open about it. When very young, she married an elderly cit who left her *very* well-to-do. He also taught her to understand business and she decided she would remarry only if her right to control her fortune was written into the marriage contracts."

"She sounds a rather odd sort of woman, but you needn't sound defensive. I have managed to latch onto the clue that you like her."

Georgi choked on a rather embarrassed little laugh. "There are no flies on you!"

"Oh, I've something other than feathers in my cockloft," said Penelope, tongue in cheek.

"Yes," retorted Georgi, "no part of *your* attic is to let."

"No, the old bone box has a few things rattling around in it."

"*My* noggin is overstuffed with extremely odd bits and pieces, or so think many of my acquaintances. Grandfather saw to that."

Both women burst into unladylike guffaws. Penelope, still chuckling, said, "We seem to have come out about even in that ridiculous contest. Tell me about your grandfather. I recall him as a rigidly stiff-backed old gentleman. I remember that I was rather frightened of him."

"Then you didn't know him. Not at all. A kinder, more caring man does not exist. I do not exclude Everhart, whom I love with all my heart, when I say there is no better man than Grandfather."

"Tell me," said Penelope, curious about her hostess—to say nothing of the fact that what she learned of Georgi would probably tell her something about Vincent—Mr. Beverly—as well. Then she not only wondered at the depth of her curiosity, but found it worrying that she'd begun thinking of the cousins by their given names. It was not done. Certainly not when one had only been introduced a day or two earlier and then under awkward circumstances.

Georgi loved talking about her grandfather and explained how she and Vincent were taken in after their parents died, all four together, in an accident. She explained that they were reared together like brother and sister, that she was allowed to join Vincent's studies with his tutor and then, when Vincent went off to school, Grandfather turned his hand to her education—once he rid Georgi of the governess her aunts hired, finding the woman at least as incompetent as Georgi had believed her to be.

". . . which was something my aunts did *not* approve. With the loss of the ladylike Miss Milton, poor Aunt Marie despaired of my ever wedding anyone and Aunt Anne was forever doing her best to curb my independence and turn me into a pattern card of respectability. She would be appalled that first Grandfather and now Everhart encourage my greatest absurdity, something we keep a deep dark secret from the aunts."

"And that is?"

Georgi straightened in her saddle, suddenly realizing she'd allowed her tongue to wag beyond what she'd meant it to do. She bit her lip, glancing sideways at the woman who rode beside her. "I believe I can trust you . . ." she said, a tentative note to be heard for the very first time in their brief acquaintance.

"You have no reason to assume you may do so, but I assure you I'll not stain," Penelope responded, using still more of the cant vocabulary she'd absorbed while following the drum.

Georgi nodded. Vincent had, from an early age, seen to her education in that regard, and there was little cant *she* didn't know. Certainly she knew all the more reasonably acceptable bits and more than she should admit of what was not!

She drew in a deep breath. "I write," she admitted, again glancing sideways. "Novels. Novels of the most absurd sort, complete with die-away heroines and perfectly heroic heroes and the most villainous of villains . . . You know the sort of thing I mean?"

"Minerva Press!" Penelope laughed. "I read them avidly. Some of us were occasionally sent those marble-backed volumes as gifts. New ones were greatly prized and passed from hand to hand, each of us awaiting our turn with great impatience."

"Then," said Georgi, "perhaps you have read mine. I will show you when we return—but here we are." She waited for the groom to help her dismount and was surprised to see Penelope already on the ground when she was released from the respectful groom's helping hands.

Penelope, noticing, grimaced. "I should have waited. I

must learn that I no longer need be utterly independent and able to do all sorts of things for myself. It was necessary in the Peninsula, of course."

An hour later they'd returned to Minnow Manor where Georgi, rather diffidently, showed Penelope her published work. Penelope admitted to having read and enjoyed one of the novels, chose a second, and, clutching its three volumes, disappeared up the stairs. Georgi, after a word with her butler, followed.

Dinner would be in less than two hours, since they kept country hours. Both women had to change from riding gear to evening gowns before coming down to it. Penelope stared longingly at the novel, wishing she had not agreed to dine with the others but might dive right into it and then, with a sigh, took out her only gown halfway suitable for evening wear, a high necked dark gray silk trimmed with tiny white frills, one arching across her bosom and the other around the hem.

Vincent changed for dinner somewhat early and descended to the library, which was the Everharts' favorite room and where they met, informally, before a family dinner. He was dipping into Georgi's latest novel, which he had not yet read, when the door opened.

The butler looked in, saw that the room was occupied and announced, "Lord Wakefield."

Vincent's head snapped up and he felt his spine stiffen. Wakefield? He was expected the next day or even later in the week. No one was prepared for him . . . especially Mrs. Garth, who, he'd been pleased to learn, meant to come down to dinner that evening.

Vincent turned. "Remington," he said, nodding. "I heard you were invited."

"Vincent . . . I suppose," said Lord Wakefield in his faintly prissy manner, "I should have guess *you'd* be here, although I'd have thought Everhart would have—" He stopped abruptly in the midst of what would have been an insult, quickly changing it. "—assumed you'd be elsewhere."

Vincent blinked. "Where else?"

"Beverly Place, perhaps?"

Why, wondered Vincent, *am I hearing animosity?*

"But then," continued Wakefield, "you are always in the midst of trouble, are you not?"

"Trouble?" Vincent felt still more wary.

"Oh yes. I think so." Wakefield's manner was still more starched up. "You thrive on controversy, do you not?" His nose lifted a trifle. "I am informed I must be prepared to meet the woman who jilted me without a word of explanation!"

"Ah," said Vincent, enlightened. "The woman who hadn't a clue she was to be forced to marry you until she was fitted for her wedding gown? The woman whose father would not allow her to communicate with you?"

"I see. Or no—" Wakefield frowned. Slowly, his tense body relaxed, but only slightly. He shook his head as if to rid it of some confusion. "—I do *not* see." A sneer grew more pronounced. "But I am certain," he said, at his prissiest, "you will enlighten me."

Vincent grimaced, but obeyed the implicit invitation. "She had fallen in love with another man. Her father forbade the marriage. She ran off with her soldier when she learned she was about to be brought, a sacrificial lamb, to the altar at which she was expected to wed you, a man she'd spoken to perhaps twice and then only in company and concerning the most trite of subjects." Vincent shrugged. "What would you have had her do?"

"Sacrificial lamb." Wakefield's heavy brows climbed his abnormally high forehead.

Vincent grimaced ever so slightly, feeling faintly absurd. "That *was* a trifle overly dramatic, was it not? How did you learn she was here?" he asked in order to change the subject away from himself.

Wakefield's brows again climbed his forehead, again joining a sneer. "Her father, of course. I see him occasionally and I stopped on my way here. I admit that I'd intended staying there the night, but his . . ." The precise voice trailed off, the man's eyes searching the room as if the right word might be hiding there.

"Ranting?" supplied Vincent.

Wakefield laughed a high strain-filled laugh. "The *least* of it. If you must have it, he was a dead bore on the subject." He cast Vincent a speculative glance and then, rather offhandedly, said, "*He* claims she was never wed."

Vincent felt himself stiffen. "I must presume that Tennytree, in his usual absurd fashion, disapproves a Scottish marriage. She *was* wed, however, and from her husband's home."

Wakefield, looking guilty, sighed. "I should not have insinuated I thought otherwise. I had a friend, a Scotsman, check on the legality of it at the time."

Vincent's brows edged nearer each other. *Why did Wakefield go to the bother of checking?* he wondered. *Everyone knows such marriages are legal.*

Wakefield laughed again, this time a bitter sound. "You will forgive me, Vincent, given your reputation, for wondering if she has succumbed to *your* well-known wiles—as Tennytree insists?" His brows rose. "Has she?"

Vincent found himself fighting to contain his temper. His teeth gritted and his eyes flashed. "She has not. My only role in her arrival at Minnow Manor was to save her from freezing to death and bringing her, at once, to Georgi."

"Freezing?" Wakefield's brows were particularly mobile and now rose exceedingly high. "*More* drama, Vincent?" he sneered.

"Nothing but the outrageous truth. Did your would-be father-in-law explain to you that he cast her from his door into a storm? With no offer of transport? That she managed to make it to the inn where she was told there was no room?" Vincent frowned. "I never learned where she was headed when I discovered her, exhausted and miles from anywhere and ready to give up. I brought her here . . ."

Penelope, standing rigid outside the library door, listened. Behind her, unbeknownst to her, Lord Everhart also listened. Penelope, very near to bursting into tears, turned and ran straight into his lordship. He took her shoulders in gentle hands and held her still.

"You are a proud woman," he said softly. "And you have done nothing of which you need be ashamed. You will go in there and you will hold your head high." He shook her ever so slightly. "I will support you. So will Georgi. And Vincent. Wakefield will come down out of the bows. I know him, Mrs. Garth, and he is not one to hold a grudge when there is no reason."

"It will be so embarrassing."

"For whom? Remington? Lord Wakefield, I should say. For my wife and myself? For Vincent?"

"For *me*."

"Ah. But not for long and then it will be over and we may all be comfortable." Lord Everhart looked around. "Georgi, come tell Mrs. Garth that Lord Wakefield is not an ogre."

"Lord Wakefield is not an ogre," repeated Georgi obediently. "He is not, I assume?" she asked her husband before turning to Penelope. "Why do you think he is?"

Penelope cast Lord Everhart a look pregnant with the embarrassment she'd said she'd feel. He chuckled. "Wakefield has arrived, Georgi, and is stoked with Lord Tennytree's vicious accusations. Vincent has been disillusioning him. I cannot promise all will be *instantly* well . . ." He gave Penelope a look filled with sympathy.

Georgi rolled her eyes. "Your father, Penelope, has a great deal for which he must answer."

But Penelope, who was no coward, had regained her poise under the soothing effect of Everhart's voice and Georgi's friendship. "Yes. But I believe I do owe Lord Wakefield an apology. I should have found a way of sending him an explanation of why I did what I did, explaining the way of it." She sighed. "My father was the obstacle, forcing me to run away as he did. He has been the serpent in my garden from an early age, always testing me, never satisfied. Some will say I failed when I ran off with my Kennet, but, at the time, I saw no other solution."

"Lord Tennytree said you'd agreed to wed me," said Wakefield from the door to the library. His tone held only a mild element of accusation.

"He lied." Penelope Garth turned, her back straight and her chin high. Faced by the man she'd jilted, she wondered how long he'd been listening.

Wakefield nodded. "I have just been told you were unaware of his plans for us, but was there no way you could tell me they were against your wishes? It seems you found it quite easy to reach your *lieutenant's* ears." Still that hint of disbelief, of long-held anger.

"*Not* easy." Penelope's straight spine stiffened. Her chin rose. "*Not at all easy.* My maid was forced to sneak away in the depths of the night. She carried two carpetbags. I followed an hour later lugging a third. If she had not reached Kennet, which she did with a great deal of resource, I'd have been in grave difficulties. My plan, you see, was for Kennet to come to where I awaited him and that we leave at once, that very night."

"But the two of you did *not* leave. *You* disappeared. That is true enough, but it was *days* before Lieutenant Garth took a leave of absence to visit his parents."

Penelope sighed. "I was very young and naïve. It was, of

course, impossible for him to simply turn away from his duty and go off with me at once. Instead he sent his batman to me and the man escorted my maid and myself north. We both wore her clothes and pretended to be the man's sisters. The Royal Mail took us to Edinburgh where he hired a post chaise and escorted us to Kennet's father's house. Kennet sent along a letter explaining my arrival and his family welcomed me. Kennet and I wed the day after he arrived home."

"That explains what I discovered as to dates." Wakefield nodded. "I will admit that I wondered about that period between your leaving your father's roof and your marriage," he said with more of that nasty sly insinuation in his tone.

Penelope remained still, her steady gaze locked with his.

Wakefield sighed. "I apologize," he said in his mincing manner. "It was true that I wondered, but unforgivable of me to say it."

She nodded. "I will accept your apology if you accept mine."

Only Vincent saw that Georgi held her breath, waiting to see how Wakefield responded. That expectant, hopeful look on his cousin's face informed him what she had in mind for Penelope—which, as his grandfather had suggested, was *not* the impossible.

Although glad his cousin did not mean to attempt to reconcile Lord Tennytree and his daughter, Vincent was, nevertheless, instantly overcome with a strong sense of denial of her true goal. *Remington, Lord Wakefield, would not do for Penelope Garth.* He was not the man for her. The feeling was so strong Vincent sat down abruptly, wondering why he felt as if he'd gone off his horse at a regular oxer, landing with a breathtaking thump well beyond the hedge-and-rail style fence.

CHAPTER 5

Penelope made a quick survey of the room. Too many, too interested, faces stared—politely, of course—and she felt heat rising up into her throat. She glanced at Wakefield who also, it seemed, only then realized they were not alone.

She turned slightly, met Vincent's steady gaze—he'd returned to his feet with no one noticing—and the blush worsened for reasons she didn't understand . . . and, once she felt the heat, didn't *wish* to understand. Why Vincent Beverly's opinion had become important to her was not important. That it had, and far too quickly, was absolutely ridiculous. He was nothing to her.

Well, that wasn't exactly true. He'd rescued her—and more importantly, her son as well—when she'd so very nearly succumbed to weariness and the cold, and had wished nothing more than to slide to the ground and sleep.

And, of course, given the weather, never wake up.

"What?" she asked, startled.

"I said that of course I forgive you," repeated Wakefield testily. "I should have insisted, at the time of our engagement, on seeing you and have demanded a period of time in which we might become acquainted. I should not have accepted your father's insistence that all be completed instantly. My only excuse was—" Wakefield glanced quickly around the room. "—the impetuosity of youth," he finished.

More than one listener, Vincent in particular, felt his lordship had censored the words on the tip of his tongue to the relatively meaningless phrase. He wondered what his lordship had almost said.

"Thank you for your generosity," said Penelope. She wondered how they were to end this embarrassing discussion and, without thinking, turned her gaze, once again, toward Vincent, unconsciously asking for help.

Vincent stepped forward. Languidly, his tone one of boredom, he said he was glad that was settled and asked Lord Wakefield if he cared for a glass of wine before dinner was announced. Taking Wakefield by the arm, he inexorably led his lordship toward a side table on which several decanters and sparkling crystal glasses awaited those wishing to slake their thirst.

"Were the roads difficult?" he demanded as he poured a ruby colored wine into one of the glasses and handed it to his lordship.

Penelope's heartbeat slowed. It would be all right. Thanks to Vincent Beverly it was over. Well, nearly over. After this one dinner she would be isolated in the nursery and need not, ever again, speak with Lord Wakefield, need never feel that . . . *hunted* feeling the intensity of his dark look induced.

What, she wondered, *does the man want with me?*

Because something convinced her that he still *wanted.* It was there whenever he caught and held her gaze. Even when he had looked his most challenging, his most disapproving, his most *superior,* there had been that . . . that *heat* that chilled her to her core. *Heat without desire.* She had seen desire in men's eyes and knew it. Recognized it. This was . . . different. She shuddered.

Dinner was nearly over when Lord Wakefield turned that gaze, once again, on Penelope. "I hope you mean to sing to us this evening," he said.

The words were polite, but there was something approaching an order in the intensity of his tone. Penelope stiffened. "Sing?"

"I recall your voice vividly. There was a depth and beauty to it that was indescribable. It has, I am certain, only improved with age."

"I have not sung since my . . . since before Talavera," said Penelope. "I have no desire to sing. I doubt I ever will again," she finished, her eyes heavy with sadness, with regret, with memories . . .

"Of course you need not sing if you do not wish it," said Vincent before Remington Wakefield could voice the thought his frown suggested was about to be expressed. "We understand that you are still in mourning."

Wakefield turned his body in order to glare at Vincent, his tight coat and overly large cravat making it impossible to merely turn his head. "You, obviously, have no understanding of the true artist!" he said, sputtering. "She *must* wish to sing, wish to express her emotions in the way she does it best. It is what drives a great musician or a poet or an artist. They *use* their emotions. Emotions fuel their talent."

"If that is true, then I am not a great musician," said Penelope. "I've no desire whatsoever to express myself musically. In fact, the very thought of trying to sing makes me feel ill." She nodded to the footman hovering at her shoulder, accepting a serving of a syrup covered compote that held no appeal but which would be an excuse to avoid more conversation on the subject of her singing.

"You must sing!"

Her spoon halfway to her mouth, Penelope looked up and across the table where her gaze met Wakefield's demanding expression. "Must?" she asked, her tone cold.

"Of course you must." One could see the man force relaxation into stiff shoulders, force calm on himself. Far more
pacifically, he added, "It would be a sin to hide such talent,"
he said, coaxingly. "You cannot do it. The world needs to
hear your voice."

"It sounds to me," said Vincent, "that it is *you* who needs
to hear it. Why?"

The blunt question brought red climbing above Wakefield's
snowy white cravat and into his cheeks. "*You've* never heard
her," he choked out. "Her voice . . . incredible. Unforgettable.
A God-given talent. It must not be wasted."

"You would have Mrs. Garth become a stage singer?"
asked Lord Everhart calmly.

"No! Of course not. I suggest nothing of the sort!" Wakefield cast a harassed glance toward his host and then turned
that piercing stare she hated back onto Penelope. "You cannot mean you will never sing again. Impossible. *I will not
allow it.*"

Vincent remembered some things about Wakefield that
brought a glimmer of light to the conversation. "I think I
begin to understand. You have a passion for music, do you
not?"

Wakefield turned the glare toward Vincent but only for an
instant. The scalding force of it returned instantly to Penelope.
"For *good* music, yes." He held Penelope's gaze locked to
his. "It is like . . . like a fire in the blood. Like good wine
singing through one's body. You must know what I mean."
There was almost a pleading note to that. "Like . . . like . . ."
He shook his head. "How to explain . . ." He hesitated before
adding, "It is *ecstasy.*"

"And you would force Mrs. Garth to provide you with that
ecstasy in spite of her wish that she not be asked to sing?"

The soft question dangled in the silence. Wakefield's mouth
tightened. After a moment, with difficulty, he said, "You do
not understand . . ."

"Obviously we do not. Perhaps it is that *I* was reared to believe people should not be forced to do what they do not wish to do—not when that thing is neither necessary to their well-being nor—"

Vincent was interrupted, Wakefield's voice louder than before. "But it *is* necessary. She is a Voice. She must use that Voice or she will be less than whole."

Vincent's voice rose as well, to cover Wakefield's voice. "—made to entertain another because the other craves entertainment." Vincent looked down at his dessert and pushed it aside. He looked up at his cousin who had been seated in silence during the whole of the argument—which was unlike her. He caught her attention and, very slightly, jerked his head toward the door.

Instantly Georgi rose to her feet. "I see you, too, have finished, Penelope. Shall we leave the men to their port?"

Penelope, thankful, followed Georgi from the dining room. Once the door closed behind them, she put her hand on her hostess's arm. "I do not feel I can face him again."

Georgi bit her lip. "I do not understand him. I thought he loved you?"

"I had no knowledge of love. From what has happened tonight, I fear it was my voice he wished to marry far more than he wished to marry *me*. If that makes sense." She frowned. "I am glad I had the courage to elope with my Kennet. If you will excuse me," she finished before Georgi could respond, "I will go up now. You will understand."

Georgi was in a quandary, her plans fallen into disarray around her. She needed time alone nearly as badly as Penelope did. "Of course." She reached up and kissed the air near Penelope's cheek. "I am so sorry you were embarrassed in that way. Truly, Lord Wakefield was not due until tomorrow."

"It was, I think, my father's doing that he arrived early," said Penelope and sighed. "I don't know if he wished to cause trouble or if he thought perhaps Wakefield could manage to put things right. From my father's point of view, of course."

Georgi had had that very notion, hoping to bring the two together herself, but it would not do. All her plans lay in tatters. She no longer believed that Lord Wakefield loved her unexpected guest or that he could make Penelope love him back but, above all, she could not believe he'd make her new friend happy.

"I understand," she said on a sigh. "We'll see you in the morning."

Georgi watched Penelope climb the stairs. Her guest looked like a much older woman as she held the railing tightly and made her slow way up them. Penelope turned a corner and gradually the sound of her passage disappeared.

"Now what?" Georgi asked of no one at all. She was as determined as ever to make things right for the widow—but stymied, for the nonce, as to how that could be accomplished.

Penelope hesitated before going down to breakfast the next morning, but it felt wrong to ask a servant to carry up meals when there was no special reason for it—she was neither ill nor incapacitated. And it was especially wrong when it meant a footman or maid must climb so many stairs when every maid and footman must already be run off their feet.

Penelope had found it nearly impossible to fall asleep the night before, the scene at dinner going through her mind again and again. When she was not thinking of Wakefield's words, she was remembering. Remembering dark nights when Kennet's friends asked her to sing to them. They had been especially demanding just before a battle, and Penelope now wondered if there was something to his lordship's praise of her voice. She recalled the songs that had been requested.

Often they were sentimental songs of home and love. Of peace and tranquility. Or humorous songs. But never, ever, had a rousing paean to battle been requested . . .

And when, hoarse, she told them she could sing no more, the men would thank her and fade into the night. And, from some small distance, hidden by the dark, there would be a rustling, a sound of furtive movement. Frightened the first time she heard it, she asked Kennet what it was and he'd told her many of the enlisted men came to listen to her as well, that after she'd finished singing they found it easier to sleep, easier to gain the rest needed before facing the enemy the next day.

"But," she told herself, "that does not mean my voice was so special. It was only that the men needed distraction, that I was the only one available, that no one else . . ."

But was that true?

She stood staring down at her sleeping son and recalled songfests during winter cantonments when a great number of good voices were raised in song. So why was it only herself who was asked to sing before a battle? Had the *men* believed there was something special about her voice?

And if there was?

"So Lord Wakefield would force me to sing for others? Because he believes my voice pleases to a greater degree than other voices can?" She shook her head. "Besides . . ." She bit her lip, forcing back that thought, but it slipped under her guard.

I cannot. No. Even if I . . .

Again she forced the thought away. She stared at her child. She felt a stirring of surprise. She had never sung for her son. Did not most mothers sing lullabies to their children? Why had she never wished to sing to Tal? Never thought to try . . .

Because she hadn't. Even on those rare occasions when

the babe had fussed or would not go to sleep or when he was so ill . . . never had she sung to him.

Why? But she *knew* why. She swallowed. Hard.

Penelope stared at Tal who stirred, made a few funny little mewling noises, and slid back into deeper sleep. Once Penelope had loved to sing. Occasionally, in those days before she lost Kennet, she had felt as Wakefield said as if she *had* to sing. That it was *essential* to her that she sing.

But that feeling had not come to her for a long time now . . .

Penelope frowned. Not since before Talavera . . . Her throat tightened.

Talavera. Kennet's last battle. He had gone off cheerfully, telling her he'd no notion when he'd return. And then, when she had managed to pull herself together and turn to packing their possessions, readying them to move quickly if that became necessary, he was back. He had taken her in his arms, smiled down at her as if he wished to memorize her face, kissed her tenderly, and, once again gone off, this time whistling the last tune she'd sung the evening before, a soft lilting Irish tune of home and fire and love and peace.

Of peace most of all . . .

Had he known? Had he somehow felt that that would be their last kiss? Surely not. Surely he could have had no presentiment that his life would end that day . . .

Once again Penelope focused on their child. She felt tears rising, drowning her eyes, and blinked rapidly. Vincent Beverly had said that Kennet *knew.* That Kennet was *happy* there was a child, a son . . . A tight smile tipped the corners of Penelope's mouth and the tears receded. Kennet *knew.*

And—she tipped her chin to a stubborn angle—if she no longer wished to sing, there was no earthly reason why she *should.*

Matty came into the room just then, carrying a pile of

Tal's little dresses, newly washed and ironed. "Mrs. Garth," said the maid, halting, hesitating . . .

"Come in. I was about to go down to breakfast. My, you have been up early to have accomplished all that," said Penelope, praising the maid.

" 'Tis a pleasure, handling such lovely things. You do really lovely needlework, Mrs. Garth." Matty touched tiny blue forget-me-nots that decorated the neckline of the top garment. "Such fine cloth. Presses up a treat, it does," she said.

Penelope chuckled. "I suspect I decorated things a trifle too much since Tal turned out to be a boy. But he'll never know, and I'll do things differently when he needs larger clothes . . ."

Matty laughed, a trilling sound that made Tal open his eyes and blink. The child looked around, saw his mother and raised his arms. Penelope picked him up, wrinkling her nose. "Oh dear," she said.

Matty reached for him. "We can take care of that problem, can't we Tal?" she asked and the boy grinned at her, going to her easily. "You go eat. It's getting late, you know."

Penelope lifted the tiny watch pinned to her bodice, grimaced, and agreed. "*Too* late. They will have cleaned away breakfast and I will find it necessary to upset Cook in her kitchen, when I steal an apple or a slice of bread and cheese."

But she was not too late. Georgi lingered over a last cup of tea and looked up, smiling to see Penelope. "Good. I wondered if you were ill. Or . . ." She bit her lip, her gaze flying to Penelope's face.

"Or if I'd decided to avoid coming down at all? I have never liked bullies, my lady. I'll not allow this one to ruin your Christmas party. Ah! Shirred eggs," she said, forcing lightness to her tone. "My favorite."

The eggs, which had been put out much earlier, had begun to dry, but Penelope found a portion that was still moist and tasty. A footman brought coffee and fresh toast only a few minutes after she'd seated herself. He poured her a cup of the steaming dark liquid before returning to his post just outside the breakfast room door.

"Has . . . everyone else eaten?" asked Penelope. She looked up from the cream she poured into her coffee, not quite as sanguine about facing Wakefield again as she'd suggested.

"The men ate earlier and went off. Vincent wished to inspect Beverly Place land, as he does whenever he is home, and I think my husband meant to check on the condition of a couple of fields he ordered drained last fall. We've been at his primary estate since our marriage during the Little Season last autumn and this is the first opportunity he's had to see how things were done."

"And my bête noire?" asked Penelope, her voice dry.

Georgi looked troubled. "He went with Everhart. Do not concern yourself. They'll not return until late."

"It will take that long for Lord Everhart to inspect the drainage ditches?"

Georgi grinned. "No, but I told him I hoped the two of them would enjoy a nice *long* ride, so I'm sure they will." Her eyes twinkled. "Others should arrive before they return."

"Which will dilute the intensity of Lord Wakefield's attentions." Penelope smiled. "Thank you. I feel better already."

Georgi sobered. "I do not understand the man."

Penelope's smile faded as well. "Neither do I. His behavior when he discussed my singing . . ." She bit her lip. "Will you think me strange when I tell you he rather frightened me?"

"Not at all," said Georgi promptly. "If he had not, *then* I'd think you strange. Or dense as a post. Since you are not at all stupid, we will discard that notion."

Penelope smiled again. She had, as they talked, eaten her breakfast and poured herself a second cup of coffee. "Tell me what I may do to help. I'm certain there are things you have yet to do . . . ?"

"Much to my surprise, everything is up to snuff. Instead, since I expect no one until sometime this afternoon, let us go for one more ride." Georgi brightened. "We will go to Beverly Place," she suggested, "so that we will not accidentally meet up with your nemesis. I will reintroduce you to my aunts and my grandfather."

"I remember them, although they may not remember me."

Because they departed quickly, they were gone when Lord Wakefield, firmly turning down all Everhart's suggestions for his amusement, returned to the house. He was furious to find his prey had escaped him and that no one could tell him where she had disappeared.

Or, he fumed silently, *would not tell.*

CHAPTER 6

Vincent, finished with his inspection, arrived at Beverly Place in time to join the aunts, Georgi, and Penelope in a light luncheon. The Ladies Marie and Anne were seated one to either side of Penelope, and Penelope was having something of a difficult time of it, attempting to listen to the one question her while, simultaneously, she tried to answer a question the other had just asked.

Vincent went around the table. He kissed Georgi on the cheek, his Aunt Marie, and then, surprising her, Penelope. He finished by placing a smacking kiss alongside Lady Anne's ear.

"You naughty boy!" scolded Lady Anne, the family disciplinarian. "You sit yourself down this instant and behave yourself."

Vincent, winking at Georgi, obeyed and, the instant his napkin was laid across his lap, asked his Aunt Marie for her opinion of Prinny's latest doings.

"We will have none of your tonnish gossip at the table," said Lady Anne sternly.

"Then, my most proper aunt, you suggest a topic of conversation—but one which will allow Mrs. Garth to taste at least a mouthful or two of this very nice fricassee. I've not had rabbit this good since I last visited," he added, looking complacently at his plate and taking another bite in the hopes of avoiding acknowledging his one aunt's irritation with herself and the other's chagrin that they had embarrassed a guest by their interrogation.

"Aunt Marie, since Aunt Anne thinks the Prince an unsuitable topic of conversation, perhaps she will allow you to explain to me why it is that our other aunt has not yet arrived with my uncle and cousins?" asked Georgi, understanding that Vincent hoped to allow Penelope time in which to recover her equanimity—although it had not seemed to her that her new friend was particularly upset by the probing questions with which the aunts pelted her, but was merely finding it difficult to satisfy the both of them and also get a bite to eat.

The conversation instantly turned to family matters. "Then if they are uncertain when they'll arrive, but perhaps not until next week," said Georgi, when the aunts finished explaining, speaking in tandem as they often did, "I must rearrange the seating at my table for day after tomorrow." She frowned ever so slightly. "Aunt Marie," she asked after a moment, "is Lady Houghten still not speaking to Mrs. Mandale?"

Responding to this question along with one or two more of the same ilk took them to the end of the meal and after saying their good-byes and giving thanks for the meal, the three from Minnow Manor joined Lord Tivington in his library.

"Lady Penelope," he said, rising as the three entered, "no one informed me you had honored us with a morning visit." He spoke to Mrs. Garth, but his eyes were on his granddaughter and one could hear that he was irritated.

"We spent an hour with the aunts, Grandfather, and then Vincent arrived in time to join us for a nuncheon. Since you do not eat at this time of day, we thought we'd wait until we'd finished before visiting with you. Besides, that way I knew we'd see you alone." Georgi grinned at her grandfather whose eyes twinkled right back at her. "Do you forgive me for asking that you not be disturbed earlier?"

He chuckled. "You are still a minx, my child, despite growing up when my back was turned and having the impertinence of getting yourself married." He sighed softly. Swallowing poignant memories of times past when his granddaughter spent hours with him, daily, in this very room, he turned to their guest. "Lady Penelope, you are very welcome. It came to my ears you were nearly lost to us the other evening, in that very nasty storm. I am very glad my grandson happened along just when you needed him."

"Far less glad than I, my lord," said Penelope promptly. "But you must call me Mrs. Garth. My father disinherited me and I feel I've no right to the title. That is no loss, however, since I would not, in any case, have used it after my marriage."

Lord Tivington nodded approvingly. He had reservations about women who married beneath their social status but insisted on keeping their titles. Although it was according to social usage, it seemed not quite the thing to his lordship.

"I have read dispatches, Mrs. Garth," he said, "in which your husband's name was mentioned. He was a brave man and a great loss to Wellington. Since I am certain you've no wish to dwell on it, I will, just this once, say I am very sorry for your loss." He drew in a deep breath and turned to Vincent. "I presume you've half a dozen things to report to me concerning the estate. Hedges that need attention. Laxity on the part of a tenant. A drain that was clogged? A barn that spouted leaks?"

Vincent threw back his head and laughed. "Georgi, I have been nicely piqued, repiqued, and capoted," he said, using terms from scoring the game of piquet. "I gracefully concede utter defeat at the hands of an expert." He sobered, the faintest of frowns appearing. "But Grandfather, if you knew exactly what I'd say to you, why is nothing being done about those and a few other more minor problems?"

Lord Tivington, one mobile brow arched, looked up. "Are you saying the work is not going forward?"

Vincent frowned. "Exactly that. Next to nothing has been done since my last visit."

His lordship's frown deepened. "The aunts fuss so if I go out in cold weather that I've not ridden over my acres since I made that inspection with you. I gave orders to my agent that work be started on each and every one of those projects. Vincent . . ."

"Of course I will check into it. I am very happy to do so for you. You know that."

Lord Tivington did know. His deepest regret was that it was his *other* grandson, and not George Vincent, who would one day inherit. Vincent loved Beverly Place with as much passion as did his lordship himself. George Elliot, his other grandson, was not only a namby-pamby wastrel but less intelligent than Vincent. His lordship reminded himself that he had manipulated George Elliot into wedding a woman who knew how to manage him, one who would *not* allow the estate to deteriorate. Unfortunately, she would maintain it for monetary reasons rather than for love of the land and would never understand the Place as it should be understood. Still, it would be saved for future generations . . .

"Grandfather?" Georgi, after a glance at the time, interrupted his thoughts, "I apologize that our visit isn't so long as I'd like, but I must return to Minnow Manor before our first guests arrive. Will you forgive me for taking Mrs. Garth away so quickly?"

"Why do you not remain and ride back with me?" asked Vincent, turning to Penelope, and then wondered why he'd made the offer. Nevertheless, he was pleased when, after his lordship made it clear he'd very much like her to extend her visit, Penelope nodded.

The winter sun was low in the sky when the two mounted up and started for the Manor. "There are several ways of riding back," said Vincent, as the two walked their mounts from the stable area. "If we go down the drive, we take the road. If we cut across that meadow, we will go up over that hill to where we will have a run along the ridge before going down to the manor from the back. And—" He pointed his crop. "—if we head that way, there will be three hedges and a stream or two to cross, but it is, I think, the loveliest ride."

"And it will, just by happenstance, take you past one of those things you wish to check for your grandfather?" asked Penelope, smiling.

"You have guessed it," he said, grinning back. "But I can easily see to it another day. The road is, of course, the fastest path if you need to reach the manor quickly."

Penelope bit her lip and sent him a quick glance from the side of her eyes. "Will you mind very much postponing your inspection? I had not realized how many hours I've been gone. I find, suddenly, that I wonder how my poor deserted son is getting on."

They spoke little as they cantered along the road toward the manor but Penelope felt more relaxed riding with Vincent Beverly than she had in a very long time. *Do I,* she wondered, *miss having a man at my side to the degree that merely having one near reassures me?* She turned her head, belatedly realizing Vincent had spoken to her.

"What?" she asked.

"We've company," he repeated and, looking forward, nodded.

She too looked ahead. "Lord Wakefield."

"Hmm. You are frowning."

"I am?" She brushed her hand over her face. "So I am."

"Why?"

"I . . . do not know," she said, uncertain how to explain why his lordship's arrival on the scene was so upsetting. That it *was* contradicted her earlier thoughts concerning Mr. Beverly. Obviously, just *any* man was *not* reassuring to her sensibilities.

"Good afternoon, my lord," she said, as Wakefield rode up and turned to ride beside her. "Have you had a good jaunt?"

"No," he said shortly. "I have been searching for you. You disappeared and no one knew where you were." He glared across her at Vincent.

"Lady Everhart and I rode over to Beverly Place. I am quite certain any number of people knew where we had gone," said Penelope with only the barest hint of acid.

"Her ladyship arrived home some time ago," said Wakefield, his tone more than a little accusing.

"My grandfather, if it is any business of yours, invited Mrs. Garth to stay on for a longer visit. He had questions concerning the army and Wellington's plans for next spring's offensive."

Wakefield ignored Vincent's intervention. "You should have returned with Lady Everhart. She was your chaperon. She'd no right to leave you alone and unprotected."

Penelope turned her head and stared at his lordship, her mouth a trifle agape. "My lord!"

"You will not wish your reputation tarnished as it must be if you are seen riding alone with—" Lord Wakefield leaned forward and once again glared at Vincent. "—a man known by all to be nothing more than a rattle-pated rakehell."

"By each and everyone?" asked Vincent, wishing to draw Lord Wakefield's ire, although he hadn't a clue why the man was scolding Mrs. Garth. "Come now. Surely it has not reached the ears of quite the whole of the world that I was, once upon a time, young and foolish."

"A man never loses the bad odor of a tainted reputation, and you must know that yours is such that a decent woman should never be seen alone with you."

"No, I did *not* know my reputation was so bad as you'd suggest," said Vincent, more than a trifle irritated. "In fact, I rather doubt it is. So what is really bothering you, my lord?"

"Is all this arguing necessary?" asked Penelope when Wakefield began blustering. "I was enjoying the splendid weather and the scenery. Lord Wakefield, I suggest you either go away or allow me to continue enjoying it. One or the other."

"You *dare* to interrupt?" his lordship asked, obviously astounded.

"My lord," said Penelope, raising a hand when Vincent would have defended her, "I do not understand you. I am not certain I *wish* to understand you. I am a grown woman. A widow. It is not your place to treat me like a child still in the nursery. In fact, although my father disagrees and, apparently, you as well, *it never was your place.*"

Penelope touched her heel to Lady Everhart's well-trained horse and the mare obliging increased her speed. Neither Vincent nor Wakefield expected the move, and neither reacted instantly. Wakefield swore softly but, before he could take off after her as he obviously wished to do, Vincent stopped him by the simple expedient of grasping the horse's bridle above the bit.

"I am not happy," said Vincent, "at your insults. I would not harm a woman. Any woman. Ever. That you insinuate I would is name-calling of the most despicable."

"You will leave Lady Penelope alone," said Wakefield, his features rigid with dislike.

"I will be polite to *Mrs. Garth* and oblige her in any way I can whenever I can. She is, as she pointed out, none of your business, my lord."

And, with that, Vincent, too, put heel to horse and took off.

"This house party," he told Black Spot Flying, "may turn out to be a far more interesting interlude than I'd any hope of." He was very nearly back to the stables, before, musingly, he added, "I hope Georgi will forgive us if we turn her house party into a battleground, but that man must not be allowed to harass Mrs. Garth."

Vincent went directly to his room, changed riding clothes that smelled of the stable for clean linen and evening wear, and then he headed for the stairs to the upper regions of the house. He paused at the day nursery door, wondering if he would be unwelcome after the scene on the road, but, deciding he wanted to see how young Tal went on, and that that was excuse enough, he knocked.

"Yes, my lord?" asked Matty.

"Now, girl," said Vincent in teasing tones, "you know I'm no lord!"

The maid cast him a naughty look. "More a lord than some who can claim the title by birth," she said, a mocking tone to her voice. "I'll tell Mrs. Garth you are here," she added, curtsied an overblown, flirting version of a maid's quick dip of the knees, and shut the door.

"Mr. Beverly," said Penelope only a few moments later when he'd been allowed in, "I want to apologize for that scene on the road."

"Why? It was not of your making. If anyone should apologize, it is Lord Wakefield. I have changed my mind and now believe the man has nursed a passion for you all the years you've been gone."

She frowned. "I cannot believe he loved me to such an extent." She shook her head, her mouth firming. "No," she said. "It was impossible that he could even have known me. I swear we had not exchanged half a dozen words when he approached my father. He certainly hadn't registered in *my* mind as a possible suitor."

"I have known men to fall instantly in love with a face or figure . . ."

Penelope looked startled and then laughed. "I was never

such a beauty as that! Even before the sun ruined my complexion forever. It also bleached my hair in this odd streaky fashion that led to an old friend accusing me of using tricks to change its color." She jerked at a strand, shaking it slightly, and brushed it back behind her ear. "No, it cannot be that he loves me." She frowned. "He has mentioned my music again and again. Surely that is the only reason for his . . . his attentions?"

"I don't know, but I do know he is behaving in what one must consider an overly possessive manner when you've given him no right to your person."

Her gaze sharpened and she caught and held his. "What did he say to you after I rode off and left you? For which I apologize, by the way."

"A bit more of the same," said Vincent, shrugging Wakefield's threats away, "and again *you* have no need to apologize." He drew in a breath and looked around. "I came to visit your son, Mrs. Garth, but I do not see him."

"Matty has taken him off for his bath and bed. The very young need far more sleep than do we—until we reach a far more elderly age than we've yet achieved."

He chuckled. "Then may I escort you downstairs?" he asked, offering his arm.

Penelope shook her head. "I am not going down, Mr. Beverly. I told Lady Everhart when I first arrived that I've no wish to join in the season's festivities and now that guests have arrived, I prefer to remain above stairs."

"His lordship will very likely think you are staying away in order to avoid him," said Vincent, his fingers stroking his chin thoughtfully.

"I care not what Lord Wakefield thinks," she retorted. "The man has no right to think anything at all!"

"I have *taken* that right," said Wakefield from the doorway. There was just a touch of a whine to his tone but it grew more prissy as he continued, "I have ordered the old piano toted up to this floor and sent off for a tuner to put it right. You will wish to practice."

"I wish nothing of the sort." Penelope, her hands going to her hips, rolled her eyes. "I have told you. I lost all desire to sing when my husband died. Will you please cease this persecution?"

Vincent took a step forward.

Wakefield turned a sour look on him. "You were told to leave this woman in peace."

"You have that quite wrong," said Vincent softly. "*You* have been asked to leave her in peace. Not I."

"Bah! You are a fool." Wakefield turned on his heel and they heard him all the way down the hall and part way down the stairs.

"Did he mean you or did he mean me?" asked Penelope when she could find her voice.

"I'm blest if I know."

They stared at the empty door for a long moment and then at each other. Vincent shrugged his coat more comfortably onto his shoulders and smiled. "Well, Mrs. Garth, if you will not come down, then I suppose I must go alone to join the company. Georgi would be glad if you will change your mind . . . ?"

She shook her head and was surprised to realize she experienced a pang of disappointment that *Lady Everhart* and not Mr. Beverly would be disappointed at her absence. She instantly pushed the awareness of that to the very back of her mind, refusing to allow herself to admit she was developing more than a trifling interest in Mr. Beverly.

Vincent sighed, nodded, and took himself off, wondering if he should have words with Everhart concerning Wakefield. Everhart could put a word to his old friend in a way Vincent, who apparently rubbed the man the wrong way by his very existence, could not. He debated with himself all the way down the stairs to the ground floor.

But once he reached the hall he was instantly surrounded by three of Georgi's young friends who herded him into the salon, chattering at him from all sides and making it impossible for him to answer . . . and, in among the jests and the laughter he, for the moment, forgot Wakefield's pestiferous manner toward Mrs. Garth.

But not for long.

Vincent crossed the room to where he saw Georgi looking for relief from someone—very likely anyone. Wakefield had cornered her between a potted palm and a stand on which resided a truly excellent copy of a Grecian urn. Her features lightened into a smile when Vincent arrived. "Vincent, will you please explain to Lord Wakefield that it is not my place to demand a guest perform?"

"Are you at that again?" Vincent heaved a theatric sigh. "Georgi," he said, pretending ennui by exaggerating nonexistent boredom, "the man was upstairs only a little while ago, demanding Mrs. Garth practice at the piano which he has ordered *your* servants to heave up to the nursery. She was not pleased."

"*Lady Penelope* has finally returned to her proper milieu and must take her place in it. That is decreed by both her birth and her talent," said Wakefield.

Something in his tone turned that into the sort of pronouncement that instantly set up Georgi's back. "Must?" she asked. "*Must?* My lord, you forget yourself and you forget Mrs. Garth's situation. She was all too recently widowed. If she has no desire to join in the season's jollities, then surely that is to her credit."

"Widowed? Widowed! Bah. A commoner. A *Scottish* commoner. She was young and foolish and must feel nothing but relief to have been freed of a union that can have caused her nothing but pain and distress!"

Georgi's mouth dropped open and she gaped. She turned wide-open eyes toward Vincent—and, surprised again but for a different reason, blinked. She had never seen such contempt for another man on Vincent's countenance.

Unconciously, she reached toward him, but he, unnoticing, turned on his heel and stalked off. She turned back to Wakefield and was again disconcerted. *His* face revealed a complacency that could only be based in such utter self-assurance it left a bad taste in one's mouth. For the first time since she could remember, Georgi hadn't a notion what to say.

"There now. You must not feel chagrinned. You, too, are very young. You can have no notion of the degradation she endured."

Georgi blinked. "Lord Wakefield, you are my husband's friend, but you will never be mine. Please find someone else with whom you may converse before I say something which both of us will regret."

Georgi pushed by the fronds hanging from the back of the palm and moved across the room to where Everhart stood talking to one of their older guests, a government man who had been a near friend of Everhart's father. She took her husband's arm and, for a moment, leaned her head into his shoulder. With effort she managed to set aside Wakefield's comments and forced herself to listen to the discussion about the cost of the war and the need for still heavier taxes.

But, although she listened, half Georgi's mind worried at the problem of how she was to prevent Lord Wakefield from ruining her very first house party. It appeared that his obsession with Mrs. Garth's voice was such that he preferred to cause a scandal rather than behave as a gentleman should.

One thing was clear however. If she had not already set aside her plot to bring Penelope and his lordship together, she'd do so now. Such a relationship would be far worse than to remain widowed for the rest of one's life. Georgi glanced up at her husband. Did he have any notion that Wakefield was such an awful man? Very likely he did not. When men were around other men they often behaved in a manner totally unlike the side of themselves they showed women.

Georgi glanced around the room. There were half a dozen men all dressed in the restrained fashion Brummell had introduced, scattered among the brightly gowned women, wives, and daughters. Did they all have a hidden side, as Wakefield obviously did, some nasty characteristic that became apparent only in some unpredictable situation?

CHAPTER 7

Vincent managed to free himself from the fluttering flock of young women by telling them he must speak with his cousin before dinner. He approached her slowly, speaking to first this person and then with that as he wended his way toward her.

"A word with you, Georgi, my dear," he said. He was standing just behind her and had leaned forward so that he spoke into her ear. He was rather surprised when she jumped, startled, and swung around to face him, her eyes wide and her mouth slightly open. "What is it?" he asked, his ever-present concern for his little cousin instantly on the alert.

She blushed slightly. "Nothing. Nothing at all. You merely startled me from thoughts better interrupted."

"Perhaps thoughts you should share, if they lead my intrepid Georgi to react in such a startled manner to merely my voice."

She grinned, her eyes twinkling. "The thought you broke into was that all men might have a secret side, such as Wakefield has revealed, one they reveal only to women. Your voice in my ear demanding words with me was, you will admit, extremely *apropos*."

The corners of his mouth twitched and his eyes gleamed. "You feared I was about to turn into a monster? After all these years?"

"Something of the sort, I suppose. What do you wish?" she asked.

"To box your ears." When Georgi looked as if she couldn't decide whether to laugh or be alarmed, he chuckled. But then he sobered. "You invited—" He named three young women. "—specifically for my benefit, did you not?"

For half a moment Georgi looked guilty. Then she looked defiant. "And if I did?"

He sighed. "My dear cousin, I know you are exceedingly happy in your marriage and wish everyone you know to feel equally content with their world, but matchmaking in such a blatant fashion is not the way to achieve your goal." He took her chin between finger and thumb, catching her gaze with a steady look of his own. "I am *not* happy to be chased by chits with more hair than wit and I already have evidence that that is their plan. I suspect they have come to an agreement that one of them will catch me during this visit. You must have words with them, Georgi—"

Georgi looked more than a trifle startled.

"—or I will move to Beverly Place and stay with Grandfather. I will not fend off your bevy of beauties for a full three weeks. Not even for you, Georgi."

"What is this? Why are you scolding my wife?" asked Everhart, coming up and putting an arm around Georgi's shoulders. "Do you need a knight in shining armor, my dear, riding to the rescue?"

"Not at all. Vincent is just being his usual stubborn self," said Georgi and thrust her chin in the air. "Very well, Vincent. I will tell them your heart is given elsewhere and you are not to be bothered."

"Georgi! I am shocked! You would tell such a tarradiddle?" said Everhart, pretending great astonishment.

"Perhaps it is not," said Vincent and, abruptly, walked off.

Georgi stared after him. "Now what could he have meant by that?"

Everhart also stared. "I don't know," he said, slowly. It had, the previous summer when he was wooing Georgi, crossed his mind that Vincent loved his little cousin with more than a cousinly love, but, for a variety of reasons, he had dismissed the notion. Now he wondered if his first intuitions had been more correct than he'd guessed. "At least . . ."

"My dear?" asked Georgi, looking up at him.

"Hmm?" He looked down. And smiled. "Nothing at all. Just a momentary bit of nonsense." He glanced around. "My love, I believe we are needed. You had better check that that is no more than a tempest in a teapot—" He nodded to where two of their more elderly guests were being coldly polite to each other. "—while I make certain that that ends—" His chin thrust to where two gentlemen were becoming rather heated in their discussion of the consequences of several decades of enclosures on the countryside. "—as nothing more than an agreement to disagree."

And, while host and hostess smoothed feathers, Vincent managed to leave the room and, finding the hall empty, took the stairs two at a time until he disappeared. Two more flights and he reached the nursery floor where he heard Tal's burbling laugh. He knocked and, at a call, entered.

"He woke up," he said, staring at the child who immediately turned onto his hands and knees and, unsteadily, climbed to his feet. Vincent reached down and swung the boy above his head to more chortles of glee before settling the boy in his arm and turning to look at the boy's mother. "May I suggest, Mrs. Garth, that, in future, you discover who is at the door before giving permission for entry?" he asked politely.

Penelope looked startled. Then she flushed. "You would suggest it might have been Lord Wakefield?"

Vincent nodded. He touched Tal's tummy and made a

buzzing sound before looking around the room. "Where is Matty?"

"She went below for my supper tray," said Penelope.

Tal patted Vincent's cheek, demanding his attention. Vincent poked his tummy again, again making that odd sound Tal appeared to find terribly amusing. "Still worse that you allow *anyone* in when you've no protection at all. A maid isn't much, but better than nothing. Most men will behave when there are witnesses."

"You are really worried about that man, are you not?"

"I have seen his harassment of you when you are *not* alone. I cannot guess what his manner might be if you were. Yes. I am . . . concerned."

Penelope bit her lip. "Perhaps we should leave. The weather has not been bad . . ."

"No. You will not take Tal into the danger of a sudden winter storm that could block roads through the more barren stretches on your way north. Travelers have been known to freeze to death." Vincent spoke sternly, but a sudden notion lightened his countenance. "What you *might* do, however, is move to Beverly Place."

"Impose on Lord Tivington and your aunts? I could not. As it is, it is too bad of me, making it impossible for Lady Everhart to feel she can turn me away."

"I believe the aunts would enjoy your company, Mrs. Garth. You would not impose, as you call it, but would give them great pleasure. Shall I arrange it?"

Penelope looked around the rather stark nursery. She thought of the small room that Georgi had gone to such lengths to make comfortable for her. Matty arrived just then, carefully balancing a tray, her lower lip between her teeth as she concentrated.

Matty. The girl was so good with Tal . . .

Vincent watched the various emotions flitting across Mrs. Garth's features. "You find yourself comfortable here and know that Georgi will not demand you do anything you do not wish to do. You do not wish to leave," he said and nodded. "Shall we leave it that, if Wakefield makes life too difficult for you, you will not hesitate to ask me to help you make the move?"

Penelope smiled. "I don't know how it is that you are able to understand without a word being said, but I thank you. And, yes, if I find I cannot bear to be so near the ogre, I will ask your aid in finding asylum elsewhere." She put out her hands to take her son. "Since Matty managed to bring up my meal, I would guess they are about to call the guests to order. You had better return below."

Vincent unwillingly agreed. He handed over Tal with equal reluctance. The child filled his arms so comfortably. More than once it had crossed his mind that the boy's mother would fill them still more comfortably. He touched the child's cheek instead of the cheek he wished to touch—and then grinned when he was forced to free that finger from the boy's strong clasp. Saying all that was proper, he departed to take his place at Georgi's table among far less interesting guests.

Wakefield, much to his surprise, found a fellow music lover among the lovelies Georgi had invited in the hopes one would catch Vincent's eye. He overheard Miss Rose Grimson speaking of a concert, one which he, too, had attended the preceding season. Unashamedly, he listened.

". . . and I thought the rebec not quite in tune," Miss Grimson was saying to another guest as Wakefield had passed on his way to the stairs to the nursery floor. He'd paused. "It is such a fault when a musician cannot bring his instrument into exact agreement with the others with which he plays."

"You have that correctly, Miss Grimson," said Wakefield in his prissy fashion. "You are speaking of the last performance of the Society for the Preservation of Ancient Music, are you not? Did you happen to attend the first or was it presented before you arrived in London this last season?"

Miss Grimson turned to Wakefield eagerly, amazed to discover another who felt just as he aught about something so important. The two wandered into the salon, Wakefield forgetting for the moment that he meant to escort Lady Penelope to the first floor so that she could entertain them all with a song . . . or two or three . . . or, preferably, *more*.

It was quite a half hour later when he realized he was enjoying himself excessively, but that both he and Miss Grimson would enjoy listening to Lady Penelope's marvelous voice even more. He said as much.

"Lady Penelope?" asked Miss Grimson doubtfully. She scanned the room for the unknown. "I do not believe I have been introduced to her ladyship?"

"No. She insists she will not join the company," he said, his tone pregnant with his irritation. "She simply does not understand that she must."

"Perhaps she is overly modest and does not appreciate her voice," said Miss Grimson, thinking of her own unwillingness to perform on the pianoforte before an audience even when she was certain she had the piece perfected. "There are those who feel they are not good enough, or are afraid they will make mistakes which will embarrass them."

Wakefield's mouth prissed up. "It is not that. She performed before she left the country with her Scottish soldier. She has some bee in her bonnet which I cannot understand." He brightened. "I know," he said. "I shall introduce you to the lady and perhaps she can make you understand. Or, alternately and more importantly, you may persuade her to allow those among us who appreciate such things to be filled with the joy of once again hearing her . . . ?"

As Wakefield spoke he edged Miss Grimson toward the door to the hall. She was almost there when she realized he had her arm in a rather tight grip. "Sir! My lord!"

"Hmm?" He very nearly shoved her another step in the direction he would have her go.

"Surely you do not mean now? Tonight?"

Wakefield stopped and looked down at Miss Grimson. "Yes, of course. Right now. At once."

"No, no," insisted Miss Grimson, digging in her heels and showing a stubborn expression. "It would be highly improper. Tomorrow I will allow you to send up a message requesting an introduction." She nodded firmly, once, and put up her other hand to pry at his fingers, which had tightened. "Sir, I protest. You hurt me."

Wakefield glanced at his hand and opened his fingers as if burnt on a hot cup of tea. "My dear Miss Grimson," he said, appalled. "Do forgive me. You have never heard Lady Penelope's voice or you would understand my . . . my *eagerness* to hear her again."

Miss Grimson relaxed. "I *can* understand such a passion, sir. It is much the same with me where music is concerned." She drew in a deep breath, determined to keep this fascinating man at her side. "Have you heard anything by that new composer? Herr Beethoven, I believe he is called? Such oddly complicated music! It is very difficult to . . ."

And they were off again. Wakefield went up to bed later that evening feeling satisfied in a way he had not for a very long time. Miss Grimson was a particularly knowledgeable young woman who had, obviously, studied with some of the foremost instructors of music available. Wakefield was tying the tie at the throat of his nightgown when he paused.

"If," he muttered, "Miss Grimson has *studied* music, does that not mean that she *plays?* Or *sings?* But if so, why did she not mention it?"

Wakefield tried to recall if he had ever heard her perform at any of the musicals of which he was a regular attendee. He was nearly certain he had not. He concluded Miss Grimson was one of those young ladies who loved music but was incapable of producing it and felt saddened by the thought.

He himself played a more than adequate cello—although he avoided playing in public. He had always told himself his music was too private to share with others and that that was the reason he played only for himself . . . but, as he climbed into his bed after turning down the lamp wick and blowing out his bed candle, he recalled Miss Grimson's speculation that Lady Penelope might fear public performances and, with something of a wry laugh, admitted, there in the privacy of his darkened room, that that was his real reason for remaining unknown as a very good amateur.

He had settled himself against his pillow as that acknowledgement ran through his head—when, quite suddenly, he sat up again. "Is that," he muttered, "Miss Grimson's reason for not playing or singing for others? Whatever it is she does?"

Wakefield lay back, his mouth puckered into a funny upside down smile. Tomorrow. Tomorrow he would discover if Miss Grimson was one who kept her music a secret—and tomorrow Lady Penelope would not again escape him. She *would* sing.

His smile faded, his blind gaze staring up through the floors toward where he thought the woman slept.

"Yes. Tomorrow," he said and slipped into a sleep in which his dreams were mixed, one woman replacing another, a voice mixed with the music of a pianoforte which would fade to a lovely contralto voice issuing from the wrong woman's mouth accompanied by the other playing as he'd never heard her play and had no reason to believe she could . . .

Wakefield woke the next morning with a headache. He was cross and angry and could not understand why. The only possible cause was Lady Penelope's stubborn refusal to sing—so why, he wondered crossly, did thoughts of the knowledgeable and interesting Miss Grimson also cause irritation?

* * *

Vincent rode across Beverly Place acres, frowning at what he saw. Retracing his route, he turned up a rutted lane to a small cottage tucked into a small wood, a stream running along one side.

Dismounting, he tied Spot to the ring in the post set near the front door. Then, approaching the door, he knocked. After a moment he knocked again more loudly. He smiled to himself at the grumbling he heard and the tap-shuffle-shuffle sound of slow steps approaching the door.

"So?" A little old lady glared up at him through a tangle of hair. And then she smiled. "Vincent!" She peered beyond and sighed. "My girlie isn't with you? No, never mind, then. A woman, she is now. And married. Hasn't time for her old nanny I suspect . . ."

More grumbling, but the words indistinguishable, trailed back as Vincent followed her into the dark room that was parlor, kitchen, and workroom. His brows rose for a moment when he saw a rumpled cot set along one side of the room, the cover thrown back.

Had Nanny been sleeping? He sighed softly. The woman had not been young when she'd come to the Place to care for him and Georgi many years ago. She must be every day of ninety. So much as ninety-five, perhaps?

"So, what can I do for you?" asked the old woman, turning from the fire to which she'd added a few small sticks.

Vincent reminded himself to bring in a load of wood and a bucket of water before he departed. He must also find someone to come each day and see to such things . . . and to check on Nanny. "I think," he said dryly, "it is more what I can do for you. But more of that later. Nanny, what has happened to the Place?"

Her brows lowered and her lips scrunched up, making wrinkles in her face like those in the shell of a walnut. Then she chuckled wryly. "What happened? Old age happened, Vincent. That's all. We all got old."

Grandfather? *Old?* Vincent felt a chill up his spine as he recognized that it was true. Something must be done and soon or—no, he'd not think of that. "More particularly, why are Grandfather's orders being ignored?"

She scowled. "Old age! I tol' you!"

Vincent frowned. "Elbertson?" he asked after a moment's cogitation. Nanny nodded. "But he's *much* younger than Grandfather."

"The man's been ill a lot this fall and winter. Doesn't like to admit he can't do his work."

Vincent sighed. "No one thought to mention it to Grandfather?"

Nanny's scowl screwed up her forehead still more and the age lines criss-crossing her face deepened into crevasses. "Did tell him. More than once told him."

"And?"

"*Old age, Vincent.* He would say not to worry, just go tell Elbertson, please, to take care of hisself." She sighed and, using a hand bent by arthritis, pushed the hair from her face. "We've all outlived our usefulness and that's the truth of it." She sighed again and looked around the room, her gaze troubled.

Vincent followed her eyes and noticed the unswept floor, the unemptied slops, the bread and cheese left out on the table . . . Half an hour later the little house looked as it always had and Nanny smiled. He noticed she'd lost another tooth and added another item to his mental list. He must purchase eggs to be delivered to Nanny regularly. Something she could fix and eat easily, something good for her . . .

"You're a good boy, Vincent, even when you pretend to be a bad boy." She grinned when he colored up. "Was always your way, lad, not wanting anyone to know how deeply you felt things."

"I didn't want to feel. To feel . . . *hurt,*" he said and added, somewhat curtly, "So I *didn't.* Feel things, I mean."

"Such a lad it is. Silly lad!" She chuckled, her sharp old eyes piercing him. "Only *hid* how much you felt—" Her voice softened. "—everything. It was all there, down deep inside you, even—" Her frown returned and her voice firmed. "—when you acted the fool."

Vincent swallowed. He hated to admit softness. He'd been soft when his parents lived . . . too soft. He'd hurt when they died, so he did his best to rid himself of the pain and avoid future pain as well—and his *best* had been quite *good.*

Most of the time . . .

But was Nanny right? Was it all there, down deep, where he didn't have to admit to any of it? *Very likely,* the wry thought crossed his mind. *Nanny has a trick of seeing things one doesn't want seen.*

"I have much to do Nanny, but I'll be back. We'll be at Minnow Manor for several weeks and maybe I'll stay on at the Place after that. For awhile."

"No maybe about it." She nodded one of her little decisive nods. "You'll be there. It's where you want to be." The frown returned. "You tell that girl of mine," she added, as Vincent pulled gloves on and put his hat on his head, "that she's to visit me. Soon."

"Yes, I'll tell Georgi, although she doesn't need telling. She's been busy organizing things for the house party, but she's said more than once she wanted to ride over. Perhaps she'll drive instead and bring Mrs. Garth and her son Tal to visit you. Some nice day when the cold won't harm the child."

"Mrs. Garth . . . Lady Penelope?" asked Nanny sharply.

"Yes." Vincent frowned. Usually Nanny knew all there was to know long before the rest of the world knew it. "Yes," he explained, half his mind wondering at Nanny's ignorance, "she's widowed. She returned to make peace with her father."

"Hah! That'll be the day," barked Nanny in quite the old way. "That old screw will go to his grave a lonely man and all for stupid stubbornness. You like her?" she finished, peering up at Vincent from under her brows.

"Mrs. Garth?" asked Vincent, pretending not to understand what Nanny was really asking. "Of course. She is a very likeable woman. Soon I must find time to see Elbertson and then think how to go about sorting out the problems his illness has caused." He held up his hand when Nanny opened her mouth. "I'll see he's pensioned off, if that seems necessary. He'll not be sent away with nothing—although," he added in a more biting tone, "he's a sensible man and has very likely put aside a tidy amount to live on in his dotage."

"You stop that right this instant, Vincent Beverly. You'll be old one day. Then you'll wish you'd not been nasty to those who now are!"

Vincent grinned. "Am I nasty to you, Nanny?"

"No. You know I'd put you over my knee and give you what for if you laid that sharp tongue on me. I'd not put up with nonsense. Especially, from you, you young scoundrel. Especially," she grumbled, "not when it is all an act. Time you gave that up." She peered up at him again. "All that childish silliness. And more than time you got on with life." She shook a bent finger at him, her frown very much in place.

"I haven't a notion what you mean, Nanny, and have no time for conundrums. I'll visit again in a day or two so you can lecture some more and perhaps elucidate."

"Don't know about this 'lucidating thingee, whatever it may be, but you see you come. Soon," she ordered, "so I can explain in simple words you'll *understand*." She shut the door in his face.

Vincent scowled at it. He hated it when Nanny made him think . . .

But think he did. Had he been playing games all these years? Was his cold withdrawal from close acquaintance nothing more than a means of protecting himself? Had it become merely a habit during those years he was too young to control his life and fate, a habit that needed breaking now he was fully adult?

But—defiance filled him and his chin stuck out—*why is it wrong to protect oneself?*

CHAPTER 8

A few days later, Georgi drove away from Nanny's in a thoughtful mood. "She's getting old," she said and sighed. "I feel guilty. I haven't given her nearly enough thought. Not recently . . ."

"You've been preoccupied with your marriage and adjusting to living with a man in your life," said Penelope, smiling. She started to point out a row of geese and a goose boy to Tal but discovered the lad slept. "It is rather . . . preoccupying, is it not?"

Georgi chuckled. "Yes. At the very least, it is *preoccupying*." She frowned. "But that does not excuse me for forgetting to check on Nanny. She has been far too important in my life for me to forget her. More than once she has saved my life."

"Do I hear a tale?"

"Not really. I have this stupid tendency to come down with an idiotic fever with almost no provocation at all. The last time was not long before Everhart and I wed. But that isn't relevant. What *is* is that I haven't once thought of how she goes on and I should have."

"She understands."

"She hasn't the sense she beat into us," said Georgi a trifle bitingly. "If she *did,* she'd have requested help long ago."

"Pride."

"Pride can be the very devil—as you, of all people, know," said Georgi, and then closed her mouth with a snap and a sideways glance at Penelope and the boy on her lap. She hoped she'd not upset her new friend.

"You refer to my father," responded Penelope placidly, not at all upset. "He is certainly a devil and perhaps it is pride that drives him, but I suspect it is nothing more than bloody-mindedness."

Georgi was surprised that Penelope said the whole with no particular emotion. "How can you speak so calmly?" she asked.

Penelope smiled sadly. "Long ago I accepted there was nothing I could do to change him. When I came home this Christmas, I suppose I had forgotten or else I was overly optimistic. I have learned my lesson. It is his loss." She looked down and touched a bit of hair that showed among the blankets in which her son was wrapped. "And my boy's I suppose, since he'll never know his grandfather. This grandfather, I mean. His other one is waiting for our return to Scotland and is angry that I mean to live in Edinburgh rather than with the family on their estate."

"I wonder if your father knew your husband came from the gentry."

"I don't think he wanted to know."

Georgi cast her a startled glance and, inadvertently, mishandled the reins. "What?" she asked, as she turned back to her horses to sort out the poor creatures' confusion.

Penelope grasped the side of the gig but didn't, otherwise, react to the pair's antics. "I'd done the unforgivable," she explained. "I made my choice of husband without consulting him," she added once the pair again trotted calmly down the road.

"And if you were tempted to do that again? Would you?" asked Georgi, all innocence.

Penelope didn't respond for a moment. "I think you are asking if I would worry about my father's reaction if I were to remarry without his having a hand in the decision?"

"Yes."

"If I loved again and—" Penelope's hand went to her son's head. "—*if* I thought the man would be a good father to my son, then I would remarry. I am comfortable with what I have and feel no need to find a husband. Any husband. I expect to raise my boy myself and am perfectly capable of doing so in such a way he'll have a good life."

Georgi had to be satisfied with that. Now her only problem seemed to be that she find the man who would fill the need. The need to love and be loved. She searched her mind as they turned into the lane for Minnow Manor but could not settle on any gentleman who might suit since it was obvious Lord Wakefield would *not*.

They had no more than turned into the long lane when Vincent trotted down toward them. "Good," he said, pulling up. "You are needed, Georgi. Some sort of contretemps in the kitchen, I believe." He reined his horse back a few steps and turned, riding beside them up and into the stable yard. "You run along in, brat. I'll give orders for your team and escort Mrs. Garth up to the house."

A few minutes later he casually took Tal from Penelope's arms and set off for the house. When he realized she was not coming along beside him, he stopped, turned . . .

"Is something wrong?" he asked.

"You didn't even think about it, did you?" she asked, a trifling bit of wonderment evident on her face.

"Think?" He frowned. "About what?"

"About taking Tal. You just, quite naturally, did it."

He looked down, his hand going to cover the child's sleeping head. "Is it something about which one needs to think? He is growing overly heavy for you to carry and I am here." A thought struck him. "Should I *not* have taken him?" He looked up, his gaze piercing.

She smiled a trifle sadly. "It is just that most gentlemen do not manage to handle a young child with such casual ease." She shrugged slightly. "I suppose it is that they've had no practice?"

"Neither have I," said Vincent, that touch of acid in his voice that so often covered his emotions. "I don't see the problem. Come along now. We don't want either of you catching an ague."

He held out his arm with just a touch of arrogance and, taking it, Penelope hid a smile. "Why," she asked, "do you attempt to hide your softer side? Did you, as you predict my son must do, find it necessary to fight the world for your place in it?"

Vincent glanced at Penelope and then away. Only a few days earlier Nanny had said something very similar, had she not? About his softer side and the hiding of it? He frowned. A few more paces and he felt her staring up at him and again turned a quick look her way.

"I apologize," she said softly. "It is just that you are very easy to talk to. It led me to speak out of turn."

"Not out of turn," he said. He drew in a deep breath and let it out again. "It is more that I haven't a notion how to answer you. I was not forced to fight, as you say, for my place. My place, such as it is, was written out for me at birth, so to speak. I am the only son of a younger son." He shrugged. "The thing is, Nanny, who you met today, asked me a similar question recently, but she had a different explanation for it. She thinks I no longer feel emotions because of the pain I felt losing my parents at an early age."

Penelope nodded. "I doubt it is that you don't feel it, but that you hide it. Perhaps you hide even from yourself. I knew a few officers like that. They'd seen too much, experienced too much, lost too many friends. They reached a point where they refused to admit they had friends, that they ever felt affection or love, or anything our poets consider soft."

"I love Georgi. I love my grandfather and, even when she is her most irritating, I love Nanny." He paused. "I feel warmth toward a handful of others whom it would pain me to lose. I do not think I hide my emotions."

"But you are very careful of those you admit to your circle?"

"That is only sensible," he said, opening the back door for her. "The backstairs are just here. Be careful. They are steep," he said, and held that door open as well.

"Only sensible."

He barked a laugh. "You say that with such aridness it is obvious you do not believe me."

"I am not convinced," she retorted, "that you believe yourself."

They turned the corner and continued up toward the next floor.

"Why? What have I done or said that leads you to say such a thing?"

She clutched the rail with one hand and her skirts with the other and took a few more steps up before stopping and turning, forcing him to stop as well. "What, you ask? You handle Tal as if he were precious. You stopped to help me when you could have ridden on, saying it was none of your business, that figure crouched by the tree. You have, more than once, interfered when Lord Wakefield became awkward. You helped Lord Everhart remove my abusive father from this house with nary a thought and no discussion between you. You are kind and considerate, whatever you think of yourself. You do not like to see others in pain or in an awkward situation, and you play with Tal with the same gentle humor you'd use when playing with a pup, which is just what he loves at this particular age. And you do it all instinctively, from a level of your mind and heart that does not require thinking. It is natural to you."

Vincent felt his ears burn. "You embarrass me."

"Because I think you a good man?"

He frowned. "Is that what all that means to you?"

"All . . . what?"

"All that . . . piffle . . . what you said."

She laughed that seductive chuckle that drew Vincent as no woman's laugh had ever done. "Piffle. What a word!"

"But . . . ?"

"But yes," she said. "I think all that *piffle* means you are a good man."

She turned and continued on up the stairs.

Down the hall from where the two had stood talking on the backstairs landing, Wakefield frowned mightily. Lady Penelope had been somewhere with that . . . that *fellow*. He'd been told she was driving out with Lady Everhart, a duty visit his hostess felt necessary to make. Someone had lied.

Wakefield was not in good humor as he stalked down the main staircase and, at the bottom, nearly ran into his hostess. "Lady Georgianna. I was told you went driving." His brows pulled together and his eyes narrowed as he awaited confirmation of the lie.

"I have just returned. Mrs. Garth and I drove over to visit my old Nanny." Georgi frowned. "She is not well. I must discuss her situation with Vincent . . ." She shut her mouth and forced herself to put on a pleasant expression. "But, my lord, did you wish something? Is there something I can do for you?"

"No, no . . ." He pulled himself up. "No. I just hope Mrs. Garth did not take a chill. Her voice, you know . . ."

Georgi's smile faded. She looked at him with an almost blank look. "Mrs. Garth does not wish to sing. You must not continue this impertinent nonsense—" Georgi felt her cheeks warm. "—or, as I *should* say, it is not polite to importune her to do something she does not wish to do."

"Her voice is special," he said in a soothing-the-simple-minded tone some adopt when explaining something they believe the listener will not comprehend. "You will understand once you've heard it."

"Has it occurred to you that she may have lost her voice?" asked Georgi, much in the spirit of casting a cat among the pigeons.

Wakefield paled and reached for the banister, grasping it firmly. "Do not suggest such a terrible thing!" He turned and stalked off.

Georgi stood there for a long minute, blinking, and thinking furiously. Finally she smiled. It was the answer, of course. Wakefield must be convinced Penelope had no voice! She tucked the notion to the back of her mind—and then forgot it.

Vincent played with Tal for a time, enjoying the child's cheerful trust and attempts at emulation. He praised the boy before rising to his feet and turning to where Mrs. Garth sat watching them. "He is a delightful boy," he said, smiling down at her.

"It is nice of you to say so, but you have not seen him in a temper or when tired and fussy and needing sleep or food. He can, like any child, make one wish to tear one's hair and leave home!" She smiled lovingly at Tal.

"Oh yes, I am certain you ever wish to leave the lad. As if you would! Admit it. *If* you left home you would take him with you."

She chuckled. "Quite true, but we must never allow Tal to know that."

Again Vincent was drawn to her by that wonderfully husky laugh. Once again he almost succumbed to the need to gather her up into his arms and hold her against him. Just hold her. Nothing more.

"I must go," he said abruptly. "I promised Grandfather I would check on a particular problem for him. It is time and more that I did so."

"Then, yes of course, you must go," she said, standing. She went with him to the door and was quite amazed at how reluctant she was to see him leave. She felt so comfortable and at ease with him. It was as if she'd known him for many years instead of a mere handful of days. She closed the door and turned, pressing her back against it, wondering at herself.

"Am I such a fickle woman?" she asked softly. "Am I falling in love with another man when the man I loved has been dead for barely two years?" She looked up, staring at nothing at all. "Kennet?"

A sudden inexplicable warmth flowed down over Penelope. She blinked.

"Kennet?"

Once again that warmth filled her.

"It is all right to love again?" she asked, her voice weak. "Oh, I am quite mad to be speaking to a dead man and thinking he has answered!"

This time it was as if the warmth contained laughter—well-known laughter. Laughter she had not heard since before the battle of Talavera. She felt the blood drain from her head and pressed her hands hard against the wood behind her.

After a moment she nodded. It had happened. Whatever it was, it had been quite real. Kennet had given his permission—encouragement even? She could, without guilt, fall in love with Vincent Beverly.

Which is just as well, she concluded after another moment's thought, *since I think I already have.*

"I feel terribly guilty," said Lord Tivington sadly.

"It is no more your fault than anyone's. He has neighbors who live much nearer who should have checked when he did not appear." Vincent sighed. "As I said, I think he died quietly in his sleep nearly a week ago. Mrs. Conley took him a dozen eggs just over a week ago and two are gone. She had meant to go again today, taking him some Christmas baking she'd done for him, but had yet to find the time. I am glad I found him and she did not have that shock."

"Arrangements must be made," said Lord Tivington, clutching the arms of his chair.

"I have given orders that I am certain you'll approve, sir."

His lordship nodded. "Yes. Of course you have. I am sorry I barked."

Vincent's sober expression lightened. "Bark away if it makes you feel better. I'll not take it personally."

Lord Tivington did bark, but it was a short sharp laugh. He sighed. "I must advertise for a new agent, I suppose. It is not a good time of year to find such."

"I agree and, if you've no objections," said Vincent slowly, "I rather wondered if I might not manage things . . . for the winter I mean. Just until better weather when you can think about looking about you for a new agent. If I work out, perhaps you need not find another."

His lordship sat up straighter. "You would stay on?"

"I have, for some time, been thinking that if you did not object, I'd like to open up the dower house. Perhaps, make a few improvements. I have reached an age, sir, when I occasionally feel an urge to have a bolt hole to which I can retreat, a place I can call my own." Quickly, before his grandfather could reply, he added, "Complete with a lease and rent and everything right and proper about it?"

Tivington nodded, maintaining a sober expression with difficulty. "A *long* lease," he suggested. "One which your cousin will be unable to break once he inherits?"

Vincent grinned. "I don't think I had *that* long a term in mind, sir. After all, I see no sign you mean to leave everything to my uncle's responsibility any time soon and I am certain my uncle has no plans that would involve Cousin George Elliot stepping into *his* shoes. No, when that time comes I am certain—"

Lord Tivington saw the tightening of Vincent's muscles and, once again, wished this particular man were his heir and not Elliot Beverly who would *not* make a particularly good landlord.

"—I will wish to be permanently situated elsewhere."

His lordship nodded, pursed his lips, and steepled his hands in that way he had. "Shall we say a ten year lease?"

Vincent nodded. "That will do. Do I have permission to see what must be done to make the house livable?"

"You do."

They discussed a few more things, mostly how Vincent should proceed, in order to carry out the orders the deceased agent should have set in motion several weeks earlier, and then Vincent rose to his feet.

"You must say a few words to the aunts, Vincent, before you leave."

Vincent grinned. "I know. At this time of year it is impossible to sneak in to see you without their knowing I have arrived. Such abominable weather makes it impossible to simply tie up my horse and come through those doors—" He gestured toward the French style windows, covered at this time of year by a heavy, draft-reducing damask. "—and then return to where I've left Spot. In this weather, someone in the stables is certain to mention I've been here to someone in the house who would pass it to someone else and, eventually, it would come to one of the aunts' ears. I would be in the doghouse if I'd not spoken with them."

He nodded to his grandfather and proceeded to the front of the house where his aunts sat, the one with her embroidery and the other reading aloud. Both were glad to set aside their current occupations and spent a delightful hour asking him questions about Georgi's guests.

". . . but you will see for yourselves, will you not?" he finished one comment. "I am certain Georgi said you were all coming, once again, to dinner tomorrow evening?"

"Yes. There is a chance our brother and his family will be with us this time," said Lady Georgia Marie.

Lady Georgina Anne cast her a sharp look. "Was that in that letter you refused to read to me?" she asked, a faintly accusatory note in her voice.

"Oh dear. I meant it for a surprise and here I have gone and spoiled it," said Lady Marie, pouting.

"The one who would be surprised is poor Georgi," said Vincent, his chuckles interrupting the lecture Lady Anne was obviously about to begin. "Her table would be quite upset would it not? Just how many extra will there be?"

"The whole family, of course." Lady Anne counted quickly on her fingers. "Six in all."

Lady Marie blushed. "How very silly of me that I did not think of that problem."

"Very silly," said Lady Anne in her abrupt manner. "Vincent, you must warn Georgianna to have two seating plans. I will send a groom with a message if they arrive in time to join us. She can then decide which seating arrangement is needed."

"I'll do that. Until tomorrow night then, the best of my aunts."

"We are all of your aunts," said Lady Marie, a trifle confused.

"No, no. I must count Lady Melicent as an aunt, even if it is by marriage. I assure you," said Vincent at his most devilish, "you are by far the best of my aunts!"

With an insouciant salute, he left them, Lady Anne obviously wishing to scold him for impertinence and Lady Marie hiding giggles behind her hand. He didn't breathe freely until he closed the green baize door to the servant's area and knew he'd escaped. Then he grinned. Even if she didn't approve, Aunt Anne had looked pleased at his compliment and Aunt Marie, of course, always liked such things.

He spoke to several of the more senior servants as he passed through the kitchens and then, sobering, put everything behind him, shuddering as the cold hit him. His thoughts turned to the dower house as he headed toward the stables.

No one had lived in it for several years and, he suspected, it was years before that when the rooms had last been painted or refurbished in any way. It very likely needed new hangings and upholstery and all sorts of things of which he'd no knowledge.

"I'll ask Georgi's advice," he said—but somewhere in his mind was the niggling notion that perhaps Mrs. Garth would have more time for such things than Georgi would.

Georgi, after all, was responsible for a houseful of guests!

CHAPTER 9

The next morning Penelope stood inside the closed door and frowned ever so slightly. "It is a very dark hallway, is it not?" she asked, a certain hesitancy to her words that had Vincent grinning.

"Why do you not simply say it is dark as Hades and be done with it?" he asked, pretending a seriousness he did not feel. "Come into the parlor. I remember that it is not quite so dark, although I make no claims for cheeriness or even gentility." As he spoke he crossed the narrow foyer to the proper door and flung it open, bowing as he gestured for Penelope to enter before him.

The room was nearly as dark as the hall and Penelope suppressed a grin.

With a mild oath Vincent strode toward a window where he pushed back drapes wrapped in protective bags. The weak winter sun crept into the room, revealing a myriad of flaws. Vincent groaned. "I had not thought it so *very* bad."

"It could be quite charming," said Penelope, moving around the room to uncover a chair here, a delicate Queen Anne desk there. She bent and lifted the cover from the sofa. Dust billowed up from it. "With," she added, once she'd controlled the series of gently explosive dust-induced sneezes, "a bit of work."

"It is dark. I dislike the dark," said Vincent, frowning.

Penelope went to the other windows and shoved back the heavy bundles, allowing in a bit more daylight. "There is too much overgrown shrubbery on this side of the house, which is part of the problem." She whirled around, glancing here and there as she did so. "The other is the dark wood and darker wallpaper. I wonder who chose that heavy red with what must, when it was new, have been a gold motif. Much too formal for a room this size."

"What would you do?" asked Vincent, curious.

"Strip off that paper to begin with. Paint everything a pale green. Order new hangings with a pale background and leaves or flowers or some other soft design. Re-cover the furniture in a slightly darker green, in a fabric that would wear well."

She put her finger to her lips, gazing around the room again and in a much more thoughtful manner. Vincent's eyes were drawn to her mouth. He felt an urge to feel its softness and took a step toward her before he caught himself. She had agreed to help him. She had trusted him enough to put herself in his power by coming here with him. He could not, *must* not, do anything that would frighten or anger her.

And kissing her as he wished to kiss her was sure to do one or the other or both.

Vincent moved to the fireplace and knelt to look up it. "Another problem. The chimney cleaners will have a job of work clearing the chimneys. I wonder when they were last seen to."

When he was certain he was back in control of himself he stood and turned . . . and found her staring at him.

"What is it?" he asked, fearing he had, somehow, given some indication of his rakish urges.

She started, blinked, and blushed ever so slightly. "Oh. Nothing. Nothing at all." She lifted her gaze to his and, suddenly, surprisingly, felt a deep connection to this man who was still very much a stranger to her. She could feel a blush heat her cheeks and lifted her hands to cover them. "How very missish of me," she murmured.

"Missish?"

Vincent took one step nearer, his heart pounding. There had been something in her eyes. Something that drew him, excited him—and at the same time drew a tenderness into him that was almost frightening in its unexpectedness.

Penelope lifted a hand.

He reached for it.

Their gazes tangled.

For a very long moment neither moved and then, squeezing her fingers, Vincent drew in a deep breath and, releasing her, moved a few steps away. "I apologize," he said, his voice slightly muffled.

"Don't."

He turned, staring, and found her smiling. "Don't apologize?"

"I have been widowed for nearly two years. I still miss Kennet. I suspect, at some level I always will. *But I am not dead.*"

Vincent blinked. Was Penelope, *Mrs. Garth,* suggesting . . .

"I am not saying I would ever indulge in an affaire—"

Vincent felt a surge of regret.

"—but I am not immune to . . . to . . ." She bit her lip, her courage failing her.

"To those feelings that can arise between a man and a woman. You have been alone for a long time now. I deserve the reputation I gained as something of a rake." He nodded. "Nevertheless, you must allow me to apologize. Those . . . feelings do not happen without some provocation. Although I did not mean to, I must, unwittingly, have . . ."

"You suggest," she interrupted, "that I am *not* the sort to rouse your rakish tendencies?" She laughed at his appalled expression when he realized he had, in a rather odd fashion, insulted her. Her voice was softer when she added, "You were merely being *you,* Vincent. I have not felt such . . . feelings for any other man but Kennet. There was no need for you to hand out lures, you see. You are, by existing, an attractive man. Still, I've no desire to become enmeshed in the sort of games that I understand are common at house parties. Please do not feel insulted if I beg you not to dangle lures before me now that I've been brash enough to admit I might . . . bite."

Vincent swallowed. A vision of attempting to fish in the Garth waters, the temptation of landing her . . . but the image of Penelope as a fish, a scaly tail behind, did not fit and he felt himself smiling. "I will do my best to behave," he said, the sardonic side of him arising. "When I forget, as I am likely to do, you must remind me."

"Hmm." Her lips twitched and she smiled. "I might, I suppose, emit a squeak."

"Or a howl."

"Or a . . . sneeze," she said, and proceeded to sneeze. There was still a great deal of dust in the air. "Or perhaps not that," she said. "It might be a trifle misleading."

"Perhaps you should merely slap my face. That is traditional, is it not?" As he spoke, he moved toward the door. "Do you wish me to return you to Minnow Manor, or will you trust me for the time it takes for a quick look through the remainder of the house?"

"You are eminently trustworthy, Vincent."

Ruefully, he wondered if that were true. But they continued their inspection, going from room to room. Vincent took brief notes of her impressions and suggestions. Finally, they came to the kitchens off the back of the house.

"My lord," he muttered, looking around. "Could anyone cook in this?"

Penelope wrinkled her nose. "I managed in worse conditions when following Kennet around the Peninsula," she said, "but here in England I do not believe I have ever seen anything quite so . . . so primitive?"

"I must strip the whole and begin again. It is the only solution," he said.

"Yes. But perhaps you should discuss how to improve it with whatever person you mean to hire as your cook."

He nodded thoughtfully. "You are correct. *I've* no notion of what is proper. I am sure the local builders would do a decent job of it, but perhaps without those niceties of touch that the person who must use the space might wish."

"You are seriously thinking of refurbishing and moving here?" she asked, curious.

It was Vincent's turn to feel heat in his neck and ears. He grimaced. "I could say Grandfather needs me and it would be true enough, but the real truth is that I'm tired of London and my life there. I need occupation and I love Beverly Place with a passion. My cousin, who will one day inherit, does not. He'll need someone to manage the place and I would be ideal if I decide to make it a lifetime occupation. He doesn't like me and very likely would try to turn me off, but his wife is far more sensible and would make it possible for me to stay on. *If I wish to.* They prefer London, the both of them, so they'd not be in my hair more than I could bear. My uncle is the immediate heir. He'll approve my staying on, although his wife will try to interfere. Oh yes—to answer your question! I mean to move here. At least for some years."

An instant of what Vincent could only call wistfulness filled Penelope's eyes, her expression, and then she drew in a deep breath. "I admit I envy you. If it were not for my estrangement from my father, I, too, would choose to live here in the Cotswolds. I missed it while away . . ."

Vincent swallowed back the advice that she should live where she pleased and ignore the curmudgeon who had tried very hard to make her life a misery. He nodded, "I, too, missed it when I was . . . gone."

She guessed he referred to his period of army service and concluded they were becoming far too serious. She asked him if he knew what the time might be.

Vincent pulled his watch from his fob pocket and snapped it open. His eyes widened. "How did it become so late? I have made you miss your lunch." He held it so she could read the time.

"Worse, once again I was not there to tell Tal a story before his nap. I always talk to him for a bit at that time. When he was a baby it was just nonsense. Or talking about his father, knowing I could say anything I pleased and no one would be embarrassed or worry about me. Nowadays I tell him little stories . . ."

"We will go."

Vincent quickly did those things that needed doing before they returned to Minnow Manor. Windows were recovered. Dust covers replaced over furniture . . . that sort of thing, but he did the work quickly and efficiently and very soon they were on their way back, arriving before the Manor at the same time as a group of wassailers.

"I will let you off here, Mrs. Garth. Georgi has a wonderful recipe and the wassail bowl will be filled with a truly delightful mixture. It includes the traditional ale and roasted apples and nutmeg, but she does something more to it. She refuses to tell even me what it is."

"No," she said, laying a hand over his on the reins, "do not stop. I will go in the back and bring Tal down to the landing where he may listen to the singing. If he is awake, that is."

"I think you will find he is already down." Vincent pointed his crop to where, just inside the door, he could see Matty holding the boy who, wide-eyed, was watching the group of strangers pass into the house.

The child looked beyond the singers into the drive and saw his mother. He squealed and reached out his arms for her. Vincent grinned at her and, resigned, she allowed him to help her down, going in the front door behind the last of the singers.

She took Tal and shushed him. He hugged her and grinned at her and then turned to listen to the old carols, the wide-eyed look back. Penelope had had no intention of joining the house party in order to listen to the wassailers, and felt a touch of chagrin that, willy-nilly, here she was. She was still more annoyed when an acquaintance, a guest who had arrived only that day, noticed her.

The young woman approached, squeezing around those crowding the entry making it difficult to move. "Lady Penelope! When did you arrive? No one informed me you were to join the party!" exclaimed Miss Charlotte Herning.

Penelope grimaced. "I don't. Amn't? Haven't?" She drew in a breath and laughed softly. "What I am saying, but not particularly coherently, is that I am *not* a part of the house party. I am here by accident, really."

Miss Herning looked bemused. "Accident?"

Penelope chuckled, but it sounded false to her critical ear. "I had meant to visit with my father over the holiday, but he didn't wish for company," she said, admitting more than she wished to do. "Lady Everhart was kind enough to offer us a roof over our heads until it is safe to travel to Edinburgh where I mean to take up residence."

"We? You?"

Penelope had forgotten Charlotte's least enduring trait. She had a curiosity that was impossible to satisfy. "Perhaps you had not heard. I was widowed at Talavera. Lieutenant Garth was Scottish and I will raise his son in Scotland."

"My poor dear!" Charlotte looked aghast. "I did not know. Then you are in mourning?" she asked.

Penelope felt irritation at the question and more irritation at the hopeful tone. "Talavera was nearly two years ago, Miss Herning. I have taken off my blacks and am in half mourning."

"Oh." Charlotte slid a sideways look at Penelope. "You will be looking about you for a new husband, then."

Did that explain Miss Herning's concern that she be in mourning? "Why would I do that?"

Charlotte blinked. "You will not?"

Penelope sighed. "I loved my Kennet. I do not think I could go into another marriage feeling anything less for the man I was to wed. Since it is unlikely I should be so very lucky twice in a lifetime, it is very unlikely I will rewed."

Charlotte eyed her. "Love." A faint tinge of bitterness crossed the woman's face. "You were lucky, I suppose. Most of us haven't any choice in the matter if we are not to wither away into old age and end by leading apes in hell."

Penelope eyed her old acquaintance. If she recalled correctly, there was a decent dowry there. Charlotte was not a beauty, but she was certainly not so ugly as to put off every man thinking of matrimony. Why had she never wed? Penelope was curious, but had better control of her curiosity than Charlotte had of hers. She didn't ask—but learned the answer anyway.

"You may wonder that I am still unwed," said Charlotte. She tittered in a most irritating way. "I was engaged. *Twice,* actually," she added with a touch of defiance. "The first time my intended had a carriage accident and died only a week before we were to tie the knot. The second time the gentleman—" Charlotte's expressive face revealed what might be anger. "—became enmeshed in a duel and was killed a mere three days before we were to meet at the altar. And then—" The anger was unmistakable now. "—I was tagged with a miserable nickname which drives any other possible suitor in the other direction rather than even *think* of wedding me."

This time Penelope found she did *not* have control. "Nickname?"

"Fatal Bride," said Charlotte, almost spitting the words

out. She drew in a deep breath. "But that is something I'd rather not discuss," she said primly. "Is this *your* son, then?" she asked, staring at Tal who was quietly resting in his mother's arms, staring at the lady with whom his mother talked. "I would like children," she added rather wistfully.

"Tal is the miracle that has kept me sane," said Penelope, meaning every word.

"He doesn't seem very old," said Charlotte.

"He was born seven and a half months after Talavera," said Penelope, her eyes narrowing. If Charlotte made any sort of snide remark about Tal . . .

She didn't. Her eyes had been restlessly searching the crowd as they talked and now she brightened. "Ah. Mr. Beverly has returned! You must excuse me. I am—" Briefly, she turned a coy look toward Penelope. "—here to be his partner, you know."

Before Penelope could comment, Charlotte had slipped between two people and moved off toward Vincent. Once she had a chance to relax the tension the woman's words had caused, Penelope was glad she had not opened her mouth and said what had come to mind. Neither Charlotte nor Vincent would have appreciated the urge she'd had to give poor Charlotte a set down for her presumption.

"And why," murmured Penelope, "was I about to do so?"

A good hostess always tries to keep the numbers even, so of course Lady Everhart chose some young woman who might keep Mr. Beverly entertained.

"Lady Penelope," the much detested voice of her bête noire interrupted her thoughts.

Penelope turned and Tal reared back against her at the nearness of the man who had spoken. "Lord Wakefield."

"You were gone all morning. Out in the cold. And you did not practice," he said, his tone accusing. He stared at the child in her arms. "Who is this?" he asked, with a hint of accusation in his tone.

"Talavera Garth, make your bow to Lord Wakefield." Penelope bobbed a bit of a curtsy in lieu of the child actually bowing.

"Garth." Wakefield's eyes widened. "*Your* son?"

Penelope blinked. "Why yes. Of course."

"You did not tell me." The accusation was clear.

"Is there some reason why I should?" she asked, holding on to her temper. She was tense, however, and the tension was communicated to Tal. The boy squirmed, frowning.

"Of course there is." But then Wakefield stopped and shook his head. "No, of course not," he contradicted himself, but his mouth pursed in a pouty look that was not at all attractive. "You will go up and practice as soon as these terrible persons leave. I know such things are traditional," he added, the prissy, faintly accusatory tone returning, "but really, such pain should not be allowed." He winced as one of the singers hit a particularly flat note. "No, no. I will never allow such goings on in any house of mine." His face screwed up as if he suffered greatly, he turned from her, headed for the door to the salon. After a few steps, however, he turned back, raised a finger, and pointed at her. "Do not forget. You must practice." And then he was gone.

Penelope shook her head. How was she to convince the man she would never sing again? She grimaced. Perhaps the easiest solution would be to try it, to show him . . . but she could not bear it.

The wassail was served to the singers and Lord Everhart passed out coins. Conversation became general as more and more people were offered and took a cup of the punch. Penelope glanced across the hall to where Charlotte hung on Vincent's arm, beaming up at him, completely ignoring the sardonic twist to his mouth that added years to his real age.

He happened to glance across at her just then and grimaced. She grinned, knowing exactly what he was thinking.

But then Tal saw him. The boy leaned in the direction of his new hero. " 'Cent! 'Cent! Want 'Cent!"

"Hmm. Time for *you* to return to your nursery, young man," said Penelope and holding the struggling boy close, she headed—not for the stairs—but to the back of the hall and the green baize covered door through which she could reach the back stairs. She could get her howling child away far sooner that way!

Penelope was rather surprised to discover she felt no particular embarrassment at her son's behavior, merely nodding at the people she passed, and noting which showed amusement and which displeasure. She had found that one learned a great deal about people by the manner in which they reacted to childish tantrums. She wondered how Lord Wakefield might behave and smiled at the horror *he'd* express. Lord Wakefield's tender ears were not meant to endure the verbal foibles of a child.

Lord Wakefield, meanwhile, had gone in search of Miss Grimson. "A child, Miss Grimson. How could she? And why must she care for it herself? It is a disaster."

"No great artist should bear children," replied Miss Grimson. "They are a distraction and a nuisance. Always falling ill just when one most needs to concentrate. And there is this odd habit a mother has of wasting time in the nursery, which is quite ridiculous. Why else does one hire a nanny and nursery maids? Surely the br . . . er, the boy does not also require the time and energy of the woman that suffered to bring it into the world."

Wakefield had never looked at the situation in quite this way. He recalled his own doting mother and how very necessary she had been to his comfort. His father had had no understanding at all of the needs of a sensitive boy who had no interest in the rowdy things boys were supposed to like. "I cannot totally agree with you. My own mother had quite a presence in our nursery." He raised his brows and cast her a knowing look. The look faded into a frown. "But surely there is no need to inflict such a very young child on company."

Miss Grimson nodded, retrieving her earlier mistake. "It is really too bad of parents who are so selfish as to think to entertain young ones at adult functions."

"Exactly," agreed Wakefield, convinced he'd changed Miss Grimson's mind about a mother's place in her child's life.

Miss Grimson had not changed one bit and was, besides, very tired of discussing a topic she found utterly boring. "Have you," she asked, "seen the latest composition by Herr Beethoven? My source sent a copy which I received only today, if you'd care to see it?" she finished, desperately wanting to take his mind from the fact that Lady Penelope had a child, something his lordship appeared to consider a revelation of great importance. "I find Herr Beethoven's music difficult but terribly exhilarating, do not you?"

Wakefield blinked, adjusted his mind to consider his real passion in life, and was soon deeply involved in a discussion of the new rage in the world of music. "You say," he said some time later, "that you have a copy of his newest work?"

They adjourned to the music room with the music. Miss Grimson seated herself at the pianoforte.

"You must," she said, suddenly worried, "not expect too much of me. I am not so very good, but I do wish to attempt the piece. It is that I cannot wait to hear *professionals* play it *properly,* but must know at once something of how it will sound."

"I understand entirely and will be patient with any mistakes," said Lord Wakefield tolerantly. "I, too, have a great impatience to discover what the German has done, this time, to set us all on our ears!"

Having magnanimously decided to put up with the defects of Miss Grimson's playing, Lord Wakefield was pleasantly surprised to discover how very good she really was. Since she had found the courage to reveal her talent, he decided it might encourage her in future if he were to reveal his own. He excused himself in order to retrieve his cello and they spent the rest of the afternoon doing their best to perfect the music.

Their best was very good indeed. In fact, when the sound of the dinner dressing bell finally cast a sour note into their playing, Wakefield laid aside his instrument and stared at Miss Grimson who, blushing, stared back. "You are very good," he said.

"Oh no," she demurred. "However, *you,* if you wished, might play with the best musicians. Herr Beethoven would be honored to hear you perform his work."

Lord Wakefield flushed. "Not true. The merest amateur," he insisted. He sighed. "It is my greatest sadness that I am such a weak musician. You however . . ."

Each attempting to convince the other of the other's talent they removed from the music room and made their way up the stairs where they were forced to separate to continue to their own rooms. Visions of years of playing duets with Lord Wakefield filled Miss Grimson's head and the satisfaction of having discovered another rare talent among the myriads of tonnish females filled Wakefield's.

Lord Wakefield, of course, had no suspicion he'd been marked for a major role before the altar in Miss Grimson's village church. Miss Grimson had, at long last, managed to find compensation for enduring the terrors of fulfilling the role a tonnish marriage required of a woman. A lifetime's production of truly excellent music would more than balance the temporary if awful pain of producing an heir.

She did pause, once, at the notion the fates might be so much against her that her first would be a girl-child. She was suddenly filled with her old fears, but, by recalling the wonderful music she and Wakefield made together, she managed to convince herself such injustice was impossible.

She returned to dreaming of duets.

CHAPTER 10

The following day Georgi spent more time than she could afford to waste convincing Penelope to join the company at dinner. "I did not wish to mention this," said Georgi, desperate to find a reason whereby Penelope would agree, "but my table will be unbalanced if you do not." She cast Penelope a chagrined look. "It is such a . . . an *unworthy* reason for asking that you go against your inclinations!"

Penelope looked startled and then laughed. She cast a quick look toward Georgi, discovered Georgi was staring at her with a hopeful expression and laughed again, this time more uproariously. She pointed, but could not control herself long enough to speak and merely stuttered a few "You . . . you . . . y . . ." before again bursting into chuckles.

Vincent stuck his head into the nursery and looked first at Penelope and then turned his gaze toward Georgi who stood, hands on hips, a frown creasing her brow, but her lips twitching. "I missed something," said Vincent. "What did I miss?"

Neither woman responded.

He rolled his eyes. "A jest and I not party to it. I cry foul."

Georgi shook her head. "It truly is not in the least humorous. I swear there was nothing at all comic in the situation. I have merely humiliated myself," she continued, putting on a patently fake expression of misery, "and all for nothing—except to provide an unexpected burst of hysteria on the part of our favorite guest."

Before Vincent could respond, they were interrupted. Tal saw Vincent and, moving with surprising speed, half crawled, half stumbled toward him, crying, " 'Cent. 'Cent. 'Cent! Want 'Cent."

Georgi's mouth fell open when Vincent swept the child up and tossed him, grinning as widely as the boy.

"Hey! He's got another tooth," he said, and turned the child into his arm so he could poke a finger into the boy's mouth. "Ouch! You little devil," he said, and poked the bitten finger into the child's tummy, which produced chortles of glee.

"My goodness," whispered Georgi. "I hadn't a clue my cousin had such a way with children."

"He is very good with Tal, is he not?"

"I suppose this ability to charm a child is part and parcel of whatever it is that makes him the favorite of all who know him," mused Georgi—but wheels began churning inside her head and her eyes narrowed.

Georgi was unaware of how Penelope interpreted the thoughtless comment. If she *had* known, she would have spent another hour she could ill afford, doing her best to undo the damage. But she did *not* know. Instead, she asked, "*Will* you come down tonight?"

Penelope's features had not been rid of a trifling remnant of the pained look that filled them upon hearing Georgi's explanation of Vincent's rapport with her child. Georgi's version was far more believable than Penelope's hope that *Vincent* was falling under *Tal's* spell. That it was the other way around, Tal under Vincent's spell, was far more realistic—once it had been put into one's mind.

"Oh dear," said Georgi. "If the notion pains you to that

degree, then of course you need not join us." Georgi was appalled by what she, mistakenly, thought she'd done.

"What? Oh. Of course I will come," said Penelope in an offhanded manner. "It is merely dinner. I need not stay in the salon afterwards."

"No, of course you need not," said Georgi—but wondered at the easy agreement when that expression had convinced her, as nothing else had done, that she had gone too far in her attempts to draw Penelope back into society. Georgi's eyes narrowed. It seemed there was something else at work here—and Georgi put her fertile mind to work on *that* possibility along with the odd notion that had crossed her mind when she saw Vincent's easy way with Talavera.

Dinner that evening was by far the most formal of those so far served to the house party. The party from Beverly Place was large. It included not only Georgi's grandfather and aunts, but Lord Tivington's son, the heir's wife, *his* son and daughter, and the son and daughters' respective spouses. Those nine along with a handful of the more important neighbors—beyond the dozen or so already under the manor's roof—filled the large dining room very nearly to excess.

The table had been extended to its maximum size and covered by the only tablecloth anywhere near large enough. One or two darns were carefully hidden under candlesticks and other items of dinnerware. And, of course, the cutlery, crystal, and china gleamed in the candlelight, distracting the company from any possible inadequacies. Besides, the servants served with a dexterity that impressed many of the guests.

Country servants were rarely so well trained, but Georgi had invented a game she played with them that *showed* them what to do instead of merely *telling* them and the good results of her rather odd method of teaching were obvious.

Georgi felt a deal of pleasure as she glanced around her table. Lady Houghten was—at least this early in the evening—

polite to Mrs. Mandale. That they were seated at opposite ends of the long table probably facilitated the unusual fact that they had *not* come to points. Yet. Georgi was not sanguine about their ability—or desire—to maintain the peace as the evening lengthened.

Her glance flitted here and there around her table. She had placed Penelope between her grandfather and her Aunt Marie, who was, at the moment, entertaining—if that was the word for it—the younger woman by repeating a great number of *on dits* which might not have come Mrs. Garth's way while she was abroad. Grandfather, obviously awaiting an opportunity to introduce a more suitable topic, listened. He would soon attract Penelope's attention, so Georgi did not concern herself with the situation.

On the other side of the table Lord Wakefield sat beside Miss Grimson, muttering to her, a dark look on his handsome features. Too often he would cast that glower toward Penelope who, since it was impolite to speak to anyone across the table, could pretend she had not noticed and pretend he didn't exist.

Miss Grimson quite obviously nursed another wish—that *Lady Penelope* did not exist. Was that a possible match? Lord Wakefield and Miss Grimson? Georgi recalled it had crossed her mind once before. She tucked the thought away for later consideration, since her original plan—to wed Wakefield to Penelope—had come to nothing.

Vincent, when she looked his way, cast her a sardonic look—one that promised swift revenge. She grinned at him. She'd known when she placed him between their Aunt Matilda and Lady Houghten he'd be unhappy with her, but one must drive the team one had and so she would tell him. He was the only possible solution to her major problem in seating her guests and he must just do his best—which, of course, being Vincent, he would do very well indeed.

Still, that look was a warning and not to be ignored. Georgi made a mental note to check the sugar in the morning and assure herself, *before* she stirred it into her tea, that it *was* sugar. And perhaps she should check her riding boots before putting them on and . . . but enough of that. She knew Vincent well. He'd not manage to take revenge on her by such juvenile tricks if she kept her wits about her.

Elsewhere around the table all seemed well and Georgi turned to her right when her dinner partner asked her a question. "I am very sorry, my lord. I was worrying about the sweet course," she prevaricated, "and didn't hear you . . . ?"

Dinner progressed. Her partner complimented her on the desserts offered, telling her she'd worried in vain—which comment had Georgi scrambling to recall the excuse she'd given him for her earlier inattention. The meal ended soon after and Georgi, casting that look all hostesses must learn, gathered the eyes of her female guests and rose to her feet.

"We will adjourn to the salon," she said, "so that we may enjoy a measure of peace and quiet before the gentlemen remember our existence and join us," she said with a mischievous look. "Peace will, of course, be at an end then, their minds still *chewing* over the movements of various armies and their *digestion* of Wellington's plans along with a *main course* of railing against our French *bête noire*."

There was mild laughter and, with a satisfied nod, Georgi led the way to the double doors, which her butler flung open. She paused in the hall, gesturing the women onward as she waited for Penelope to come out.

"Will you change your mind?" she asked.

Penelope hesitated and then nodded. "I had better come for coffee before I go upstairs," said Penelope, pointing a discreet finger. She added a smile for Lady Houghten who approached with much the style of a warship. A top of the line ship of course, and under full sail with a good following wind! Penelope lowered her voice. "I've a notion that if I disappear before enduring Lady Houghten's catechism, I will bring down her wrath upon your head . . ."

"Never mind that. If you want to . . ."

Penelope shook her head and, holding out her hand, greeted her ladyship politely if without excessive enthusiasm. She was borne off to a corner of the salon where Lady Houghten proceeded to ask more questions in ten minutes than most people could think up in an hour. Penelope remained patient until a final question was too impertinent even for her tolerant nature.

"No, he has not," she responded, her voice icy. "I doubt my father either knows—or cares—that he has a grandson," she added, her bitterness obvious. "And speaking of my son—" She brightened at finding the necessarily polite excuse. "—it is time I check on him." Lady Houghten expressed shock that Penelope felt any such need. Penelope, patience at an end, smiled sweetly and added, "Yes, I really must go. It is possible that, if I stay here, I will find myself unable to remain polite in the face of—everyone's—curiosity."

She nodded and escaped before Lady Houghten probed under her pleasant tone to the meaning of the words. When she'd discovered the insult, her ladyship turned so quickly, in order to send a glare after Penelope, that her turban, unable to maintain its position, twisted to one side and tilted to an odd angle.

Georgi, watching them at that particular moment, hid a grin at what was Lady Houghten's mortification. On the other hand, if something were not done, it was likely the woman would retaliate by spreading all sorts of venom about the region concerning Penelope. Georgi excused herself to the small group with which she was speaking and crossed the room.

"Did Mrs. Garth become overly tired again?" Georgi pretended chagrin. "It was too bad of me to ask her to fill in at the table when she has not fully recovered."

"Recovered?" asked Lady Houghten, glaring down her long nose at Georgi.

Georgi's brows rose. "You are unaware she came very near to dying in that recent storm? Her father, you know. Lord Tennytree refused her admittance to Tennytree Hill, but only after she had paid off her job coach and sent it away. He also refused her and her son transport to the village where, when she finally reached it on foot, she discovered there was no room in the inn. She was making her way to a friend's house when the storm caught her. She became confused, lost, exhausted, and very nearly gave up."

"My goodness," said Lady Houghten, blinking. But then she recovered. "An affecting tale," she sneered. "You—so very young and innocent of you, me dear—believe it, or so I must suppose?"

"Since I helped her from snow encrusted clothing, boots soaked to the point they were ruined, and worked very hard to assure she did not come down with an ague, I assure you I believe it." Georgi had trouble retaining a pleasant manner but forced herself to do so. Penelope had suffered enough. She must not be made to suffer Lady Houghten's vituperative tongue.

"She insulted me," said Lady Houghten, drawing herself up.

"As I said, she still tires easily. If she snapped at something said to her, then I am sure she will be sorry for it. It is my fault for encouraging her to join us this evening when she was not yet ready to do so." She hoped word of the long rides Penelope and she had taken never reached Lady Houghten's ears. The quickly invented excuses, though with a basis in truth, would be seen as the soft soap they were if her ladyship were to do so.

"Ah." Her ladyship mulled over the excuses along with weighing her anger and, finally, managed to be generous. "I suppose answering *polite*—" She glared down her nose, forbidding disbelief. "—questions concerning her father *is* difficult for her when the man is—the man he is," finished Lady Houghten rather lamely.

Georgi's brows rose. "You brought that man's name into the conversation? The man who came near to killing her and her son by his heartlessness?" Georgi stared at her guest with such conflicting emotions flickering across her features even she was unsure of what she really felt. The surprise was false. The outrage was real. But other sensations roiled through those two making such a stew of her emotions that she made no attempt to define the ingredients.

Spots of color touched Lady Houghten's cheeks. She hurumphed and then, obviously relieved to hear them arrive, was able to turn toward the doors through which the men, in twos and threes, entered the salon. "Now we will have some entertainment, will we not?" demanded her ladyship, her nose once again elevated and her glare directed down the length of it.

"Of course we will," agreed Georgi, wafting a prayer of thanks heavenward that the men arrived so opportunely. "I have had tables set up in the connecting room for those who wish to indulge in a hand or two of cards. As will my aunts, for instance. The card players, however, will not be so isolated from this room they cannot hear the music one or two of the guests have agreed to provide."

She nodded to Lady Houghten, who, at the mention of cards, brightened. Her ladyship swept into the other room and to the table farthest from the salon. There she waited, gathering her usual partner and the couple with whom she liked best to play. Her liking was based on the fact that they did not play so well, so that she often won. Lady Houghten did *not* like losing.

Lord Wakefield, after a quick search of the salon, came directly to Georgi's side. "Lady Penelope. Where is she?"

"She tired and returned to her rooms, of course," said

Georgi, and cast a look toward her husband who immediately joined her. She took Everhart's arm and drew in a breath. "Now, I've asked several of the young ladies to perform for us. And two of the gentlemen have agreed to sing a duet. Is it possible that you and Miss Grimson might play for us? I heard you practicing . . ."

Wakefield looked appalled. It had not occurred to him at the time that he was not only revealing his secret to Miss Grimson, but that the *world* would become privy to it as well.

"No, no," he said. "I would embarrass myself forever. No. I couldn't." He backed away and went in search of Miss Grimson who was staring sourly at the young lady searching through the music on top of the pianoforte.

"Lady Penelope will not sing," he said, abruptly, his scowl at least as nasty as Miss Grimson's although for different reasons.

"Nor will Miss Phisby, although she *tries*," she whispered in return. "I cannot bear to listen to Miss Phisby mangle one more ballad."

"I am so disappointed I do not believe I could pretend polite attention." He tugged at his nose, a mannerism he rarely allowed himself when in company, but he was exceedingly upset and didn't think how it would look. "I know. Let us go to the library. It is far enough from this room that, perhaps, we will not have our ears tortured by wrong notes and shrill voices." His brows arched and he offered his arm.

Miss Grimson hesitated, but then she heard Miss Phisby squeal and say something to the effect of "the very thing" and immediately agreed—although she knew it was wrong to go off alone with his lordship.

Why, if we are found together . . .

Her eyes widened at the thought and, half guiltily, she too sent a prayer wafting heavenward. Hers was to the effect someone *would* come searching for them, would *find* them. Alone. Together. *Behind closed doors . . .*

So, with that thought in her head, she was chagrined that Lord Wakefield left the door half open. She sighed.

Still—she brightened—*we may discuss music and not find ourselves enduring impossibly amateur attempts at making it.*

And so they did.

Penelope stared into the day nursery fireplace. Tal was abed, asleep, so she was safely able to pull the heavy woven wire guard from before the hearth. She watched for pictures in the flames but found that she was unable to indulge her favorite form of relaxation. However much she tried to concentrate on flames and embers, her mind allowed her no peace.

Finally, she replaced the screen and moved into her room. She went to the desk she'd not expected to need and wrote a note of apology to Lady Houghten. Returning to the nursery, she found Matty yawning over her mending and sent the maid down to find a footman who would deliver the note to her ladyship. That done, she returned to her fire watching and found, to her satisfaction, that there were lots of pictures to be seen.

Vincent, after a quick glance proved his suspicion that Penelope would not be present in the salon, stifled a sigh and moved to stand near his grandfather, thereby outmaneuvering two young ladies who hoped to gain his attention. Miss Herning, however, was made of sterner stuff and less easily convinced her company was unwanted. She took up a position very near the group of men with whom Vincent talked, and maintained it patiently—quite as patiently as Vincent listened to older men propound theories, make pronouncements, and carefully contradict each other in the politest possible manner.

Vincent would, he was determined, stay there for the whole of the evening if he must. Miss Charlotte Herning's antics to attract him were a dead bore and it was too bad that polite usage denied him the right to tell her so.

Unfortunately, Georgi called the company to order, announcing that Miss Phisby would play and sing a few folk songs for their entertainment. The men, reluctantly, ceased their conversation and, politely, turned to listen.

It was Miss Herning's cue to step forward and take Vincent's arm. "There is a sofa just there. Shall we . . . ?" she asked brightly.

Without speaking he escorted her to the sofa, helped her seat herself, and then, pretending to seat himself, but catching himself, he bowed. "I see my cousin wishes something of me. Please excuse me." He turned on his heel and hurried over to Georgi's side and whispered in her ear. "Pretend to send me off on an errand and I will forgive you for seating me next to Lady Houghten at dinner."

Georgi, glanced up at him, saw he was serious, and gestured toward the door, pretending to give the order but really telling him he was a villain to desert such a desperate young woman as Charlotte.

"She has taken it into her head that we will suit. I can find no polite way of telling her we will *not*."

Georgi bit her lip to stifle laughter but her eyes danced. "Poor Vincent," she murmured. "Off you go," she added, giving him a little push.

He went. To the library—from which he hurriedly backed when he saw that Lord Wakefield and Miss Grimson were deep in what looked to be an intensely personal conversation. Would there be an announcement there, he wondered, and, unable to think of another room that Georgi had not given over to the party, he went up to his bedroom where he found coat, hat, and cigar. Using the back stairs so he'd avoid guests, he went through the kitchens and out into the protected kitchen garden where he could enjoy a smoke. It was the only possible excuse he could make that would not too badly contravene polite conventions.

Vincent leaned against the brick wall surrounding the garden and stared up at the top floor. Lights showed dimly through the day nursery windows. Mrs. Garth was there.

Penelope.

It is a nice name, thought Vincent. *Penny?* He considered and shook his head. *No. Penelope fits her. She has that calm that Odysseus's wife must have had. And another of that particular heroine's qualities as well.* He felt a trifling regret at this thought. *She is loyal to her husband.*

Vincent stared at the windows, occasionally taking a puff from the cigar. He threw away the butt and wondered if he'd been gone long enough that Miss Herning would have found another man to entertain her. He feared she had not, but forced himself to return to the salon anyway.

He reached the hall at the same time as Matty. "What is it, child?" he asked.

"Mrs. Garth, she wants this taken to Lady Houghten," said Matty. She looked flummoxed, finding no footman where she'd expected one to be.

"Give it to me. I'll take it," said Vincent. Even Lady Houghten was better than Miss Herning. He'd seen her ladyship earlier when he'd glanced into the card room and was not surprised to discover she was still there. He stood near the table while her ladyship lectured her partner on how he should have played his last hand. Assuming she'd been doing so the whole of the evening, which was likely, Vincent was not surprised to see the man rise stiffly to his feet and excuse himself to the others all the while glaring at his partner.

Lady Houghten's glare was far fiercer, but then she'd had far more practice. Vincent debated whether he should attempt to deliver the note just then or wait until her mood improved. It occurred to him that one might wait a long time to discover her ladyship in a truly benign mood and moved forward.

"My lady," he said, and found the glare turned his way.

"You! Ha!" She pointed across the table. "Sit."

Vincent's brows rose, but from the corner of his eye he saw Miss Herning hovering in the doorway. He sat. "My lady, as I began to say, I found the nursery maid in the hall. She was looking for a footman to deliver this note to you." Vincent handed it across the table.

Lady Houghten told the lady on her right to deal while she read. She proceeded to untwist the note. "Hurumph," she said when she finished . . . but Vincent thought there was a faint relaxation to the woman's harsh features. She looked up and the glare returned. "I hope you are not one of these modern young men who have never attempted to learn proper whist," she said.

Vincent smiled the faintly self-deriding, faintly cynical smile that settled into his features far too often. "My grandfather," he said, his voice dry, "would never have forgotten such an important part of my education, my lady."

"Well." Her brows rose. "We shall see, shall we not?"

Vincent saw Miss Herning disappear from the doorway and, breathing a sigh of relief, settled himself to play. Lady Houghten was, he knew, an excellent player, one who did not tolerate stupid errors. Grandfather had been equally intolerant during those winter months in which, with one of the aunts taking the fourth hand, their grandfather had, with stern determination and great thoroughness, taught Georgi and himself the finer points of the game.

They finished the first set and her ladyship actually, if grudgingly, gave him a compliment. Vincent reminded himself to thank his grandfather for all those hours of patient—and occasionally not so patient—teaching.

Upstairs, an old and dog-eared deck in her hands, one that had traveled back and forth over the Iberian Peninsula,

Penelope laid out still another hand of Patience. She stared at it blankly for a long moment, wondering what Tal's 'Cent was doing, and then, with a sigh, played out the game.

And then another.

And another . . .

Her candle guttered and she looked up from the game she was just then laying out. *How,* she wondered, slightly shocked, *has it gotten so very late?* Feeling something akin to mild guilt for wasting candles and lamp oil, she put away the cards and prepared for bed.

And then lay there in the dark room, staring into nothing at all, and wondering why she felt so restless, so unsettled . . . and perhaps even a little unhappy? She absolutely refused to admit that it had anything to do with her decision to escape Lady Houghten by coming upstairs, that there was any reason whatsoever she might have wished to remain with the company . . .

And then she did.

Admit it, that is.

The time had come. A proper time for putting away her pain and distress at losing Kennet. Not to *forget,* but time to find quiet enjoyment in what she had. And, if that pleasure included time spent with a certain gentleman—well so be it.

Another, less satisfying thought followed the first. Perhaps that pleasure would result in *more* pain? Later? Once she went north to her new home in Edinburgh? Once she could no longer enjoy the gentleman's company?

She sighed. That, too, was something with which she could deal. When the time came. As it would . . .

With another sigh, Penelope drifted into a deep sleep in which a certain gentleman played a large role. When she woke the next morning she had no recollection of dreaming, but something bothered her. The reason for her sense of irritation escaped her, however, and Tal's morning antics soon wiped away the last lingering traces of frustration.

CHAPTER 11

Several days later Vincent woke to the new day feeling as if he had had only a few hours sleep. Since he had been in his bed for nearly seven he knew that was wrong and could not understand why he felt strung out, tense, and slightly unhappy. He leaned against the pillows his valet propped for his back and sipped his morning tea while staring straight ahead. Actually, he sipped only once. The rest chilled and, taking a long delayed sip, he cast the tea an unbelieving look— but went back to staring.

The watchful valet took cup and saucer and set them aside before holding out a wildly colored banyan made of a heavy silk, a hint of the oriental in the styling. Vincent's tailor had discovered the silk tucked away in a corner of a warehouse and suggested Vincent might like a robe made of it. Vincent, his odd sense of humor tickled, had not only agreed, but taken a hand in the design—which was extreme in several ways, not the least of which was that it showed off his ankles and more than a trifling length of hairy leg. The full skirts swung nicely when he strode and the palm-sized silk-covered buttons running down the front drew a smile whenever he touched them.

Bunsen, his valet, could not like the robe. He had no sense of humor whatsoever and could not see its attraction. However that might be, he did like his master, so had not given into his earnest desire to find some means of—accidentally, of course—destroying the thing.

Vincent remained far more quiet than usual as Bunsen shaved him, something his master usually did for himself. Nor did Vincent comment on the suit of clothes laid ready for him. It was not riding dress, his preferred morning attire, but he'd no intention of riding. Instead, he meant to borrow either Everhart's gig or his curricle so he ordered his heavy cloak readied for the drive. He meant to attend to some of his grandfather's orders—but, more importantly, he hoped Mrs. Garth might be free and willing to aid him further in the planning of the changes to the dower house.

As he was helped into the tight coat that went with the long trousers, he mused over the preceding few days. They had had a mild day for the former agent's funeral, which was lucky. His aunts would have been against Lord Tivington's attending it if there were wind, rain, or snow, so there would have been a distressing argument if the weather had *not* co-operated. His lordship had every attention of showing honor to the man who had worked loyally and well over several decades, and would not have been gainsaid, however much the aunts said against it.

The service itself was distressing enough. The vicar saw fit to include a homily about neighbors who did not take time to be neighborly and a less than gentle chiding concerning the length of time before the agent's death was discovered. It was a lecture appreciated by no one.

The funeral was a turning point in Vincent's life. From that day he was accepted as his grandfather's new agent, and had been busier, actually, than he either expected or liked. Between authorizing various repairs, setting them in motion, overseeing how they went on, *and* arranging to have the dower house brought up to snuff, *and,* along with all that, managing to do his duty as a guest at Minnow Manor, Vincent was feeling a trifle harassed.

Worst of all, he discovered he lacked time to pursue a certain very personal interest, one that, as time passed, grew more and more urgent. Vincent went down to breakfast that morning and was further annoyed to discover that Everhart had already broken his fast, gone out, and was, therefore, unavailable to be approached with regard to a carriage. He scowled at his shirred eggs and the slice of ham until Georgi, who had eyed him as she talked to some of the female guests, excused herself and moved to a chair beside him.

"What is it, Vincent?" she asked, concerned.

"I am finding life a trifle hectic at the moment, brat, that is all," he said, erasing the frown and turning his usual heavy lidded sardonic look her way. "Why? Do I seem particularly preoccupied that you feel it necessary to ask?"

"Preoccupied is perhaps too gentle a word for the expression you wore. Are there more problems than you expected over at the Place?" she asked.

He shrugged. "There are problems. I fear Elbertson allowed the work to slide for far longer than we realized and there are other, more personal, problems with which I must deal. The dower house is something of a mess, you know. The rest would not be difficult if I were not also attempting to put it in order and doing my duty by you. Have you any notion of how much work is involved? How many decisions one must make?" he asked, rhetorically.

Georgi, however, did not merely smile and change the subject. She nodded. "When Everhart began the work here it was the same. You must remember what the manor was like before the workmen were brought in. It was months before one could walk down any hall and not fear to trip over a tool or kick over a bucket of paint or find the floor just refinished and not yet dry, which meant one could not get to the room one wanted."

"Months?" Vincent cast her a look pregnant with disbelief. "Surely you exaggerate."

"I think you will discover otherwise. Good morning, Mrs. Garth," she said, glancing up at the new arrival. "Oh dear, did you not sleep well last night?"

Penelope, rather heavy eyed, smiled. "I think my rest suffered from one or two dreams. That is unusual for me."

The young women, all of them avidly waiting a moment in which they might draw Vincent's attention to themselves, instantly and simultaneously found an excuse to join the conversation. Each attempting to outdo the next, they rattled on and on, relating their very worst nightmares.

Vincent, wishing they would go away, but knowing they would not—not while he was there—excused himself. He immediately found a spot where he was not visible but where he could see the breakfast room door. He put a shoulder against the wall and, his eye glued to the crack where the hinges of the partly open door gave him a spy hole, awaited a glimpse of Penelope. While he waited, his mind traveled the route he meant to take that day.

The other women left the breakfast room first—much to his relief—a chattering bevy of brightly colored chits, their holiday "feathers" brightening up what looked to be another dull winter day.

Penelope was not long after them. She had, while following the drum, learned to be a quick neat eater and the habit lingered. Besides, she had discovered that Lord Wakefield had not yet breakfasted and wished to be gone before he arrived.

"Oh," she said, when Vincent joined her in the hall, "you startled me!"

"I apologize," he said, "but I wished to ask if you might have time today for a more detailed tour of the dower house. The workmen have pretty well finished stripping off old paper and I must make final decisions concerning paint color and fabrics. I know of no one I would rather ask than you."

Penelope felt herself coloring up—and then her neck and ears heated up still more at the embarrassment of discovering that she was embarrassed. She compressed her lips.

"If it is inconvenient . . ." began Vincent, worried by her expression.

Penelope interrupted. "I would happily give you any aid I could if I were certain you were not merely being kind."

Vincent frowned. "Kind? To ask you to do a great deal of work in my behalf? My dear Penelope, you have the strangest notions of kindness!"

Penelope blinked, thought of telling Vincent it was improper of him to use her name, and then, just as quickly wondered if he thought of her that way. In an instant, she decided she'd do better to just ignore it. "I guess I feared you had discovered that I once felt I had a knack for that sort of thing," she said. "I thought you were allowing me to take part because you knew I'd enjoy it no end."

He chuckled. "And how was I supposed to have known any such thing? But I am *delighted* to have the opportunity to indulge you!" He adopted a hopeful look. "When could you begin?"

She shrugged. "I've nothing planned for today. Anytime you wish."

Vincent nodded. "I will ask Georgi if we may use the dogcart. If Everhart were available, I'd borrow a fancier carriage, but he is not and I do not wish to take a vehicle he may need. Half an hour?" he asked.

Penelope frowned slightly. "An hour? I spend a bit of time playing with Tal first thing each morning. As he gets older I will begin teaching him his letters."

He nodded. "An hour."

He returned to the breakfast room where he knew Georgi remained. Penelope moved through the servant's door to the backstairs, knowing she could avoid running into any of the guests that way.

Especially, that she would avoid one particular guest!

Since drapery had been removed so that the work could begin, the rooms were not quite as dark as before. Vincent looked around and grimaced, but turned his gaze to Penelope.

"I will leave you to make notes, then," he said, when he couldn't convince her her decisions would be acceptable. "And I'll return as soon as possible in order to discuss them with you, since you feel I should." Vincent sternly repressed a desire to touch the wisp of hair that lay against Penelope's neck. "I know the aunts would enjoy our joining them for a bite to eat in midday. I will do my best to be in time so that we will have finished here and can go there."

Penelope hesitated and then nodded.

"You are reluctant," he said in the same frank way Georgi would have made such a personal comment. "Why?"

She smiled a wry smile. "You have caught me out. I did not dress to go into company, but to work here where, as you know, it is not so clean as one might wish. I will take that dirt into your aunts' very pleasant dining room and feel awkward doing so. Especially since so much of your family is in residence." She shrugged. "It is just that I do not wish to make a guy of myself."

"Of course you will not wish to be seen in all your dirt! I should have thought of it. Ah!" he said, instantly finding a solution to the problem. "I shall stop in the village and ask for a basket at the inn. We shall dine here. You must order a decent fire made up in whichever room you think we might use for our picnic," he said and, with a nod, left her.

Forced himself to leave her.

It was, he discovered, becoming harder and harder to behave sensibly in her presence and he wondered why.

Perhaps, he decided, *it is because I have never before felt the need to move with such care in a relationship.*

Always, when he found he'd an interest in a woman, he'd shown that interest and reacted as the woman indicated was her pleasure. If his interest were returned, he and she, whoever she might be, would enjoy an interlude of a shorter or a longer length, and when the interest faded, the interlude was ended, politely and with grace.

Vincent did not dare approach Mrs. Garth in the same fashion. It was not that it was inappropriate to think of her in terms of dalliance. Widows were often freer with their favors than many a straight-laced matron thought proper, so it was not that—although she had admitted she did not wish to indulge in an affaire. Still he might . . .

He shook his head. It didn't feel right.

Vincent searched his mind and heart to discover the source of his difficulty. His left brow arched nicely and his smile twisted when he realized this particular relationship was far more important to him than was usual. The discovery that he actually feared she would send him to the right about and that he'd then be allowed no further opportunity to convince her how very well they would deal together was more than a bit of a shock.

Too, sneaking under his guard from time to time, was the very odd notion that he did not wish his usual sort of affaire with this woman. There was the added problem, therefore, that he was uncertain what it was that he *did* want.

It was all very confusing and Vincent disliked confusion. Therefore, he refused to be rushed into . . . anything. Whatever that *anything* might be.

But, he fretted, *I wish I knew.*

Vincent was gone for no more than half an hour when

Penelope heard voices in the entrance hall. Her head jerked up and she clutched the pad of paper on which she'd been jotting down notes concerning color and fabrics for the small library—or perhaps it should be called an office—below the notes concerning what might be kept of the heavy old-fashioned furniture crowding the room and what needed discarding or replacing. For a moment the strange voices frightened her, but then she recalled that Mr. Beverly had hired two maids who were working somewhere in the house. She relaxed.

No longer afraid, her curiosity drove her to the door where she could listen more easily in order to determine who had arrived.

"The drawing room is quite adequate for the boy as it is," said a loud, rather harsh feminine voice.

"Oh no," said another, softer one. "I fear Vincent would be quite unhappy, living with such dark decor."

"He will put up with whatever I decide," said the first voice. "He hadn't the courtesy to discuss his rash decisions with the pertinent parties and he will find he must live with whatever comes of it. I have decided this is fine just as it is."

Penelope bit her lip. Who were they? What were they discussing? And, come to that, what right did anyone other than Lord Tivington have to interfere in what Vincent did or did not do?

"I believe Vincent did discuss it," said the second voice. "With Lord Tivington." Penelope heard a dry note she liked. "My husband's grandfather mentioned it to me just last evening."

"And why would he discuss such a thing with *you?*" This voice, the first one, carried sarcasm soaked in bitterness, and seasoned with enough venom that Penelope did not like it at all. "It is *my* husband who will inherit. And I cannot think it will be so long now." There was a very brief silence. "And, of course, my husband's aunts will then require the dower house.

I do not know why Vincent is even thinking of living here. It will be no time at all before he must find accommodation elsewhere."

This time Penelope heard something more positive, but equally unlikable. It sounded very much like triumph. Who in heaven's name was speaking? Penelope's thoughts settled on the woman's reference to her husband and she searched her mind, coming up with the name. *Lady Melicent.*

Penelope sighed as she recalled how the woman had looked down her nose when they were introduced before the dinner she'd been rash enough to attend. What was she to do? Could she possibly remain hidden? A clatter from the upstairs where workmen were still stripping ancient wallpaper from one of the bedroom's walls, caught everyone's attention.

"What is that?" asked Lady Melicent—and Penelope heard determined footsteps climbing stairs.

"My lady," said the other voice, "do you think . . ."

"I think my nephew has gone far beyond his allowed responsibility and actually had the gall to order in workmen. *That* is what I think. Who will pay for it, that's what I want to know?"

The bitterness in that was unbelievable. Could Lord Tivington's son be in such financial difficulties that her ladyship feared there would not be enough to sort out his problems, when—not soon one hoped—the time came he did inherit? Surely not . . .

"My lady, please. Do come down. I really think we should return to the house and discuss this with his lordship."

"I will not have that man ruining all. He is in his dotage. He *must* be, assuming he allowed this. I will have him declared incompetent."

"I think not," said Vincent. He had come quietly in the back door. "Grandfather and I discussed, in detail, what is to be done. I will thank you to *not* stick your overly officious nose into any of it."

The steps, louder and more hurried, returned to the hall. "You! You mean to feather your nest at my expense. I know you do!"

"Aunt, sometimes I think you are escaped from bedlam, the ideas you take into your head. Besides, whatever you wish to believe, there is nothing you can do. Grandfather and I have signed a lease for my use of the dower house. It details my responsibility to see it is modernized and kept up. Since that expense will be on *my* shoulders, I believe we have nothing further to say."

Consternation had given her pause—for a moment. "The lease expires, of course, upon the date of Lord Tivington's death," said her ladyship snidely.

"It does if he lives for exactly ten more years minus three days," said Vincent, that dry sardonic note so common to him more obvious than ever.

"Nonsense! Where are your aunts to live if you have selfishly taken over the dower house?" Again there was that terrible triumph in her tone.

There was silence.

Penelope heard an odd sound and realized Lady Melicent had stamped her foot. "You cannot expect my husband to house them, feed them, and care for them!"

Again silence reigned.

"I will not have it!"

"And you called me selfish," said Vincent softly. "You would turn the aunts out of the only home they have ever known? At their age? It is not myself who is selfish, Aunt Melicent. Good day to you. And to you, Cousin Alicia. Perhaps *you* would care to come another day and I will tell you what I have planned?"

The emphasis on the "you" in that invitation made Penelope smile. She heard the women leave, Lady Melicent complaining loudly and swearing revenge and Alicia speaking soothingly but with no obvious result. When the door shut behind them she waited a moment to make certain Lady Melicent did not return and then moved into the hall.

"Mr. Beverly?"

He turned, glaring, and then, seeing her, wiped the frown from his forehead. He forced a smile. "Penelope—Mrs. Garth, I mean . . . ?"

She felt herself color but did not give him permission to use her name as the faint querying note she heard suggested she do.

"You heard?" he asked after a moment.

Penelope nodded. "You have no notion how very glad I was to hear your voice. I feared I would be discovered and would have been asked to explain my presence here. I do not think your aunt would have accepted anything I said and would certainly have disapproved. Do you think informing her that you mean to pay for the improvements will—once she has thought about it—satisfy her?"

"No, because she does not like me. She knows Grandfather prefers me to her son, which hurts her pride. She also knows I will do an excellent job as Grandfather's agent and that irks her still more. And—" He frowned again. "—I very much fear that threat to banish my other aunts from the Place once she is mistress there was not merely hot air, but a very real threat. I would house them myself—there is room here, although it might feel a trifle crowded. That is not such a very large problem, but the fear that they would be unhappy anywhere but in what they must consider their home—now *that* I consider a problem of major proportions."

"Could she really be so cruel?"

"Aunt Melicent is very jealous of her rights, of her authority, of all sorts of things you, who possess a heart, will never understand. But it is true that, if the aunts stay on at the Place after Grandfather's death, it will be hard for them to change, to discontinue giving orders as they've always done. The servants will go to them when they've a problem, another thing that would anger Melicent. Unfortunately, she is the sort who, when in a temper, does not *think*. She might actually try to give the boot to someone who has been in service here for decades." He sighed. "She could not do it, of course. My uncle would never allow it, but the fact she tried would count against her. Despite her many faults, Aunt Melicent is aware of most of them—and although one must disparage her methods, one must admit her reason for attempting to set things *just so,* is so that she is less likely to fall into the briars."

"She would evict your other aunts. Just like that. So that they would not be a problem. *For her.*"

Vincent nodded.

Penelope groaned. "Do you—" She, pretended a brightness she did not feel. "—think there is a school where people like your aunt and my father go to learn their nasty ways?"

Vincent laughed. "Perhaps. The school of hard knocks, do you think?"

She smiled but shook her head.

He offered an alternative. "The school of *giving* hard knocks perhaps?"

That had Penelope stifling a chuckle, but she searched for a way to change the subject. Her eye fell on the basket Vincent had placed on a table near the baize door to the service rooms. "Is that, by chance, our picnic?" she asked.

A sudden rumble from her stomach brought her eyes to Vincent's face to see if he'd heard. He had, and attempted, but failed, to hide a smile. She sighed dramatically.

"I opened up the breakfast room," she continued, ignoring his twinkling eyes, "and found rather yellowed linens for the table. Shall we take your basket there and see what we've been offered in the way of a feast?"

"Instantly," he agreed. He offered his arm, picked up the basket as they passed it, and swung open the door to the breakfast room. His brows climbed up his forehead. "Well . . ."

"Is it?" she asked, giving the word another meaning. "I found the roses in a protected corner of the brick walled garden. It seemed a pity to leave such beauty hidden away like that."

Vincent bit his lip, creases reappearing on his forehead. "That's another thing, isn't it? I must find a gardener to bring the garden under control. I wonder why I thought it would be such a good idea to take this house for my home."

"Because you needed more freedom than living up at the Place would give you, but need to be nearby. That's why. Really, it will not be so very bad," she said encouragingly, "and you will be pleased when it is finished."

"Yes, but Georgi threatens me with chaos for *months,* and I doubt I've the patience to put up with it."

"That is perhaps an exaggeration. This house is, after all, not so large as the Manor. Come to that, perhaps Lord Everhart would allow you to live there while the work is done here," she suggested absently, far more interested in emptying the basket of the good things the inn's cook had packed for them than in their conversation.

"Now that is a truly ingenious notion," said Vincent, "I wonder why I did not think of it?"

Penelope looked up and found him watching her. "Think of what?" she asked—but her mind was caught up with wondering why Vincent stared with an intensity of gaze that was rather unsettling.

After a moment he said, "Did you say something?"

Her gaze still entangled by his, Penelope blinked, and, with effort, managed to turn away from him. "I . . ." She touched one of the plates she'd set out for their meal. She straightened. "I haven't a clue what either of us is talking about. Shall we eat?"

Vincent, watching her set out the food, her hands efficient but gentle, had suddenly realized just exactly what it was he wanted of this woman. He swallowed. Hard. He, who had thought he'd never wed, was suddenly determined he *would*. Somehow, he must convince this one particular woman she could not live without him, that she must become his wife . . . But how did one convince a woman she should take a second husband when, two years widowed, she still thought only of her dead love?

"Mr. Beverly?" asked Penelope.

Vincent's jaw tightened. "I am behaving like a complete and utter idiot. I am sorry. A problem I must solve . . ." He relaxed, smiled, and gestured. "Shall we eat?" he asked, speaking lightly. The table onto which she'd unloaded the food awaited them. "It looks wonderful and I find I am very hungry."

If it was a hunger that food would not satisfy, Vincent was too old a hand at the game of hearts to give away his feelings and allowed no hint of them to cross his features or his tongue. He would, he knew, have to think very hard about how to solve this particular problem . . . So, before she could ask him *what* problem, as he feared she'd do, Vincent began telling her of his work among the tenants, and, when he finished, he asked how far she'd gotten in her plans for the dower house.

Penelope, putting aside her curiosity about that long intense look, talked for the rest of their meal about her notions, occasionally referring to her notes. When they finished, she suggested they leave the remains for her to clean up later, so that she could show him. Later, when she returned to the breakfast room, meaning to take the dirty dishware to the kitchen and pack the remnants of food in the basket for return to the village, she discovered the room had already been cleared.

"What . . . ?"

Vincent grinned. "You have forgotten that I hired maids."

"No I hadn't. I met them earlier and was very thankful for their existence when I first heard strange voices in the house. When your aunt arrived . . . ?"

Vincent smiled. "Then I am doubly glad I had them come immediately. My reason, however, was that there will be constant need of them until the workmen finish making messes. Besides, now the chimneys have been cleaned, I wish someone to build fires in the rooms each day—to drive out the damp, you know?" He adopted a thoughtful look for a moment, then nodded before adding, "But your concern when you heard my aunt talking to my cousin's wife . . . I wonder if such young girls might find the house big and lonely. They've a brother who might like a winter job as footman— to carry coals and do the heavy work."

"He could also begin polishing wood paneling you don't wish painted, or washing it where it *is* to be painted. Here in the breakfast room, for instance, a good scrub and polish may be sufficient. Except that that sideboard is far too large and ugly and must be replaced and that there is a need for new curtains in a lighter pattern, I believe the room may be left alone. Assuming the walls come up to be the color I think is there."

"Smoke stained?"

"Something. Perhaps simply years with no attention . . . ?"

"The preceding tenants, you would say, did not take proper care?"

"They were old, were they not? They may not have noticed. And it is likely they had few and perhaps elderly servants?"

"Very likely. I suppose I must return you to Minnow Manor," he said, feeling cross at the thought.

Penelope stifled a desire to sigh. "Yes. I worry about Tal when I am gone too long—" She cast him a rueful look. "—even though I have had to conclude he *prefers* Matty's attentions!"

"I doubt if he would prefer them if he never saw you. Is there anything we have forgotten?"

Penelope picked up her tablet and put her pencils in her

reticule and looked around. "I believe that is everything—if someone else is tending to the basket?"

"They are. Will you object to driving by the sisters' home? Now that it has occurred to me they will feel safer if their brother is here, I think I should arrange it at once. And so I will feel safer—*for them*."

"I've no objections . . ."

In fact, the notion pleased her. Penelope scolded herself for being thankful for the extra time in Vincent's company. It was truly silly to feed the attraction she felt for him. If only he would give a hint that he returned her interest, then perhaps she might find the courage to hint in return that she would not object to a . . . a warmer relationship?

Penelope sighed. Softly. So he'd not hear and ask about it. She was well aware she hadn't the courage to engage in such behavior. She had already told him so.

But . . . oh how she wished she did!

CHAPTER 12

"I do wish you would not take Lady Penelope out into the cold as you do," complained Lord Wakefield to Vincent as the two men started down the stairs for the evening meal. "You have no consideration for her voice!"

"I have yet to learn she has a voice." In a spirit of mischief, Vincent added, "Has it occurred to you that she does not sing because she *cannot* sing? That something happened in the Peninsula making it impossible that she sing?"

Wakefield froze. His skin paled. "Do not suggest such a thing," he said, his voice harsh. "Impossible!" His hand closed over Vincent's arm. "No. Not to be thought on!"

Vincent's brow arched. He had known Wakefield had strong feelings about Penelope's voice, but this strong? "Give me another reason she will not sing," he challenged. "You sat beside her in church. Did she open her mouth for the hymns?" Vincent still felt mild animosity toward his lordship for managing that particular trick when he'd intended that honor for himself.

Wakefield was more than a trifle upset that she had not sung. He had deliberately maneuvered those attending services so that he shared a hymnal with Lady Penelope and had nearly burst into angry complaint right there in the middle of services, in the middle of a verse, when she did not join in. Afterwards, when he attempted to speak to her, she had not been where he'd expected her and he'd been unable to find her.

"I see you do recall it," said Vincent in his driest tone. "Hadn't you better give it up?" he asked and, gently removing Wakefield's now lax fingers from his arm, walked away before his lordship could find his voice.

Miss Grimson, who was hovering nearby, approached Wakefield and laid *her* fingers on *his* arm. When he stiffened she jerked away. "I'm sorry," she said, her eyes growing huge at the insult.

He blinked, shook his head ever so slightly, and blinked again. "Sorry? My dear Miss Grimson, I am certain you've nothing for which *you* must feel sorry." He offered his arm. "My dear, I am much in need of good music. May I importune you to oblige me?"

Miss Grimson stifled a sigh of relief when it appeared her plans were moving in the direction she meant for them to go. She smiled. "Of course, my lord. For *you* I will play at any time. I know you forgive me my errors, and that I may count on you for good advice concerning phrasing and tempo."

She continued talking in much the same strain all the way to the music room, where she did not object that Wakefield shut the door on the rest of the party and forbore to mention that they might be compromised by his action. In one small hidden part of her mind, she again hoped that someone *would* enter and find them, heads together, reading the music, or his hand on her shoulder as he reached in front of her to show her a fingering . . .

To be forced to wed was never a good start to a marriage, but Miss Grimson was an impatient soul and quite willing to take any route to that much-to-be-desired end. So, while she played something she knew quite well, she dreamed of the day when they would make duets together with nary a care if the door was tightly shut against the world.

"He's a delight," said Georgi, smiling at Tal's antics as the tot chased a ball across the room. Or, more accurately, the boy chased after a pup that chased the ball. "I knew they'd do well together."

Penelope smiled, but there was a rueful touch to it. "I can see us now," she said, giving her words stress by gesture and dramatic tone.

Georgi turned. "See what?"

"A loaded carriage." Penelope drew a picture in the air with her fingers. "A fussy child, tired from the long day's travel. *And* a pup that must be walked regularly if we do not wish to travel in a pungent miasma of dogginess. And," she added as if just thinking of it, "it is bound to rain. That will be a wet dog and, when wet, the smell unavoidable." She rolled her eyes, sighing—and then caught and held Georgi's gaze. "It *will* be an interesting journey, will it not?"

Georgi bit her lip, her eyes sparkling. Penelope's words limned a picture in her mind that had her smothering laughter. That she had not foreseen the problem was rooted in her determination to find a husband for Penelope. One who would see that her new friend lived somewhere far south of Edinburgh. If Penelope disappeared into Scotland, Georgi feared she would never be seen again! It wasn't to be borne.

"I see you understand," said Penelope, her eyes bright with shared laughter. "Would you try to find a reason why the pup cannot make such a journey? Perhaps you can convince Tal that the creature is far too young to leave its mother?"

"But that would be a fib, would it not?" asked Georgi, her lips sternly restrained from smiling. "We must not lie to the child," she added, working hard to remain serious.

Penelope nodded and with equal difficulty retained a sober expression. "That *is* a problem, is it not?"

"A problem?" asked Vincent from the doorway. He was frowning, wondering what new difficulty had reared its head.

Penelope looked at Georgi who stared back. For half a moment each managed to remain expressionless. But then they burst into giggles. Tal looked around at the sound and, seeing Vincent, shouted, " 'Cent! 'Cent!" Abandoning the pup, the boy half walked half crawled toward his hero. He held up his hands and Vincent, with a grin, picked him up, tossing him lightly and catching him.

"More! More!" squealed Tal.

The women watched Vincent play with the boy, smiling, each thinking he was a natural father. Georgi's thoughts went further. She thought it was a shame he was *not* a father . . .

Tal's father.

Georgi's eyes widened. She looked from the woman to Vincent, saw a certain softness in the gaze Penelope directed at the two, watched Vincent's open smile and laughing eyes, the absence of the sardonic expression that rarely allowed deep lines to disappear from beside his mouth, saw him glance toward Penelope, saw them exchange a *look* . . .

Georgi, with a great deal about which she must think, rather absently excused herself, and went below. A small miracle occurred, in that she found her husband all alone by himself in his library with nary a guest in sight. When he turned at her entrance, she walked straight into his arms, which closed around her, holding her close.

"To what do I owe this honor?" asked Everhart. Her hair tickled his nose as he bent to nuzzle her neck just behind her ear.

"I think Vincent has fallen in love." She raised shiny eyes to meet his quizzical look. "Truly he has. With Penelope."

"With her son, more like," said Everhart, just a trifle of Vincent's cynicism to be heard in the older man's voice.

"Yes, that too."

Everhart frowned slightly. "Georgi, you aren't thinking of matchmaking in that quarter? Are you?"

"I'm not?" She opened her eyes wide, the innocent look Everhart had, even in their brief marriage, learned to distrust. "Oh but, my love, you . . ."

"No." His interruption was brief but stern.

Georgi freed herself and backed away from her lord and master. "No?" she asked. Her fisted hands pushed into her hips, arms akimbo and a scowl narrowing her eyes.

"Georgi, don't interfere."

She tossed her hair. "I wouldn't think of interfering!"

"Because you already have?" he asked instantly.

She pursed her lips and scowled. "You, my lord, are far too perspicacious."

"Where you are concerned, my love, one requires a quick and keen wit," he said, his voice dry. "I really must insist, Georgi. *You are not to interfere.*"

For a long moment her eyes dueled with his. His remained steady and she sighed. "It would be so perfect."

"Would it? Vincent has something approaching a competence, but given the manner in which he lives, no more. Mrs. Garth has what amounts to a reasonable dowry, since you tell me her widow's portion was settled on her. They could, I suppose, live comfortably if quietly—but think, Georgi. How could they provide for a family? The Garth portion would be kept safe for Talavera—" He grimaced at the name. "—but what of other children they might have together?"

Georgi's chin rose. "Grandfather will provide for Vincent."

"The entail will prevent him from doing much," said Everhart, his voice a mixture of kindness and sadness. "Vincent should marry money." He watched her stubborn look appear. "You know it is true, my love."

Her chin rose a notch higher. "I know nothing of the sort.

Unless the couple would be in dire need, love is far more important. With love all can be conquered."

"You have never attempted to live under the pressures of poverty, Georgi. You know nothing of the difficulties facing a couple, a *family,* that must make and scrape and is never quite even with the world. Love has a way of evaporating in the quarrels and the hidden debts and the fears and . . ."

"You are very stern, my lord," said Georgi, who had begun to wish she'd *not* found him alone.

"I am attempting," he said, still stern, "to make you understand why you must not attempt to bring about this particular marriage."

"Her father . . ."

"Her father disinherited her. Her father is a stubborn man—if not worse—and unlikely to change his mind."

Georgi bit her lip and cast her beloved a look from under her lashes. "I saw his lordship take several surreptitious peeks her way in church Sunday."

"At her? Or at Wakefield?"

That rang true and Georgi's hope that Tennytree was softening toward his daughter faded. "You think he hopes that Wakefield will wed her? Even now?"

"It seems likely. It is what he wanted, after all. He will be unhappy all over again if she once again refuses."

"Assuming Wakefield offers!"

Everhart cast her a startled look. "What can you possibly mean by that?"

Georgi adopted a smug look. "You'll see. At least I hope you'll see. It would be so perfect . . ." She turned away, moving in her quick way to the door. There she stopped. Her hand on the handle she turned. "You seriously think a marriage between Vincent and Penelope will not do?"

Everhart, about to state emphatically that that was exactly what he believed, paused. "My love, no one can look into another's heart. I cannot say it would be a disaster because I do not know. I do know, however, that it must be their decision and must not be brought about by trickery or over-encouragement of one or the other, or by suggestion, if the thought is not already in either mind . . . What I am absolutely certain is true is that *you* must not interfere."

Georgi sighed. "I suppose I swore to love, honor, and *obey* you, did I not?" She tipped her head. "You know, Everhart, I am very glad you are not one to hand out orders right and left. I don't know if I *could* obey if I were constantly required to go against my own desires in order to do so."

With that parting shot, Georgi whisked herself out of the room and went off to consult with her housekeeper concerning the day's requirements.

Vincent, the boy, and the pup romped around the nursery, watched by Penelope and Matty. The maid shook her head. " 'Tisn't the way of a tonnish man," she muttered.

"Playing with children?" asked Penelope, unsure of Matty's meaning.

"The men ignore the babes, can't be bothered with them . . ."

"It appears this man not only can be bothered, but enjoys their antics."

As if in proof, Vincent laughed as the pup bit into Tal's skirts and pulled the boy to the floor, the child's wide spread arms and equally wide-eyed surprise the cause. Tal started to screw up his face, about to cry and, instantly, Vincent knelt beside him. "You are not hurt," he said, his voice slightly stern.

Tal blinked, his tears held back. He appeared to think about it—although his fond mama was certain the boy couldn't have understood more than Vincent's tone. But however that was,

Tal appeared to decide Vincent was correct. He turned over, put his hands on the floor, pushed his rear into the air and, wobbling only a bit, attained his feet. The pup bounced up, leapt, and licked Tal's face.

Penelope and the maid started forward. Vincent held up his hand, stopping them. Tal, not certain he liked the pup's action, looked questioningly at Vincent.

"The pup gave you a doggy kiss in apology," said Vincent. Tal seemed to puzzle over the words, decided he was being told that the lick was okay, turned and toddled off toward the other end of the nursery, the pup lolloping along beside him.

Vincent rose to his feet. "If you make too much of such things, the child begins to fear the cause. There is nothing to fear in a lick or two. If the pup tries to bite—and he likely will—then he must be stopped. Quickly, but without heavy punishment," he added, with a stern look at Matty. "Simply take hold of the dog's muzzle immediately. Firmly tell him no. But remember, it must be right then when it happens or the dog won't understand what is meant." He turned to Penelope. "He needs a name."

"The dog?" She looked startled. "Oh dear. I suppose he does." She sighed. "I suspect I haven't quite accepted the permanence of the creature's existence in Tal's life!"

"A name?" asked Vincent.

Penelope bit her lip, turned to stare at boy and dog. Then she grinned as, crowing loudly, Tal chased the pup back toward them. "I think the name obvious," she said, tongue in cheek.

"It is?" asked Vincent a trifle cautiously. "Tell me," he added when she said nothing.

A grin twitched the corners of her mouth, although she kept her lips tightly closed. When Vincent's brow arched in query, she gave in. "Tally's Ho, of course."

"Tallyho?" Vincent frowned. "As in fox hunting?"

"Not quite. *Tally's* Ho, as in a Ho belonging to Tal?"

Vincent grinned. "You have found the exact name for him. Ho it is."

"Tally's Ho," she reiterated.

"Yes, and how long before that is shortened?"

"Maybe I'd better find another," she said, looking again at the playing duo.

"I fear it is too late." Vincent grinned. "Tally's Ho it is."

Penelope sighed.

"To take your mind off the problems a pup will cause you, why do you not put on a habit? I will take you riding," said Vincent. "Requesting your company on a ride was my original reason for coming up. I do not quite know how I got so far off the scent."

Penelope grinned. "Nostalgia," she suggested.

"Nostalgia?" He glanced at Tal but the dog drew his eyes by leaping and turning in a futile attempt to reach its stub of a tail. "Ah. You mean the pup. No, I didn't have a dog of my own. So it is nothing so simple as a longing after a long ago childhood." His eyes narrowed and he smiled his lopsided, self-deriding smile. "Perhaps wishful thinking? *Wishing* I had had such a friend as Ho in my infancy?"

She nodded. "Perhaps more than you know," she said softly and turned away before he could respond. At her door, she turned. "I'll not be more than twenty minutes—assuming you watch those two imps while Matty helps me?"

Matty cast Penelope an astonished look that she'd expect such a thing of a man—but he simply nodded and waved the two away. Matty stood gaping at him until Penelope drew her attention by tapping on the maid's shoulder. Matty followed Penelope into her mistress's bedroom, but her head was turned, eyes wide, to stare at Vincent—until the door shut and she could not.

Not quite half an hour later Penelope and Vincent trotted off down the lane toward the road leading to Beverly Place, a

groom following at a discreet distance. Vincent, perhaps belatedly, had decided he must have a care for Penelope's reputation. He wanted no one making hurtful comments about
her, as they would, if she were to go off alone with a man.
They would do so if she were to ride with any man and no
chaperon in sight, but the tattle would be especially vicious,
given that his reputation was not the most spotless in the
world. Dirt clung to those who associated with the scandalous
even when no scandal was meant or made.

Until it occurred to him he wanted her for his wife, the
problem had not crossed Vincent's mind, but with his accep-
tance that he loved came a strong need to protect the beloved.
Not that *he* would care if her reputation were smutted. After
all, considering his own, that would be more than a trifle hypo-
critical, but the widow Garth might balk at wedding him—or
any man—if she felt she could not bring a spotless character
to the marriage. Chaperonage was a problem he was capable
of solving, unlike others he foresaw in his courtship of the
widow.

Penelope, however, saw the groom as merely another indication that Vincent wished to assure her she'd nothing to
fear from his attentions. Attentions she *wished* to experience.
Ruefully, she admitted, silently, in the privacy of her own
mind, that the wish had surfaced to consciousness far more
often than she liked to acknowledge.

The week progressed slowly, the company occupied with
those things organized to please a houseful of guests at Christmas, and then came the day set aside for Georgi's children's
party. Tal clutched his mother's shoulder and stared, wide-eyed,
around the salon. The lad had never seen so many youngsters
all together in one place or heard so much childish noise.
When Penelope tried to put him down, he threw his other
arm around her neck and would not let go.

Vincent watched.

So did Lord Wakefield who, against his better judgment, had agreed to lead the children in singing several old familiar carols. Miss Grimson, hearing Georgi cajoling him into it, offered to play the pianoforte. Georgi was pleased. She was unaware that Rose Grimson was in accord with the plan that she marry Lord Wakefield, but, because the young lady's suggestion fell nicely in with *her* plans for the couple, Georgi instantly acquiesced, gesturing a footman nearer. She ordered the instrument moved from the music room to the salon, thereby aiding and abetting Miss Grimson's earnest hopes for the future.

"Why," muttered Wakefield into Miss Grimson's ear, "does Lady Penelope feel it necessary to hold that child? See how the brat clutches at her, crushing her gown, and mussing her hair! Surely there is a nursery maid whose duty it is to see to him."

"It seems," said Miss Grimson carefully, "that some mothers actually enjoy dealing with their offspring. I cannot understand it myself, but I am assured it is true."

Wakefield cast her an appalled look. "You would say Lady Penelope is such a woman?" He instantly clarified his meaning. "Not that she does not *enjoy* her child, of course, and spend time with it, but to actually have a hand in the *caring* of it? She is a lady!"

"Is she?" asked Miss Grimson doubtfully. At his shocked expression, she, too, felt the need to make clear her meaning. "I refer," she said, "to all those years she followed the drum. Is it not possible she adopted, from choice or because she was forced to do so, several, er, unladylike attributes?"

Wakefield turned his rather protuberant gaze back toward Penelope. "Surely it cannot be possible." A touch of horror colored his voice.

"I do not see why not," said Miss Grimson only a trifle

pettishly. "Life must have been very difficult a great deal of the time and not at all nice at any time and . . ." She watched his expression, realized she'd moved into depths in which she floundered, and was very glad of an excuse to wade into shallower water. Taking a deep breath, she said, "Do look. I believe Lady Everhart is organizing the singing?"

Miss Grimson seated herself on the chair set before the piano, very glad to be given a reason to leave behind what she feared might become an argument. She placed her hands on the keys and, softly, began one of her favorite Christmas songs.

"Come, children," Georgi encouraged, leading two of them toward the piano. She hid a smile as she saw Lord Wakefield involuntarily step back, putting himself next the piano on one side and the wall on the other. He was trapped—and, after a moment, realized it. He cast wild glances around, seeking a way of escape, before his gaze dropped back to the youngsters gathering around and, politely, eyes wide, awaiting his direction to begin.

"Er . . ." Wakefield turned to Miss Grimson. The title of every carol he'd ever heard was flown from his head.

"Might I suggest 'I Saw Three Ships,' which everyone is sure to know?" asked Miss Grimson softly.

Wakefield breathed again and, after clearing his throat a couple of times, began singing. Stiffly. His voice not at all relaxed. It took Georgi's joining in and then Vincent, whispering in the ear of a young choirboy before the children, raggedly, added their sweet young voices.

"Look. You can see it in his face. He is surprised at how well they sound," whispered Vincent into Penelope's ear.

She glanced at her bête noire. Wakefield's eyes bugged a trifle, but his lips were twisted into his most pronounced ironic look. She sighed. "Lord Wakefield is and always will be a snob, I fear." She hummed half a line when the next carol was begun but stopped abruptly. Biting her lips, she turned away. Tal patted his mother's cheek and she smiled at him, misty eyed.

Vincent, who was standing near enough he'd heard those few cracked notes, stared at her thoughtfully. *Poor dear,* he thought, understanding instantly that it hurt her deeply that, for some reason, her voice was not what it had once been. He wondered what had happened that it was *not* and why she did not simply tell Wakefield that she didn't sing because she *couldn't* . . .

And how, he wondered, could anyone make up such a loss to one who must have felt it to the darkest depths one could feel . . . ?

CHAPTER 13

Several days later Penelope was once again at the dower house. She came alone this time with only a groom in attendance, meaning to check on the progress of various projects. She discussed the work of the young man hired as a footman, praising him for a job well done in the breakfast room and setting him to polishing the wood paneling in the hall. A vinegary odor drifted from the room where his sisters scrubbed windows that looked as if they'd not been washed in years. They appeared to know their work, so she left them to it.

Penelope had felt it necessary to come. The painter's interpretation of pale blue for an upstairs bedroom was such that she decided she must oversee all mixing of paint in the future. He was to do the salon today and they were arguing about the tint. The painter was insisting it was much too pale when the front door was thrust open and Lady Melicent stalked in. Her ladyship cast a disparaging glance around the hall but refrained from telling the footman he was not using enough elbow grease. It was just as well, since such advice would have been unappreciated. The wood's condition was not the young man's fault, but too many years of neglect.

Hearing voices, Lady Melicent continued on in to the salon. There, she stopped absolutely stalk-still. "You." There was a world of contempt in the sound.

Penelope sighed softly. She turned. "Lady Melicent," she said, straightening her shoulders and preparing for a fight. Her last experience of Lady Melicent had led her to believe there could be no other response to the woman's interference. Her ladyship's next word proved it.

"Whore!"

Penelope blinked, restraining her temper with difficulty.

"Strumpet!"

"Why do I suspect you've been talking to my father?" asked Penelope, adopting a bland tone.

"Out!" Lady Melicent pointed a finger that trembled with emotion toward the door.

"Oh no. Not yet," said Penelope. "Not until I've finished all I came to do."

"You are impertinent!"

"Am I?" Penelope tipped her head and adopted a thoughtful look. "But then, when conversing with you, my lady, it is difficult to be otherwise, is it not? Or have you found most people with whom you, umm, *speak,* fear to be, as you say, impertinent?" Outraged silence followed. "I suppose I should apologize and explain that life in the Peninsula beat such nonsense out of me?"

Lady Melicent literally shook with rage. "You will not be allowed to run free on Beverly Place property whatever Lord Everhart sees fit to do at the manor. I'll not have anyone's fancy-piece *here.*"

Penelope's head reared back. "My husband and I were married from his family's home. *Legally* married. I am not now, nor have I ever been, anyone's mistress." She threw up her hands in disgust. "I don't know why I bother to explain," she ended on a sour note. She turned back to the workman, who had listened, his eyes wide. "If you will not accept my word as to the color, then you must wait to begin until Mr. Beverly arrives. He, too, will tell you that is quite dark enough a green."

"Barely any color a-tall," muttered the man, frowning.

"Exactly. Merely a *hint* of color is wanted."

He sighed gustily. "Do like a bit of pretty color," he said wistfully.

Penelope chuckled. "I'm certain you do," she said, thinking once again of the blue bedroom and wondering what she could do to tone it down. *Lots of white,* she decided as she turned away.

She had forgotten Lady Melicent's presence or, wishful thinking, had hoped she'd gone. Seeing her ladyship stopped Penelope's movement toward the door. "I thought you'd gone," she said, her irritation making her speak with more than a trifle of exasperation.

"She is about to do so," said Lord Tivington blandly.

His lordship had entered through the rear of the house and come silently through the baize covered door where he'd listened to the exchange between his daughter-in-law and the woman he hoped would wed his grandson. At his words, Lady Melicent turned. He added, "Are you not, daughter?" His lordship's left eyebrow climbed in an arc up his forehead.

The expression, a clue Penelope was quick to note, explained where Vincent had learned a similar, slightly sardonic, habit.

"You've nothing to do here. Have you, Melicent? *Nothing at all.*"

Her ladyship's head snapped up, her nose nicely in the air. "Once you send that . . . that . . ."

"Careful, daughter. Mrs. Garth is a friend."

"Friend." Melicent glared. *"Is she indeed?* Men are such fools."

"Are we?" asked the lady's father-in-law. "Or is it perhaps that we do not find ourselves so easily threatened by another's existence?"

Melicent took a moment to sort through that suggestion and then glared. "You have never understood how difficult it is for me."

"Since you bring most of your problems on yourself, Melicent, by insisting on your own way on every and all occasions, I see no reason to attempt to understand you. Learn to compromise now and again and I will think about it. Now do go away. I wish to speak with Mrs. Garth." He turned his back on his daughter-in-law. "Vincent informed me, my dear, that you would be willing to give me a tour and show me what has been done and what is planned . . . ?"

"I would enjoy that." For half a moment Penelope thought of offering a polite invitation to Lady Melicent. She decided against it when it occurred to her the lady was the sort who would take one up on what was merely a polite gesture instead of denying herself a treat for which, in any case, she'd no desire. So, instead of speaking, Penelope folded her hands before her and, her eyes holding Lady Melicent's, waited for the woman to give up and go away.

"Blast and bedamned," said a new and very angry voice. "I didn't believe Roland!"

"Vincent?" asked Lord Tivington, turning a surprised look toward the door. "I thought you were overseeing the work on that drainage ditch this morning."

"Aha!" crowed Melicent, finding a new target for her acid tongue. "I told you you could not trust such a coxcomb."

Vincent turned a glare her way. "And I told *you,* you were not to come here. I explained in words of one syllable that you are not welcome. When the groom told me you were on your way here, I was *forced* to follow you in order to evict you. It is your stubborn determination to stick your long nose into everyone's business, my lady aunt, which keeps me from my work. Not dilatoriness on my part. Now, *go*. And do *not* come back."

Red spots appearing on her cheeks, Melicent turned to her father-in-law. "Will you allow him to speak to me in that tone?"

"Oh, I don't know . . ." said the old gentleman musingly. He pretended to think and then, slowly, said, "I cannot make up my mind . . ." He pretended to think some more, then nodded firmly. "I have it. I must order him to speak still *more* plainly, since you do not seem to understand common English words."

Lady Melicent stared, her eyes goggling. "You . . ."

"Yes?" Lord Tivington.

"You are impossible!"

"Only *you* feel that way," said Vincent, bitingly. "So perhaps there is something in *you* which is the problem and not in my grandfather?"

"I believe you've gone far enough, Vincent," said Lord Tivington. "Melicent is just leaving. She will *not* return."

Her head high, Lady Melicent stalked from the room. When the front door slammed, his lordship turned to Penelope. "I apologize for my daughter-in-law. Her behavior is, I know, unforgivable. Not just in this particular case, but on nearly every occasion one is forced to deal with her. For the most part, we find that we deal best by simply ignoring her."

"I feel rather sorry for her," said Penelope softly. "She must be a very unhappy woman."

"If she is . . ."

"No," said Penelope, interrupting Vincent's biting tone, "it is not *all* her fault. I believe that some people, from early childhood, find the world a terribly unsettled and unsettling place. Such people grow up needing to control every aspect of their own lives, but to do so, must control that of everybody about them. They are trying to assure that there will be no more chaos, no surprises. They truly do *not* understand why anyone objects."

"There is a great deal of wisdom in that comment, my dear," said Lord Tivington, leaning a trifle on his silver headed cane. "You have known such a one, perhaps?" His eyes smiled at her, a kindly, interested look.

"Obviously," she retorted, smiling back. "My father cannot bear that anyone other than himself make a decision, since, if they do, that means he is not in control. He must control everything."

"Or?"

Her lips tightened. "Or his world will become such that he cannot bear it—as it did when my mother died. Or when I refused to wed the man he chose for me?" She shrugged. "Shall we begin our tour, my lord? Mr. Beverly, I am convinced, wishes to return to his drainage ditch. Besides, you and I will get on much faster without him?"

Lord Tivington grinned. "That, Vincent," he said kindly, "was a suggestion that Mrs. Garth and I will do very well without you."

"I *fear* that is true."

Tivington's brow arched, this time expressing a query as to what the emphasis implied.

"I am fast developing a very odd desire to *be* necessary," muttered Vincent half under his breath. Giving that odd little salute characteristic of him, he disappeared.

"Did that make sense?" asked Penelope, afraid to hope it might.

"Oh, I think so." His lordship smiled. "I had *hoped,* but hadn't a notion the lad had such good sense. Now tell me . . ." continued Lord Tivington, changing the subject to that of the projects going forward in the house.

They inspected what had been done and discussed what was planned, leaving the painter free to—looking guiltily around himself as he did it—add just a tiny bit more color to his paint. Not so much as he wished, but enough it would look *green* once it was on the walls. And then he felt guilty and added more untinted paint. He still ended up with something darker than what had been approved and quickly, before Mrs. Garth could return and complain, began brushing it onto the walls.

Once they'd been throughout the house, his lordship's questions relevant and his praise more than satisfying, Penelope realized she felt a trifle peckish. She lifted her watch and was startled to see the time. "I must return to the manor, I think," she said.

"Ah! And I have interfered so that you've been unable to accomplish whatever it was you came to do today."

"Nonsense. I came to see that the color was correct for the salon paint. Unlike that in the blue bedroom, which, as you saw, is far too intense. We had perfected the green tone when her ladyship arrived, so I was very nearly done at that point and if she had been only a little later, I'd have been gone."

"And, here alone, with no one to stop her, she'd have done her best—which is very good indeed—to see that all your orders were overturned." He sighed softly, but before she could respond, added, "I have not seen Georgi for several days. Would you object to my joining you on your ride back to the Manor? It is particularly mild today, so my daughters will not object, assuming you do not . . . ?"

"I would enjoy your company, my lord."

Penelope spoke the simple truth, not merely a polite social comment. Not only did she enjoy his company for its own sake, but she had the satisfaction of learning still more concerning Vincent—and Georgi, too, of course. Small bits of information which, when added to what she already knew, only intensified her desire to know her new friend—*friends*—still better.

"No, of course you are not too late for a bite to eat," said Georgi, when they arrived. She was shocked that anyone would think they might not order a snack at any time they pleased but, in this case, it was unnecessary. The luncheon was still spread out over the sideboard. "Grandfather? Will you indulge in ale? Or a glass of wine?"

Georgi ushered them into the breakfast room where two of the younger women dawdled over cold meat and cheese. They looked up, hopeful, when the door opened, but both sighed when they saw who came in. Both were polite young ladies, however, and well trained—and besides that, they were calculating enough to hope that if they impressed the old gentleman, he might put a good word for them into Mr. Beverly's ear—so they made an attempt at entertaining the newcomers with bits of gossip that interested neither.

Until one of them said, "Has anyone else listened to Miss Grimson and Lord Wakefield practicing?"

"Are they practicing new music?" asked Georgi, when no one else said anything. "I have noticed they spend an inordinate amount of time in the music room but was unaware they did more than enjoy themselves, playing duets. My surprise was that either of them *could* play. Has anyone else ever heard either perform for company?"

The discussion resulted in some rather pointed comments about young ladies who spent so much time occupying the time of such an eligible young man. "It would not be so bad of them if they would entertain us of an evening, but they will not do so," said one woman. "Not even when asked. Miss Grimson colors up and shakes her head and instantly disappears. Lord Wakefield merely shakes his head, puts on a sour look, and says no one would be interested. But that is not true. I will admit—" Spots of color appeared in Miss Herning's cheeks. "—that I have hovered in the hallway when they play. They are very good," she said, pouting. "Far better than I, and I do not become missish when asked to play and sing."

Miss Grimson and Lord Wakefield, upon hearing their names, had stopped in the hall to listen. They looked at each other. Silently, they stole away. "They don't understand," said Miss Grimson when it was safe to do so.

"I, certainly, am not missish," said Wakefield, attempting a jest—but it sounded sour.

"Do you believe," asked Miss Grimson after a moment, "that we should attempt . . . ?"

"No." Wakefield realized how rude that sounded. "We do well enough when alone together, but would you care to chance that we should be equally lucky when we *know* someone is listening?"

Miss Grimson shuddered. "I am sure I would not be at all proficient. My fingers would stumble and my phrasing would be all wrong and I would make a terrible fool of myself. I doubt it would be the same for you. You, my lord, are so very good. You always know exactly where one should pause, where the tempo must be increased . . . I would enjoy listening to you play for the guests and I know they would find you worth hearing."

But Wakefield shook his head. "You are very kind, my dear, but it would not do."

Miss Grimson nodded. "For myself, I certainly agree."

"Shall we . . . ?"

Miss Grimson nodded again, more firmly. "Yes, please." She accepted his arm and they returned to the music room, forgetting they had meant to see if there was a bite to eat remaining in the breakfast room.

But, in the very back of Miss Grimson's mind, tentative plans formed to make it possible for the rest of the company to hear his lordship, possible for them to discover just how good he was. She wanted the whole world to understand what it was she saw in him, so that when she went against her long voiced intentions of living her life as a spinster everyone would understand why she'd changed her mind.

Christmas Eve arrived. The party at Minnow Manor spent the day quietly, everyone resting or playing cards or running a few balls around the billiards table—or simply napping or talking of this and that as they waited through the long hours until it was time to board the several carriages harnessed up to take them to church for midnight services.

Vincent, alert to avoiding Miss Herning's plots for the short journey to church, nearly missed Penelope's quiet arrival among those waiting to find a seat in a carriage. She had a sleepy Tal in her arms and it took a little adroit maneuvering for him to garner a place in the same carriage in which the two rode.

Not only did he manage that, but he had previously seated Miss Herning in another, one so full it had no room for himself. Vincent was quietly pleased with himself—especially when he noted that Lord Wakefield and Miss Grimson were directed by Everhart to still another rig. Vincent relaxed back into his seat—only to lean forward when the jerky movement of the carriage, as it started off, awakened Tal. The boy fretted, pushing against his mother, but quieted instantly when Vincent took him.

"Here now," scolded Vincent softly. "What is this? A big boy like you?"

The admired voice instantly took Tal's attention, silencing him, and the novelty of riding in the carriage along dark roads soothed him. Vincent began singing carols in which other voices joined, the soft music further intriguing the boy—who, when the singing ceased, patted Vincent's cheek, silently requesting more.

"Not now, Tal. We are coming to the church. You must be a good boy and patient," he warned, looking into the child's eyes. "There will be singing, but there will also be talking. You can go to sleep if you wish."

"You talk to him as if you thought he could understand," said one woman, sounding amused.

"Of course. He understands the tone and he will learn the meaning as time goes on. If one only talks silly nursery words, then that is all a babe learns. Or so I've always thought," he added in a slightly embarrassed tone.

"An interesting theory," said the woman thoughtfully, but still with a touch of that amusement. She was known as a patroness of an orphanage in one of London's poorer districts. "I must remember to discuss the notion with Matron . . ."

The carriage pulled to a halt and the conversation ended. Vincent continued carrying Tal, which put a flush on Penelope's cheeks. She worried about what others would think of his odd behavior, wondered if they would jump to conclusions. Wrong conclusions. Vincent was merely being kind. He was not attempting to hint his interest in a widow with a child.

She sighed when he proved it—by handing Tal to her once she seated herself in a pew near the back. If the boy fussed, she thought, she would take him out and across the road to the inn without disturbing anyone.

But, when Tal did begin fussing some time later, she discovered it would not be necessary to leave. As before, the boy quieted when Vincent took him. Man and boy stood near the wall, Vincent softly talking to the wide-eyed Tal, pointing out the candlelit altar, the pulpit, the choir, and other such things . . .

When they returned to the house, Vincent was twitted by several of the younger men about his ability to charm the lad. When, slyly, one asked if he had equal success charming the boy's mother to his hand, Vincent frowned.

"Mrs. Garth is a woman of whom one does not speak. Not in *that* tone," said Vincent, his voice rather harsh.

Surprised silence followed his words. "Beverly, old man," said one of his nearer friends, "can it be possible that you've finally been pierced by the arrow of love—instead of merely using love's arrow to the mutual satisfaction of . . ." He threw up his hands in mock alarm. "Here now!"

"I said," said Vincent, "that Mrs. Garth is not a woman about whom anyone will jest."

He turned on his heel and stalked away, the silence behind him heavy with questions. Away from them, he hesitated. Then, unable to stop himself, he took the stairs two at a time, rounding on upward at each landing until he reached the nursery floor.

But, once there, he stopped, asking himself what he thought he was doing. Very slowly and carefully, he dropped to the top step and put his head in his hands, his thoughts rampaging. He had, surely, given away his sentiments and before men who would not let it rest. If word reached Penelope, what would be her reaction?

Vincent groaned, fearing he'd not have the time he needed to court her, to bring her around to thoughts of him as something more than her rescuer, something more than a friend.

Thoughts of him as a man, *a desirable man,* a man she might even think of wedding . . . given time . . .

Vincent drew in a deep breath. He must warn her she had become the object of speculation—but not, he decided, tonight. It was far too late. She'd be preparing for bed—or already in it. He, too, would go to his room, rise early, and catch her before she could possibly hear anything she might find upsetting . . .

Yes, that was the thing to do.

CHAPTER 14

Penelope sighed. "I had hoped to avoid this," she said, looking squarely into Lord Wakefield's eyes.

Wakefield had heard rumors Vincent Beverly was more than a trifle serious about the widow, and, fearing to lose her, had rushed his fences. His already straight spine stiffened. "Surely . . . ?"

"Surely I do not mean to turn down your offer? But I do." Hurriedly she continued with the words taught all young women who might find it necessary to decline a man's offer of marriage. "Although I am aware of the honor you would do me, I fear we would not suit."

The words tumbled off her tongue as would a memorized recitation of a schoolboy and were, obviously, unappreciated by the listening man. She sighed.

"Sir, there has been no change, has there? You are the man you were then and I the woman. A marriage between us would have been a disaster for us then and it would be still more a disaster now." She held out a hand, a gesture that suggested a pleading for understanding. "Please do not persist."

"I must. You refuse to understand."

Penelope turned away, her head high. "To the contrary. I understand all too well. It is not *me* you wish to wed, but the voice you recall from those days in Bath. You are obsessed by it. Will you go away and leave me alone if I tell you that voice no longer exists?"

"Nonsense!"

She turned and once again caught and held his gaze, hers steady. "*Truth.* It is not something of which I care to speak, but the painful truth is that my voice is gone. *I cannot sing.* I will never sing again. My voice was . . . damaged beyond repair."

He looked bewildered. "It is not possible. It must *not* be possible."

"Because you will it otherwise?" she asked, her voice as dry as the dust she'd known during hot summer days crossing Spanish plains.

He bit his lip, true distress in his expression. "But it was such a wondrous voice. How . . . ? Why . . . ?"

"It is not enough that I admit I have lost it? Since your sole reason for pursuing me is gone, you will now go away and leave me in peace."

Penelope was having more and more difficulty retaining her poise and wished he'd just *go.* She had never spoken of the terrible day she was told Kennet was dead. Told that he died instantly, heroically, leading a charge into a breach . . . Nor had she spoken of the screams she heard. Heard as if from some distance, some odd place that didn't exist, a place where *she* didn't exist . . .

Again she turned her back on Lord Wakefield, her voice was a strained thread of sound. "Please. Go away. Now."

He hesitated. It was impossible to believe he'd never ever hear that wonderful voice again. But there was something in Lady Penelope's stance, in her voice, in the pain he read in her eyes that forced one to accept *she* believed she'd never sing again . . .

Hesitating, his voice faltering, knowing she wanted him gone, still he persisted. "Have you consulted a doctor? Someone," he added quickly, "other than a military man?"

"I have," she said. She thought of the London doctor who had directed a light down her throat by the use of a lamp and a mirror. He had peered into her mouth—and stood away shaking his head. She had, to that point, hoped some healing would happen, that by some miracle she *would* sing again.

"You are very sure?" he asked, worried.

"Very."

"I . . . see."

She heard him swallow and turned, fearing the pity she'd see in his face. There was no pity. In fact, what she saw was something approaching anger. She frowned.

"Mrs. Garth, I am thankful you were wise enough to refuse my proposal," said his lordship, his head high, "I am very sorry to inform you of this sad fact, but I'd be forced to withdraw it if you had not. I was under a misapprehension. I presumed that you are perfectly healthy. I dare not wed a woman who is *not*."

Penelope's eyes widened. Her mouth began to spread, her lips widening against her better judgment into a tight smile. Then, worse, she giggled. "Thank you," she managed, her hands going to cover her mouth against further laughter. *That* action had his eyes bulging. "For being *honest* and *frank* with me," she said, tongue firmly in cheek.

His lordship looked astounded, then worried, and finally insulted. "You find humor in the knowledge my bride must come to me intact?"

"No no. Thank you for—" She spoke with only a touch of sarcasm. "—having the courage to admit it would not do." For one brief moment Penelope thought of reminding him that a widow and a mother could hardly be thought of as "intact," the old way of referring to virginity, but such a comment would only set up his lordship's back.

More than she'd done already, that is.

"I think," she said carefully, "that I was not laughing at you, my lord, but at myself. I had not thought of myself as, hmm, less than healthy, you see, but whatever the case, and whoever is at fault, it is still true that we cannot wed. Good day to you, my lord," she said.

She had heard Matty open a door farther down the hall. Very soon the maid and Tal would appear. A yip sounded and she smiled.

"My son is about to return to the nursery, my lord, along with his unruly puppy and his nursery maid. I believe you will be happier elsewhere?"

He cast a startled look toward the sound of renewed barking, and making hurried adieus, left the day nursery only half a moment before Vincent walked in the door leading from the night nursery—followed by the pup.

"You were speaking with someone?" asked Vincent, glancing around curiously.

"Where is my son?" asked Penelope, avoiding an answer.

"Getting his soaking skirts changed."

"Soaking!"

"He slipped and fell into a puddle." Vincent shrugged, a smile lurking in his sleepy looking eyes. "No harm done, except that poor Matty must attempt to get the mud out of his coat and leggings. I am quite certain I heard another voice . . . ?"

Penelope sighed, bit her lip, and turned away. "Yes. I'd a visitor," she said shortly.

"Wakefield." The sleepiness disappeared in a feature-hardening expression. His already prominent cheekbones seemed nearly harsh.

Wondering at his reaction, she nodded.

"What did he want this time? To harass you still again?" Vincent realized he sounded angrier than he'd a right to but could not help himself.

Penelope became a trifle angry as well. Silently she acknowledged that it was a reaction to an attraction for this man, which she believed she should not feel. "If you must know," she retorted, "he asked me to wed him."

Vincent felt a core of ice settle into his gut. "And?" he asked. This time there was an even greater harshness. "Am I to wish you happy? You won't be!"

She straightened. "I had thought you my friend, Mr. Beverly."

He glared at her. "You do not say if . . ."

Mild temper turned to outrage that he'd assume she'd agree to marry Wakefield. "I see no reason why I should. Not when you are so very rude and for no reason."

"Oh, I've reason," he retorted.

For once she could not tell where his sarcasm was directed.

His look changed to one of hunger and then, turning abruptly, he left her.

His exit caught Penelope unprepared. She stared after him. Suddenly she realized he had gone while still believing her engaged to Wakefield. She raised her hand—but the door had shut with a slam. She started for it, but then heard her son cry out and veered toward the night nursery. The dog yipped and Tal chortled. Penelope turned back to the hall door, opened it, started down the hall . . . but she was too late.

He was truly gone.

Vincent stalked out of the house and toward the stables. He could not believe the woman he'd thought he knew so well was so foolish as to engage herself to that posturing idiot. Wakefield! It was impossible . . .

And yet . . .

He gritted his teeth. She had a son. She had no more than the veriest competence from which she must find not only funds for daily living, but, somehow, save for the boy's future. Why would she *not* feel the offer of marriage to a wealthy peer an offer of help in a time of need, help that would forward her son's ambitions, help the boy get on in life? Married, she would, of course, have no need herself for her dowry income. She could tie up her small fortune for the boy's future, so that even if Wakefield refused aid for another man's son, the boy would be safe . . .

Without thought, as was his habit, Vincent thanked the groom who brought him his horse. He always thanked servants for their service, but, this time, he'd have no memory of doing so. He mounted and, putting spur to flank, fled Minnow Manor as if pursued by hellish fiends.

As, perhaps, in his despair, he felt he was.

Wakefield, on the other hand, smarted from the knowledge he'd, for the second time, been turned down by the only woman he'd ever asked to be his wife, despite his—yes, he could admit it—his ungentlemanly attempt to save face by withdrawing the proposal.

Music.

He needed music. He headed for the music room where he uncased his precious cello. Seating himself, he laid the bow across the strings, hesitated, and then dropped the point to the floor

"It cannot be possible," he muttered. "Surely it is not possible she has lost that voice." He reset the bow—and again found he had no music in him. Music. The one thing that had never failed him, never failed to soothe, to make right a world that refused to conform to his wishes.

The door opened and, humming, Miss Grimson tripped into the room, carrying a parcel that looked as if it had come through the post. She closed the door as she entered and went directly to the pianoforte where she set the package on top. Carefully, wishing to save it, she began undoing the string.

"What have you there?" asked Wakefield.

A tiny squeak of surprise escaped her and she turned quickly, steadying herself against the piano. "My lord!"

He blinked. "You do not answer," he said, his voice harsh

and accusing. He'd had enough for one day of women denying him!

"Sir?" Miss Grimson turned eyes toward the package. "Oh! Of course. You will be pleased, my lord, to learn that I've been sent more new music. Do join me. Let us see what treasure has been forwarded to me."

Wakefield, feeling as if there was nothing in the world worthy of the name treasure, sighed. Carefully laying aside his precious cello, he rose to his feet. "Well?" he said as he approached. "Open it then!"

When she turned back to picking at the knots he sighed still again, took a penknife from his pocket and reached around her. He slipped the knife under the string, cutting it.

As he did so, the door opened. He heard a gasp. He dropped the knife, which, unnoticed, slid down behind the pianoforte. He turned on his heel and faced a woman he should know but could not, at that moment, put a name to. All he saw was the outrage in the lady's face, her obvious misinterpretation of what she'd seen.

"Good day," he said, bowing—hiding the fact he was gritting his teeth at what he feared was to come. When Miss Grimson clutched at his arm he very nearly shook her off. Resignation swept through him and he didn't bother attempting to release himself.

What difference does it make? he wondered. *Since I cannot wed Lady Penelope . . . ?*

"My lord," whispered Miss Grimson at his side. She feared he would not do the gentlemanly thing, that she would be left with her reputation in tatters, unwed, on the shelf, an apeleader, leading apes in hell . . . and there was not a single thought in her head that that was *exactly* what she'd meant to do with her life, that she had expected to remain a spinster to her death—right up to the moment she decided that if marriage was the only way to have Lord Wakefield's musical abilities at her side, then she would wed him.

But what if he . . . ?

"Well!" said an outraged Lady Houghten, interrupting Miss Grimson's rampaging thoughts. Her ladyship had arrived rather early for Lady Everhart's Boxing Day party, and in her usual manner, arrogantly set off to explore the manor, curious as to how the young bride had redecorated. She was very glad she had. Such goings on! Of course she had suspected that the Everharts were overly *fast,* that they were the sort who would allow loose behavior, perhaps encourage it . . . !

Wakefield sighed again. His jaw set. He cast one quick warning glance at the wide-eyed, white-faced chit clutching his sleeve to the point of damaging it and sighing one last time, straightened. "I don't know who you are, madam, but will you be the first to wish happiness on my chosen bride? Miss Grimson has just agreed to wed me."

He felt the girl relax and cast another quick look at her. She was smiling broadly. Too broadly? His eyes narrowed. Had he been tricked? Had she planned it? He shook his arm in such a way she was forced to release him.

"So, if that is settled," he said, his tone sour, "I hope you will excuse me." He bowed toward the stranger and then, almost insultingly, toward Miss Grimson, and stalked from the room.

Lady Houghten's eyes narrowed. "Just engaged, are you?" she asked, her tone still more sour than Wakefield's had been and exceedingly suspicious with it.

"Very happily engaged," said Miss Grimson. Whatever it was that sent his lordship from the room in such a snit, the deed was done. He had, before a witness, announced that they were engaged. "Now, if you will excuse me as well? I must go, at once, to my mother . . . ?"

Lady Houghten shrugged. "You do look pleased . . ."

"Oh, I am. Very pleased."

"But his lordship's expression was not equally happy . . . ?"

"I assure you, he will be the happiest of men," said Miss

Grimson, trilling a very slightly shrill laugh. "We make such wonderful music together, you see." She gestured to the pianoforte. "It will be a lovely life," she added, her enthusiasm clear to be heard, "filled with all the music anyone could want."

She curtsied and fled the room, wondering where Lord Wakefield had disappeared . . .

Vincent rode randomly until, finally, he found himself in the village. Someone exited the inn and voices, raised in a raucous chorus of an old song, burst forth through the open door. Vincent shrugged. There was nothing else to do . . . So, for the first time since his ill-spent youth, Vincent Beverly did his very best to get as drunk as a man could manage.

The landlord, surprised by the oddity of it, dithered. This was very unlike the man he knew and admired. *Very* unlike . . .

"Boy," said mine-host to his middle son. "You just run up to the Place and give Cook a message for Lord Tivington. Now, mind you don't go agabbing about this—" He thrust his chin toward where Vincent sat in the corner of the settle, downing yet another glass of blue ruin. "—to just anybody. You speak only to Cook."

Cook was the landlord's cousin by marriage and a trustworthy soul. She also had a soft spot for Vincent Beverly. She'd see there was no gossip—although how one was to stop the mouths of the gapeseeds here in the taproom . . .

The landlord shook his head and sighed. His son disappeared, taking to his heels, delivering the message as fast as he was able. He was another who thought a great deal of Vincent Beverly.

Over half an hour later, Lord Tivington and his son arrived at the inn. Quietly and with no fuss, they joined Vincent at his table. Each ordered a mug of the landlord's good ale. When

Vincent raised an unsteady finger—a silent order for another glass of gin—his lordship gestured at the mug and Vincent, too, was brought ale.

"Don't think," said Vincent carefully, his eyes on the mug, "that will do the trick."

"Good."

Vincent raised his head, settled a bleary eyed gaze on his stern looking grandsire. His forehead creased into deep frown lines. "She's wedding the idiot," he said. His eyes glistened and he blinked rapidly before dropping his gaze back to the table.

"I don't believe it," said Lord Tivington.

"Don't believe what?" asked his son. Lord Beverly felt utterly bewildered. No one had informed him Vincent was, in his idiosyncratic fashion, courting someone and the poor man hadn't a clue as to what was going forward. He did know that Vincent was not a toper, however, and was shocked to see his nephew so well above par, so very nearly pickled . . .

"Asked her," said Vincent.

"Asked what?" asked Lord Beverly, but was ignored.

"But," asked Lord Tivington, "did she reply?"

"Didn't deny it," muttered Vincent.

"Deny what?" Lord Beverly was again ignored. He stared from his father to his nephew and back again. Slowly he rose to his feet, put both hands on the sticky tabletop, leaned forward between the other two men, and, speaking distinctly, asked, "What the devil has put Vincent in such blue-devils he's dipping deep into blue ruin?"

"The woman he loves has, he believes, accepted the suit of another man," said his father patiently. "I doubt very much that that is true, but our Vincent obviously thinks so."

Vincent once again raised a finger, catching the landlord's attention, and wagging it. The landlord turned his shoulder. Vincent, at that level of inebriation where a man who is determined to drink himself under the table will not be denied, very carefully rose to his feet. He steadied himself, took a step, another—and found his elbows grasped on either side.

Lord Tivington and Lord Beverly led him, complaining, from the taproom and into the cold. "We will take him to the dower house," decided his lordship.

"That old ruin?" asked his son, startled. Another thing about which no one had bothered to inform him was that Vincent was now his grandfather's agent, or indeed, any word of the lease and what had been accomplished toward making the dower house habitable. Lord Tivington proceeded to explain as Lord Beverly tooled the overcrowded curricle along the lanes.

"A very good idea, that," said Beverly. "The place badly needed work. If Vincent is willing to do it, then you are very lucky to have had him agree to it," said Lord Tivington's son.

"He will act my agent, as well . . . Lady Melicent is not particularly happy about the situation," added his lordship, leaning slightly forward to look around Vincent's slouching body at her ladyship's husband. "I understand her primary objection is that your sisters will require the use of the dower house when I am gone and you are in charge."

Lord Beverly stiffened. Then he sighed, slumping into his side of the seat. "I sometimes wish you hadn't merely informed me she would become a shrew, but that you had firmly put your foot down and refused to allow us to wed," he said bitterly. It was the first time he had ever made such a complaint.

Vincent snorted. His head was swimming, but not to the extent he couldn't follow the conversation. On the other hand, he'd drunk enough he hadn't the sense to keep his mouth shut. "Woman's a shrew and idiotic with it." He spoke too clearly.

"But you must not say so," said his grandfather, severely. "You will hold your tongue."

"Why?" asked Vincent who was in that somewhat belligerent stage that was quite willing to cause mischief.

Lord Tivington sighed. "Because you have a heart and do not truly wish to hurt anyone."

"He cannot hurt me by speaking the truth," objected Beverly. "She is a shrew. I was . . . wrong to give in to her. From the beginning, I mean. All I wanted was peace and, to achieve it, I allowed her her own way until she came to think it was her right to have it. On those few occasions when I've put my foot down, she has made life exceedingly difficult for me. It takes a great deal for me to go against her."

"As you did with regard to your children's marriages," said Lord Tivington, his tone approving.

"Yes, I did the right thing then—but she was not at home to interfere. She was here with you so it wasn't so difficult. Still—" Beverly straightened his shoulders, set his jaw, and spoke firmly. "—I must put my foot down about this as well." He was silent for perhaps as much as a quarter mile. "My wife abhors the country," he said then. "She would spend very little time here, could very well spend none at all. It is absurd for her to object to my sisters living out their lives in the only home they have ever known."

Lord Tivington relaxed. He had thought his son would not give in to his wife with respect to this particular problem, but he had not been certain. Now he was. His daughters would not spend the last years, perhaps decades, of their lives in misery, denied the comforts of a home they had made exactly the sort of place they liked best.

"Good uncle," muttered Vincent, his voice slurred. "I'd have 'em, but they wouldn't be happy . . ." He slumped farther down in the seat. "Tired . . ." he muttered. And, suddenly, went to sleep.

"Good heavens, hurry them along, will you?" asked Lord Tivington, doing his best to hold Vincent upright in the seat between them.

It took the young man Vincent had hired as a footman along with Beverly and some help from Lord Tivington, to get Vincent into the dower house and up to his bedroom. There they propped him in a chair while the maids made up a bed and ran a warming pan between the sheets. Then the three men stripped Vincent to his shirt and tucked him into bed.

Lord Tivington looked down at his favorite grandson and shook his head. "Surely he has gotten hold of the wrong end of the stick . . ."

Lord Beverly turned his father away and led him from the room. As they went down the stairs, he asked for an explanation.

Lord Tivington compressed his lips and then spoke slowly. "I am guessing at a great deal, but here are the facts and speculations . . . Vincent has fallen in love with Lord Tennytree's widowed daughter who is a guest at the Everharts. Also a guest is Lord Wakefield, the man Mrs. Garth was said to have jilted when she eloped with Lieutenant Garth. That much is clear. Wakefield has been harassing Mrs. Garth to sing and, for reasons that have yet to be explained, she will not do so. From something Vincent said there in the inn, I think Wakefield has, once again, asked Mrs. Garth to wed him. Vincent thinks she accepted his lordship."

Lord Beverly cogitated on all this. "So. If he cannot wed Mrs. Garth, then he will drink himself into oblivion?"

His grandfather nodded.

"Silly cawker."

Lord Tivington grinned.

"No woman is worth it."

At this bitter comment Tivington halted. "You don't mean that," he said gently.

Beverly cast him a stubborn look, which, after a long moment, faded. "No. There are many good women in the world. You would say that this Mrs. Garth is one of them?"

"I think she is. And I also believe she is *not* so foolish as to have engaged herself to that idiot, Wakefield." He stopped, his cloak half on and half off. "Son, will you drive me over to the Everharts'? I wish to ascertain the truth before I go further."

"What can you do?"

"Convince Vincent his life is not blighted by the loss of a woman who is *not* lost, perhaps?" His brow arched in that way it had. "But *first,* one must assure oneself she is *not.*"

Beverly, who had no particular desire to return to Beverly Place where Lady Melicent had been dropping all sorts of hints that, previously, he had not understood, was happy to spend more time with his father and away from his wife. Facing her down, giving her the word she would not have her way in her latest plans, was not something to which he looked forward.

It was never easy convincing Lady Melicent she would not get her way in something she desired. In fact, even once she *was* convinced, as with the marriages of her children to life companions not of her choice, she would continue to do her best to throw spanners in the works. Luckily their son and daughter knew her well and rarely allowed her to stir the pot—although there had been one or two occasions and Beverly had had to be vigilant to see his wife did *not* succeed.

It was such a boor, this having to keep a tight rein on his wife . . .

"Hmm," said Lord Tivington some little time later. "A skating party. I would not have said it has been so cold as all that."

Beverly spoke after sending only a glance toward the laughing couples making good use of the recent cold snap. "I see my son and daughter have joined in . . ."

"So they have. And their spouses. I am always surprised at how good at such things Sedgewycke is. He so often has his head up in the clouds and appears so awkward when preoccupied, one forgets he is actually a well coordinated man . . ."

They drove on up to the door where the Everhart butler

took their wraps and settled them in the library, the only room that was not occupied by houseguests. He then proceeded at a slow and dignified pace to the top story of the house where he informed Mrs. Garth she had company.

"Guests?" She looked startled.

The butler bowed. "Lord Tivington and his son, Lord Beverly, have come to call and requested the honor of your presence if you are available to receive them . . . ?"

CHAPTER 15

Penelope, frowning, checked that her hair was neat and that she had not crushed her gown too badly while playing with Tal. She had not. Or not so badly she felt it necessary to change. As she left the nursery floor, she wondered what had brought his lordship and his lordship's son to visit.

It occurred to her that something had happened to Vincent and she hurried her pace a trifle. In fact, she hurried it so much that it caught the attention of Lady Houghten, who, hearing unexpected guests arrive, lurked in the hall to discover the who and the why of it.

"My lords," said Penelope before she'd even closed the library door. "What is it? What has happened?"

And then she shut the door and Lady Houghten, fuming that she could hear no more, dithered as to what she might do next. Catching sight of the butler, she sailed toward him, beckoning him nearer as she did so.

"My good man, who has put our good Mrs. Garth into such a dither?"

The butler, knowing her ladyship's reputation, set his nose

just a trifle higher and looked down over the tip, silently asking what business it was of her ladyship's.

Her ladyship, recognizing rebellion when she saw it and knowing she'd get nothing of interest from the fellow, shrugged and went off to find someone with whom she might speculate on this latest interesting event. She only wished the door had not shut behind Mrs. Garth before she'd managed to garner more. It crossed her ladyship's mind that perhaps she should mend fences with Mrs. Mandale. Mrs. Mandale was one of the few local women who really knew how to contemplate such things properly . . .

Penelope, leaning against the door, looked from Lord Tivington to his son and back again. "My lord?" she repeated herself.

"All that has happened, according to my grandson, is that you have affianced yourself to an irritating fellow and—what was his other adjective, my son?" His brow arched. "Ah. Yes. Idiotic. Engaged yourself, in other words, to Lord Wakefield."

Penelope sighed and, straightening away from the door, she strolled nearer. "I feared he left thinking that."

"It is not true?"

Penelope cast his lordship a mild glare, noted the twinkle in his eyes, and shrugged. "Your grandson, my lord, has a most irritating habit of coming to a conclusion—"

"I think," inserted Lord Tivington, "you mean *leaping* to conclusions."

"—and then running off before one has the satisfaction of ramming his mistake down his throat," she finished. "And yes. Leaping is a much better word for what he did. He leapt from the one thing to the other with no thought and certainly no attempt at finding out the truth of the matter."

"I still wished to ascertain that my grandson spent an

hour or so pouring blue ruin down his throat for no good reason."

"Blue ruin?" Penelope's eyes widened. *"Gin?"*

"Gin. My son and I put him to bed, but I am not absolutely certain he was quite so jug-bitten that he will stay there—" Lord Tivington's brows clashed together. "Oh dear." He turned to his son. "Perhaps we should not have left him. He was top-heavy to the point he might do something foolish!"

Penelope turned on her heel and headed toward the door.

"My dear, where are you going?"

"To change into a habit. Your grandson is obviously a fool and must have his head put right before he puts it so far wrong there is no fixing it!"

"We will wait . . ."

"Please do not," she said, her hand on the door and the door ajar. "You go on and I will follow with a groom in attendance. Vincent Beverly is, according to his own tales, the sort of fool who enlists in a line regiment when in a tantrum."

She opened the door farther and found Lady Houghten far too near.

"My lady," said Penelope, dropping a curtsy that was more an insult than a courtesy. "Have you heard sufficient or do you demand clarification?"

Lady Houghten drew herself up to her full height, her impressive bosom thrust forward and her nose drawn back. "Well!"

"It is because all is not *well* that I require you to move so that I may exit this room."

For half a moment Lady Houghten did not move. Then, realizing Lord Tivington was looking at her with that sardonic expression she abhorred, even though she could never understand the cause of it, she stepped back. Her occasional suspicion that his lordship found either disgust or amusement in any of her doings must, of course, be foolish beyond permission.

"My lord . . ." she gushed, but he too stepped beyond her—with no more than a nod of his head—requesting his coat and hat from the Everhart butler. "My lord," she repeated, speaking to Lord Beverly who also stepped into the hall. "A moment, please," she said, laying a hand on his arm . . .

But Lord Beverly had had long years of dealing with a difficult woman and Lady Houghten was not nearly so difficult as his wife. He merely looked down his nose in obvious surprise and was, himself, unsurprised when spots of color appeared on her ladyship's cheeks as she stepped away, quickly dropping her hand.

Penelope fidgeted while she waited for the groom to saddle a horse for himself. She had, as she changed into a habit, dreamed up half a dozen different calamities that might befall a despairing man too much in his altitudes for good judgment. She had seen him in her mind's eye, lying beyond a high gate, his neck broken and his horse galloping. She saw him in a dim building, hanging by the neck from the rafters. She dreamed of him sitting at his desk, a still smoking pistol on the floor beside him . . . all that and several other equally dismal scenes.

"I didn't know I had so much imagination," she scolded herself.

"Ma'am?" asked the groom, turning from the cinch he was, at that moment, tightening.

"Nothing. I have merely become so eccentric I speak to myself. Are you not yet ready?" And then she apologized for snapping, but was quite impatient enough to lead her mare to the mounting block and climb into the saddle herself—except the groom came to her, cupped his hands, and helped her up. Then he rose into his own saddle and, surprised at the speed with which she set off, followed her rapidly disappearing mount down the lane.

Not half an hour later—her groom never quite catching

up with the fleet-footed mare borrowed from Georgi—Penelope dropped to the ground and hurried into the Beverly dower house.

"Fred," she said to the footman who was awaiting her, "where is Mr. Beverly?"

He pointed to the stairs, opened his mouth to explain that Lord Tivington and his son had already gone up and come back down again, but closed it when she turned at the first landing and disappeared. He scratched his head, decided the nobs were all cracked, even the best of them, and returned to putting a polish on the floor workmen had recently sanded and refinished.

Penelope didn't slow until she reached the door to the room Vincent had decided would be his. Then, her hand on the doorknob, it occurred to her that she was behaving in a decidedly unladylike manner. Instead of opening it, she knocked. And waited.

And waited.

No one called out. No one said a word. There was no sound whatsoever from beyond that door. Once again her heart jumped into her throat. She thrust the door open—

Vincent, sitting on the edge of his bed, cast her a bleary eyed look and closed his eyes as if in pain.

—and rushed into the room.

"Where is his lordship?" demanded Penelope.

Vincent lifted his hands to his face, scrubbed it, and then, his fingers running up through his hair, opened one eye. "You . . . ?" he managed.

"Where is your grandfather?" asked Penelope, speaking slowly as if to a child who was not quite bright.

"Grandfather . . ." Vincent cast a vague look around the room.

"I thought to find him here."

"Here."

"Vincent Beverly, are you *still* more than three sheets to the wind?" she asked, exasperated.

Vincent squeezed his eyes shut. "Penelope?"

"Yes. Penelope. Why are you alone?"

"Alone." He heaved a sigh. "All alone . . ." Another sigh. "Forever."

"Not if you do not wish it so," said a frustrated Penelope. "Vincent, must you play the fool? Now? When I want you sober and listening to me?"

Vincent finally realized that it was Penelope Garth and not some phantasmagoria there in his bedroom while he, bare-legged, dressed only in his shirt, sat staring like a cabbage-head. "You shouldn't be here," he said.

"I *wouldn't* be here if you hadn't been fool enough to drink yourself under the table and be put to bed."

"Shouldn't be here," he repeated in the single-minded fashion of the foxed.

Penelope sighed. There would be no getting any sense from or into the man until he sobered up. She turned on her heel and went to the head of the stairs. "Fred," she called. When he responded she ordered, "Coffee for Mr. Beverly. And while your sister brews it, bring up a mug of heavy-wet."

She moved back to his room and found Vincent on his feet, not quite steady, but obviously stubbornly determined on doing something. "Sit down," she ordered, going to him and giving him a slight push. He sat, but one hand came out and grasped her arm, pulling her down against him. He stared into her face as she, lying half across him, stared up at him.

His mouth came down, crushing hers, his arms surrounding her and pulling her close. After a moment, he realized she was not struggling, that she returned his kisses . . .

"Penelope?" he asked.

"About time," she muttered. "Or maybe not. Your footman will be here any moment and I'd better not be found this way . . ." She pushed against him and, the fumes clouding his head beginning to fade, Vincent allowed her to rise.

Just in time.

Carefully carrying a tray on which rested a mug of home-brew, Fred appeared in the open doorway. He cleared his throat, fearing he'd spill the ale if he were to release an edge of the tray in order to knock.

"Come in." Penelope took the mug and handed it to Vincent. "And hurry back with the coffee. Mr. Beverly will be dressing, so just bring it in to him when you arrive," she said, casting a look toward Vincent that warned him he'd better be dressing. "I'll go down to the breakfast room, Vincent, and await you there."

Half an hour later, still a trifle worse for wear, Vincent joined her.

"Are you sober?" she asked.

"More or less," he responded, a rueful look twisting his mouth. "I believe I forgot to congratulate you earlier . . ."

Penelope rolled her eyes. "You are impossible."

"Why? Because I feel you've made a huge mistake? Because I wish you had not?"

"Because you are wrong?" She came nearer and stabbed him in the chest with each word. "Wrong wrong *wrong.*"

He stilled, his eyes widening, their usual sleepy look disappearing as a distinctly alert expression took its place. "You are *not* engaged to Wakefield?"

"Look at that! The man has returned to his senses," she said, pretending to be awestruck.

He grimaced. "Then why did you not say so?"

"Because, you ninny, you so instantly jumped to the utterly ridiculous conclusion I had, and hadn't even the courtesy to *ask.* You *told* me I was engaged to that fool. The insult was beyond . . . beyond . . ."

"Beyond anything," he said, contritely and then, tentatively, put open palms on her arms near her shoulders. "Penelope, can you accept my apologies? Or did I put myself beyond the pale?"

She tipped her head ever so slightly and cast him a look from the corners of her eyes. "Well . . ."

He grinned—a quick sardonic grin very much in his usual character. "I have," he added, tipping his head and studying her, his eyes once again hidden in that heavy-eyed look that was also much in character, "some vague recollection that I kissed you. Upstairs. Should I apologize for that, as well?"

Penelope's head swung up and she glared. "Don't you dare!"

"It is true I'd rather not. In fact," he said, tugging her a trifle nearer, "I'd very much like to do it again." The rueful look returned. "Now I may have a better recollection of it . . . ?"

Penelope put her arms around his waist and raised her face. "Please," she said.

Georgi burst into the nursery. "Is it true?" she asked.

Penelope looked up from the book she was reading. She had managed to find time to reach the third volume of Georgi's gothic tale and was not pleased to be interrupted just when the tale was at its most exciting.

"Is what true?" she asked.

"Are you engaged?"

Penelope lay aside the book. "Am I engaged to whom?"

Georgi paused, blinked. "Er . . . ?"

"According to Vincent, before he ran off in a snit, it was to Wakefield, but I have heard, since, that *he* is engaged to Miss Grimson?"

Georgi was torn. She both wondered what had happened that Vincent would ever suggest such a terrible thing and enjoying the excitement of having Miss Grimson announce her engagement to Lord Wakefield—among rumors that Wakefield was not pleased to have it so.

She decided to begin with Miss Grimson's announcement. After agreeing the two were engaged, she added, ". . . I have tried to determine what actually happened, but Wakefield only pokers up and looks down his nose and Miss Grimson merely giggles and covers her mouth with her hands. I did, however, catch Lady Houghten telling secrets to Miss Herning, but Miss Herning just blushes and shakes her head. Miss Herning, unfortunately, is the sort that, when she promises not to tell, as she undoubtedly did, does just that."

"Tells?"

"Keeps her promise. It is the one thing that makes her curiosity endurable, but is also most frustrating when it is your own curiosity needing answers. So." Georgi had had enough of Lord Wakefield and Miss Grimson. She eyed her guest. "Is it true? Are you and Vincent engaged?"

Penelope's eyes dropped to her hands. "Georgi, will you think me very strange if I ask that you *not* announce it to all and sundry? I would much prefer that Vincent and I manage the whole without a great deal of fuss and bother. We have discussed it and he is agreeable. Once your house party is ended, we mean to ask that the banns be read. We will wed as soon as the three readings have been accomplished. Vincent hopes he'll have the dower house in shape by then that we may move in, but I think that a hopeless dream. Lord Tivington suggested that perhaps you and Lord Everhart would allow us to rent Minnow Manor until the dower house is ready?"

"Let us have no talk of *renting*, but of course you may use it." Georgi returned to the engagement. "Why must you be so secretive? I have been making all sorts of plans. A soiree at which we could announce it. Better yet, a country ball. Grandfather would allow us to use the Place with its ballroom. In fact, he would like that. Vincent, you know. He is very fond of Vincent."

Penelope shook her head. "A great deal of bother. A great deal of expense. And far too much fuss. We are neither so enamored of making a show of ourselves that we wish anything of the sort. I suppose," she added, "that some sort of wedding breakfast will be necessary after the wedding . . . ?"

"Oh yes. And you must go to London to order your bride clothes. Let me see. My guests begin leaving soon after New Years . . . I think we might find ourselves alone by the fifth or the sixth—" Georgi brightened. "—and then you and I could go up to Town where I can introduce you to my . . . What is it? Why do you shake your head?"

"I will purchase a few new things, Georgi, since I wish to put away my mourning garments—except for the mauves— but I do not require a large wardrobe. We mean to live quietly here in the country. Vincent will be acting as Lord Tivington's agent and because of that we'll receive few, if any, invitations that require full dress." She shook her head. "Such a waste of money. I'll not do it."

Georgi eyed her. *"Fiddle,"* she said.

The mild term made Penelope smile. "Fiddle?"

"I cannot very well say what I *wish* to say," said Georgi, exasperated. "First you deny me the pleasure of feting your engagement properly and then you deny me the fun of all that shopping and you would also say you mean to turn yourself into a . . . a . . ." Georgi threw up her hands. "I don't know what!"

"Vincent's wife and Tal's mother and, with luck," added Penelope softly, "the mother of a large brood of children to follow. Why do you look so sad?" she asked.

Georgi's hand went to her tummy. "I do wish . . ."

"You've time. As I understand it, you've been wed only a few months . . . ?"

Georgi sighed. "It is just that I wish for a large brood as well and want to start on it as soon as may be. I don't want my children to be alone as, without Vincent, I might have been. I mean if something should happen to Everhart and myself." She sighed one more sigh and put thoughts of a child from her. "So, if you will not allow the party and you will not allow a shopping spree, what *can* we do?"

"We can forget doing anything at all until your party disappears so that I need not face their curiosity and the . . . the snide knowing looks that the gossip my father has started would lead to." It was Penelope's turn to sigh. "I wish there was something I could do about that man . . ."

"But there is not. Will you join us tonight when we celebrate Miss Grimson's engagement?"

"Not Lord Wakefield's engagement?" asked Penelope, her eyes twinkling.

"I have yet to determine if Lord Wakefield feels celebratory!" With that Georgi whisked herself from the nursery— only to put her head back in. "You did not say you would join us?"

Penelope, after a moment, nodded. If she did not begin, on occasion, to join the company, then once her engagement to Vincent was announced, there would be some reason for talk—even if wrongheaded reason. Against all inclination, she decided she must join the Everharts' company whenever she was free of the work she was doing at the dower house . . . especially in the evenings, when she'd have no good excuse for hiding away.

A thought crossed Penelope's mind and she brightened. With Lord Wakefield engaged to Miss Grimson, she no longer need concern herself with his harassment.

At least, she hoped she did not.

CHAPTER 16

Lord Tennytree once again burst into Minnow Manor. This time he had an embarrassed-looking constable in tow. "I demand my grandson. Give him to me. At once!" yelled his lordship.

The over-loud voice brought a number of people into the hall. The first, moving far more quickly than was consistent with his dignity, was the Everhart butler, his usually imperturbable manner obviously strained. From the music room, Wakefield and Miss Grimson appeared, their music ending on a sour note caused by the startled reaction of two people entirely unfamiliar with such impolite noises. Lord Everhart, accompanied by one of his older guests, arrived from the direction of his lordship's study.

"I tell you I want my grandson. On the instant!"

Georgi appeared at the top of the stairs, her eyes wide with distress. She started down—but stopped as Penelope appeared behind her. She turned to look at her friend, but Penelope, a paper clutched in her hand, looked so stern and forbidding, Georgi merely pushed the back of her waist into the banister, allowing her guest space to stalk down the stairs.

"Whore!"

"Making your usual insane pronouncements, my lord?" asked Penelope quietly.

"Trollop."

"You know very well it is not true."

"I'll have my grandson. No light-skirt will raise the boy. I'll not have it, I tell you. Constable, do your duty."

"One moment," said Penelope firmly.

She unfolded the letter. Finding her place she raised her hand for silence and the muttering among the guests arriving in the hallway one after the other ceased.

"Here it is. I quote from a letter received from a solicitor a month or two after I married Kennet Garth: *this is to inform you that Lord Tennytree disavows his daughter, disinherits her, and wishes nothing further to do with her or hers.*" She looked up, her shoulders squared and her head high. "It goes on at some length, but the end of it is that Lord Tennytree *has* no daughter. If he has no daughter then he has no grandson."

She turned on her heel and trod firmly back up the stairs, the letter, crushed in her left hand, the only sign of her perturbation.

"Bravo," said Vincent softly, from just behind Lord Tennytree.

Vincent had entered the hall from the outdoors just as Penelope asked for silence, which had rather interfered with his firm intention of once again ejecting Lord Tennytree from the premises. Which was too bad, since this time, he'd meant to do so far less politely than he and Everhart had done on an earlier occasion.

"I believe," he said when Penelope's father turned, glaring, "that that letter says it all. You have no further business here, my lord." Vincent bowed slightly, gesturing with both hands to the exit, silently inviting his lordship to use it.

"I want my grandson! I will have my grandson!"

"You have children, perhaps? Someone about whom no one knows?" asked Vincent softly. "Because the woman who just read from that letter is *not* your daughter. You, with all the authority of the law behind you, denied her *and* hers."

Lord Tennytree gobbled, unable to form words in his own defense. Since he continued to want his own way, he was equally unable to accept the logic of the situation.

Lord Everhart stepped forward. "You had your chance at knowing the boy, my lord," he said, drawing the surly man's glare. "You had him thrown into a storm in which he nearly died along with his mother. I believe you have forfeited all rights to the child. Or, for that matter, given the existence of that letter, to his mother. You will leave my home, my lord, and you will cease all persecution of the woman you once called daughter. If you do not I will contact a solicitor in her behalf and see that you are forced to do so."

The constable looked from one man to another and finally, silently begging for direction, his gaze settled on Vincent. Vincent tipped him the wink, jerked his thumb toward the door, and moved half a step back, allowing the poor man to escape. Which he did on the instant. It meant a long walk to the village, but he much preferred that to staying where the obviously mad Lord Tennytree might make further unwarranted demands on him.

Vincent looked at Everhart who shook his head ever so slightly. "Well, my lord?" asked Everhart.

Tennytree made an obvious effort at control. For perhaps the first time in his life he was almost willing to admit to error. His desire for the grandson to whom he might leave his estate, which was unentailed, was so great it forced him to make an effort to be reasonable.

"But he *is* my grandson. Whatever that letter says. Is he not? I only just learned of his existence. She cannot deny my right to the boy. She cannot flout me so!" With each word his voice rose until, with the last few he was, once again shouting, his fists waving wildly in the air.

"My lord, you know you have brought this situation on yourself," said Georgi, scolding. She had, gradually, moved down the stairs and now stood at her husband's shoulder. "You not only denied your daughter upon her marriage to a man not of your choice, but you came very near to murdering her when you forced her into the storm when, wishing to introduce you to her son, she came to visit you. You will notice I do not say your grandson. You have made that an impossible relationship, have you not?"

Tennytree's face turned bright red with his fury. "How dare you speak to me so!"

"She has said nothing which is not true, my lord," said Vincent. The instant Georgi began to speak, he'd moved to stand at her side.

With Lord Everhart on one side and himself on the other, she was unlikely to find herself in grave difficulties, but Vincent would not put it past the bully confronting them to try to harm her. If not right now, then later.

He must remember to warn Everhart to have a care of her. Tennytree tended to hold grudges right into eternity. Since it was a *woman* who had the temerity to, in his twisted mind, insult him, someone far weaker than himself, he would not conveniently forget he wished revenge.

It did not soothe Vincent's concern one whit when, very suddenly, Lord Tennytree's temper faded and he calmed. In fact, that only increased Vincent's worries.

"Very well. As usual, everyone is against me. I will seek my grandson through the courts, which is what I should have done from the first." Tennytree cast one last glare around the hall, seeming, for the first time, to realize he'd an audience. "Hurumph," he said and turned all around. "Where is that useless constable? I'll have words to say to him, I can tell you."

"I wouldn't," said Everhart. "I am certain the word of any number of people who have witnessed your outrageous demands will prove the man was brought here under false pretenses and merely returned where he belonged once it was clear there was nothing he could or *should* do."

Tennytree's face once again became alarmingly red and then, with great effort this time, he achieved that unnatural calm. "We will see," he said, his tone frighteningly mild. "And," he added, his goggling eyes settling on Georgi, "you need not think I will forgive you your insults, either!"

"Since when is the truth an insult?" asked Georgi promptly.

"Truth! The truth is I've a grandson. *I will have him.*"

He stalked from the house, down the steps, and climbed into his carriage. The coachman whipped up the pair pulling it and, once again, Vincent pitied the beasts. But there was nothing he could do. What he *could* do was have a word with his cousin. He took her arm and marched her off toward the library—and was surprised when he was unable to shut the door.

Lord Everhart, having followed them, wished to join them.

"I wish you would go elsewhere for a time," said Vincent, a sour note to be heard under his usual sardonic tone. He had not released Georgi's arm, although she pushed at his fingers.

"And I wish to go to Penelope," she said. "Poor dear. She must be totally distraught. Do let me go, Vincent!"

"Not until we've had a few words. That man is dangerous, Georgi. You have roused the beast in him and he will not forget. He'll want revenge. You have made an enemy, Georgi, and you must have a care. Not just for a week or a month, but *forever.*"

"Unfortunately, I agree," said Everhart when Georgi would

have objected. "If he is not mad, he is the next thing to it. There is no predicting what he will do."

Georgi looked from one to the other and sighed. "If I promise to take care, will you please allow me to go to Penelope? Or perhaps—" Her eyes narrowed. "—Vincent, it is *you,* is it not, who should go to her?"

"I go to her now. Now *you've* been warned to take care. You might occupy yourself by seeing your guests fully understand that what occurred here this morning is not food for gossip. Mrs. Garth has suffered enough at that man's hands." Vincent stalked to the door and slammed it behind him.

"No, Georgi," said Everhart as she moved to follow. "Let him go. I think this is far more his business than yours or mine."

Georgi, about to ignore her husband and follow anyway, suddenly stopped. She turned on her heel and stared at him, her mouth slightly open and her eyes wide. Did he know? As a certainty? Had Vincent told him too?

"Because . . . ?"

Everhart smiled, his eyes narrowing and bright with something approaching laughter. "I told you not to interfere. Are you not glad you did not?"

Georgi relaxed, wishing very much to discuss Vincent's engagement—but only if her husband had been told, only if he *knew* . . .

"You think . . . ?" she asked, encouragingly.

"You will have your wish, Georgi—assuming Vincent can manage to bring the widow around his thumb and get her to agree to have him."

"Oh, my dear," breathed Georgi, pretending anxiety, "surely she would not . . ."

"Deny him?" He grinned. "You think Vincent such a complete rake he cannot fail? You forget, my love, that Mrs. Garth is armored against him by her love for her Kennet."

"But it has been two years . . . or very nearly."

Everhart's head came up and he sobered. "And, if I were to die, would you forget me so quickly, my dear?"

Georgi ran to him, very nearly knocking him down in her concern to convince him she would never forget him. Ever. And that he was not to allow anything to happen to him, because she could not bear it . . .

There were tears on her face when she raised it from his chest and stared up at him. "How could you suggest I would forget you?"

"I do not believe any such thing, but," he added softly, "I would be very sorry if, at the other extreme, you were never to recover. I would want you to—not that you forgot me, my dear, but that you would not waste that wonderful capacity to love that is in you, that you would find a new love *as well*."

Georgi's lip trembled. "Do not say such things."

"I must. Since I upset you so badly, I must make you understand how I feel. And what I feel most strongly is that you should never waste the life you have been given. If, God forbid, I were to die, you must not mourn beyond reason. That would be—" He searched for a means of expressing himself that would make the whole clear to her. "—a sin, I think."

"Please? Let us speak of other things?" Georgi spoke in a very small voice that was quite unlike her.

He smiled. "I've no intention of dying, you know."

"Thank goodness." She broke away. "And now I must attempt to turn our guests' thoughts to better things. Many will entertain their friends with a description of that scene. There is no hope they will not, but one *may* hope they'll do so with kindness toward Penelope . . ."

Lord Everhart stared fondly after his disappearing wife. He shook his head. And was startled when a figure rose from a chair to one side of the room. "Sir?"

"I felt decidedly de trop," said Lord Tivington peevishly, "but could find no tactful means of allowing the three of you to know of my existence. I suppose I should have come into

the hall when Tennytree arrived, but I cannot bear the man."
Tivington sighed. "I came to bring invitations to you and your
guests to a soiree," he added, and handed over the stack of
cards his daughters had written out in their neat script. "You
are correct, by the way, about Vincent and Mrs. Garth. If you
can manage to keep Georgi's pert little nose out of the situation, then I have hopes he'll manage to bring the widow up
to scratch."

"You *hope* he will?" asked Everhart, his eyes narrowing.
"I have seen it coming, but am worried by it. You do not feel
it would be a not particularly good match for him . . . ?"

"You mean they neither are in possession of a fortune?"
Tivington shrugged. "I doubt you need concern yourself. Vincent will never be outrageously wealthy, but thanks to his
friendship with Aaron Sedgewyke, he has made any number
of excellent investments and is quite beforehand with the
world. He doesn't discuss it, of course, or parade it in the usual
way, since wealth has never been an object with him, but
he'll have no difficulty supporting a family and providing
Mrs. Garth with the elegancies of life."

"I admit I worried about it. Not for my sake, of course,
but for Georgi's. She'd have been terribly distressed if he'd
married unwisely and suffered for it."

Tivington nodded. "I understand. My granddaughter has
far too soft a heart and, at the same time, a headstrong manner. Betwixt the two, she has a tendency to find herself in the
briars far more often than one would wish."

"So I have discovered," said Everhart ruefully. "Whatever
catches her attention, she jumps in with both feet before ascertaining how deep the water! I have always supported a
dame school in the village near our main estate, which I
thought sufficient local charity. Georgi disagrees. She convinced me I must take a seat on the poorhouse board. I was
to see that the poor are not exploited as is often done." Ever-

hart's expression changed to one of rue. "She was in the right of it. Our poorhouse has had a stocking operation in which the women participate and for which they *now* receive wages. Until I insisted, they did not. The able-bodied men are being taught fine carpentry. With trades, some have hope of escaping the poorhouse." His rueful look became more extreme. "She also finds it abominable that such people are punished for merely being poor—the least permissible ration of food, husbands and wives separated, never allowed time alone together. *That* last practice she claims is a sin. And I think," he added, thoughtfully, "that she has the right of that as well. No man is, after all, to put asunder a legally wedded pair! I've made a number of changes . . ." His voice trailed off.

His lordship smiled. "I have done much the same here—at her insistence. There will be other projects in which she will attempt to interest you, my lord," said Tivington in a kindly tone. "It will be up to you to weed out the possible from the improbable and impossible."

Upstairs, Vincent stood outside the nursery door, dithering. He wanted nothing so much as to go to Penelope, take her in his arms, and tell her he would protect her and Tal, and that she must trust him to do so from now on. Unfortunately, he knew her for a proud woman, and he feared that she would tell him not to interfere, that she would see to Tal on her own, that her father could not get the best of her.

Suddenly, it occurred to him that she had appeared very opportunely, letter in hand, and he wondered at it. His curiosity cut through his uncertainty, and he knocked. Matty opened the door, looked back into the room, was obviously given permission because she then opened the door more widely. As he passed in, she exited.

Vincent wondered at it. He supposed Tal might be consid-

ered a chaperon of sorts, but doubted the old biddies would
agree, assuming they discovered he'd visited Penelope without Matty present. Still—there was that curiosity . . .

"How did you know to bring that letter down? How did
you find it so quickly?"

Penelope rose from the floor where she was helping Tal
stack blocks. "I had it by me. I know my father, you see, and
I wondered how long it would be before he'd convince himself I am no suitable mother for his grandson. There was a
time I'd have wrung my hands and bleated as they hauled my
son away." She grimaced. "I am no longer that lamblike little
daughter who fears tantrums and will do anything to avoid
them. Those years in the Peninsula," she finished on a dry
note, "did a great deal toward teaching me independence."

"And you value that independence," he said, doing his
best to give no hint of his feelings as he spoke.

"I value it in that it will make it possible to fight my father
in this. I will not allow him to take my son from me."

Vincent was silent for a long moment. "Will you allow
others to help you?" he asked after a long moment.

She looked at him, catching his steady gaze and holding
it. "I will accept all and any help that is necessary to protect
my son."

Vincent relaxed. She did not mean to act foolishly. "I will
be the one who helps you. You and Tal." Tal had managed, by
then, to reach Vincent's side and, holding onto his idol's trousers,
had pulled himself up. Vincent leaned down and picked the
boy up. "He is a delight. I'll not have that man destroy his
bonny nature."

Penelope smiled. "Bonny?"

He smiled back. "It seems an appropriate word. Since he
is Scottish."

She laughed. "My bonny boy."

Vincent sobered. "Penelope . . ." When she did not object,

he drew in a breath and began again. "Penelope, you have given me the right to protect you from everything—as is conventional. What concerns me is that I might do something to upset you, take to myself something you feel you yourself should handle. Will you help me learn what you will and will not accept from me? As your fiancé and soon your husband?"

"Would you think me terribly forward if I admit that I will appreciate your aid and the comfort of your—presence?" At the last moment she found she could not suggest she wished for his embrace. That his arms around her would soothe her and put a balm over the wounds her father continually inflicted.

"Comfort?" he asked after a moment.

She smiled. "I love Kennet. I always will. But I believe a heart is large enough to hold more than one love. When I gave you my promise to wed you, Vincent, that included the offer of my heart."

Vincent closed his eyes and heaved a great sigh. "Thank God."

Tal patted his cheek, a frown marring the tiny brow. " 'Cent?"

Vincent smiled at the boy. "Tal, I want to hug your mother now. You go play with your blocks and, in a moment or two, I will come help you build the highest tower ever."

Tal frowned.

"Go, now. I'll come in a moment," said Vincent, and pushed the boy gently toward the fireplace.

Tal pouted, looked from mother to Vincent and back. When Penelope nodded at him, he sighed and toddled off toward the blocks. Penelope didn't wait to see that he reached them, but turned to Vincent who opened his arms. She went into them.

The kiss was all a kiss could be. To their surprise, the second was even better. And the third ended only when Tal, impatient, came back to pull at his mother's skirts. " 'Cent! Want 'Cent!"

Vincent looked down at him. "Say please," he ordered.

The boy ducked his head, looked up through his lashes and managed, "Peas."

Vincent's arms tightened for a moment around Penelope. "You'll marry me? Soon?"

"We'll discuss exactly when later," she said, apologetically. "When the imp is settled for a nap and we need fear no interruption."

His heart free of pain and bubbling with anticipation, Vincent went to build Talavera the highest tower possible with the blocks available. A tower Tal gleefully toppled the moment he was given leave to do so.

Later, Penelope and Vincent discussed possible wedding dates. They took Georgi into their confidence, but again asked that she not speak of it. They bundled up against the cold and, borrowing a carriage, drove over to tell Lord Tivington, from whom they also asked silence.

"You wish a quiet wedding with little or no nonsense about it?" asked his lordship.

"We'll post banns once the Everharts' guests are gone," said Vincent. He held Penelope's hand, tightening it slightly on the words. "We wish to avoid Lord Tennytree's interference and, since he rarely comes to church, he is unlikely to . . ."

"Vincent, do not be naïve when I know you are not." Tivington's eyebrow arched. "*Gossip* will reach his ears. If you truly wish a quiet wedding, the only way you may achieve one is to buy a license. His lordship will make trouble if you do not."

"I don't like that idea," said Vincent, eyeing Penelope who frowned, biting her lip. "Would not a license, in itself, rouse the gossips to, hum, nasty thoughts?"

Tivington did not mince words. "You think they will suggest you *must* wed if you wed by license. Time will prove the error in that speculation, will it not? And you will be *wed*. There would be no setting it aside or postponement as Tennytree might attempt if you post banns and he enters objections. Besides, if the two of you are together you will be support for each other as you could not if you were living separately."

"But he *cannot* object," said Penelope, ignoring his lordship's soothing words. "Not only am I fully of age, but he has, in writing, denied that I am his daughter . . ."

"He could find ways of tying you up in knots for some time to come. Present him with a fait accompli and there is nothing he can do but rant and rave—which he will do in any case."

"Penelope, I must agree with Grandfather. His suggestion has reason behind it. Also, once we are wed your father has fewer grounds for suggesting your son is not being reared as he should be. You will have a husband, Tal will have a father, and the both of you will be protected . . . ?"

It occurred to Penelope that her father *would* still object—thanks to Vincent's reputation. She flicked a glance toward Lord Tivington. The old gentleman's lips twitched with humor, but he shook his head ever so slightly. Penelope realized Vincent had not thought of that problem.

"You do not answer," said Vincent, a sad look in his eyes.

"What you say makes sense," said Penelope quickly, "except for one problem. My father is completely irrational. He will make trouble no matter what we do."

Vincent's eyes smiled and his lips twisted in that way they had. "But we will marry by license? Soon? You agree—even if reluctantly?"

She smiled. "I agree—reluctantly."

Several days later, while Vincent and Penelope consulted with the foreman at the dower house, Matty played with Tal, laughing at his antics as he tried, again and again, to catch up with Tally's Ho. The boy had tumbled over his own feet once again and was pushing the pup away. Ho, however, was determined to give a thorough lick to Tal's downy cheek.

The door burst open and Matty turned, curious. She rose instantly to her feet and started toward Tal, reaching him and snatching him up just before the rough looking man who, followed by a second even rougher sort, reached them.

"Who are you? What do you want?" Matty clutched Tal and the boy, catching her anxiety, grasped her tightly around the neck. He stared with big eyes at the men.

"We've come for the boy. Now hand him over and no one will get hurt."

"Just like that?"

"Yes. Just like that."

"And who will care for him?" asked Matty standing straight, stretching her four feet eight inches, to face down the much taller man.

"None of your business. Now give him here."

She held Tal more tightly. "He needs changing," said Matty a trifle slyly. "Are you certain you want to carry off a very wet baby?" She sniffed. "Maybe worse?"

The first man hesitated and cast a glance toward the second.

"You're lying. Give him here," demanded the second.

"And then you take him away? No nappies. No feeding cup? No toys?"

The second man, feeling a trifle flummoxed, looked at the first who nodded. "Get the nappies. And the cup. Hurry."

Matty, moving slowly, headed for the night nursery. At the last moment she rushed, turned to slam and lock the door . . . but was too late.

"Good try, missy," sneered the second man. "Now get the boy's necessaries and no more nonsense."

Matty bit her lip, looked from one determined man to the

other. She looked down at the pup that stood, half behind her skirts, barking.

"Now. Or we'll take him as he is—regardless."

Matty turned to the cupboard and, using one hand, pulled out a stack of nappies, some other clothes and let still others fall to the floor. The taller man tried to take Tal, but the boy only clutched Matty tighter and began to cry.

"Blast it all, we haven't all day," said the second, looking over his shoulder in a worried fashion.

"Missy," said the first, "if we take you too, will you hurry? I swear we mean the boy no harm."

"You're from Lord Tennytree, aren't you?" asked Matty accusingly—but she hurried a trifle, wrapping Tal in a blanket and grabbing her shawl. She looked around. "His cup."

"Won't need no cup," said the rougher man, looking more nervous.

"It is in the nursery," said Matty in as soothing a manner as she could manage given how fearful she was. She headed back into the other room. The first man followed, the clothes and nappies under his arm. "Here," she said and thrust the special cup with its drinking spout at the fellow. She looked around, leaned over, and picked up the pup. "You'll want some way of keeping him happy and I assure you, the pup is the only thing that will help. Not that he'll *be* happy. Not without his mother."

Scolding all the way, hoping to see a footman or a groom, Matty allowed the men to guide her down the servant's stairs, out the back door, and then, each holding one of her arms while she held the bundled up Tal and the squirming pup, she was rushed across the kitchen garden, through a small woods, and thrust into a carriage that stood in the rarely used lane beyond.

Tal, once they were settled, poked his head out of his wrappings, and looked around. "Want Mama," he said. He stared at the man. "Want Mama," he repeated, firmly, his little head set at an arrogant angle. When the man simply frowned, Tal cast a look at Matty, a glare at the man, and began to howl. "Want Mama, want Mama, want Mama . . ."

"Shut him up or he'll have reason to want his mama," said the man. Unfortunately, the other, the softer of the two, was driving the carriage. Matty soothed Tal and his sobs quieted. But he continued to mutter that he wanted his mama.

Matty wondered how Lord Tennytree thought to get away with kidnapping the boy. She wished there had been some way of leaving word for Mrs. Garth as to what had happened. Messing up the boy's clothing would be one hint and the bedding dragged every which way when she'd pulled the cover from the cot would be another clue that all was not well . . . and perhaps the missing cup would be noticed, and surely the pup's absence would mean something?

Matty closed her eyes and prayed someone would figure out where they were before she was thrown out of the house by Lord Tennytree who would want no one around who knew the boy. He'd not care if Tal were unhappy, his routines destroyed, his mother not there to soothe his tears—his " 'Cent" unavailable to gently reprimand him when he fell into one of his mild tantrums . . .

Matty opened one eye, stared at the mean-looking man watching her narrowly, decided she'd not prayed nearly enough, and sent still another anxious prayer heavenward.

CHAPTER 17

Penelope, grasping the ball topping the newel post, swung around the landing corner and rushed headlong down the stairs.

Lord Everhart, who happened to be standing at the bottom talking to one of his guests, caught her as she reached him. "What is it?" he asked the white-faced woman clutching his arms, her staring eyes raised to meet his gaze.

"Gone. . . ." She panted, her hands moved to clutch his lapels. She shut her eyes tight, opened them, a strained look to them. *"They are gone."*

Everhart stiffened. "Mrs. Garth, you must control yourself. I cannot help you if I do not understand." But he very much feared he did understand. He covered her hands gently where they clutched his coat, and patted them reassuringly . . .

Penelope stilled. She closed her eyes and drew in a deep breath. Gradually tight muscles relaxed, even the fists ruining the press of Everhart's favorite coat. She stood away from him, straightened, and, with a touch of a lieutenant reporting to a senior officer, said, "I arrived home moments ago. When I reached the nursery, it was silent. I thought perhaps

Matty had taken Tal and Tally's Ho outside—but then I went into Tal's bedroom . . ."

Her hand went to her mouth and again her eyes widened, her fears for her son overcoming her control once again.

"His bedroom," said Everhart, sternly.

Vincent arrived just then. Penelope saw him, turned to him, reached for him. "Penelope?" He came to her, taking her into his arms as he cast a questioning look toward Everhart.

"I haven't gotten the meat of it," said his lordship.

"He's gone," wailed Penelope into Vincent's chest, her words muffled.

"Tal?"

She nodded, her forehead rubbing against his neckcloth, adding creases to it that would send any halfway decent valet into a spasm were he to see it.

Vincent took Penelope's shoulders and forced her away from him. He tipped her face so he could look into it. "Slowly. Tell me."

She drew in a deep breath and tried again. "I went into the night nursery. His clothes. Hanging out of the cabinet, strewn around the floor. His bedding. Pulled about and a cover missing. Tal has been kidnapped. I *know* he has. My father . . . !" Tears, previously held back, traced rivulets down her cheeks.

A muscle jumped in Vincent's jaw and his eyes flew to meet Everhart's. "You are certain?"

"I do not see what else it can be." Penelope, now the worst was out in the open, managed, once again, to control herself. "I think Matty managed to go along, or perhaps my father had enough sense he ordered the nurse taken with the child—although I doubt that. Tally's Ho is gone too. He's too young to have followed, running along behind, so Matty must have managed that as well. Bless the girl. Perhaps Tal won't be too upset . . . ?"

The muscle turned over again in Vincent's jaw, but he

nodded reassuringly. In his mind, however, he was asking whether Lord Tennytree had enough sense to keep the girl with the boy or if he'd fear the girl would try to steal Tal away . . . Again his eyes sought Everhart's. "What should we do?" he asked.

"I think the first thing must be to check whether anyone saw anything. That the child, a nurse, and a dog could be stolen away from here and no one notice anything seems impossible, but I agree that the clues suggest it happened. Mrs. Garth, we will get your son back for you. One way or another. Do not despair."

A footman appeared in the hall just then and Everhart called him over, gave a series of orders that startled the young man a great deal, but, when asked if he understood, he nodded and set off to obey. "My butler will check the inside servants. My coachman will see if anyone among the grooms or gardening staff saw anything. And now . . ." he continued, looking about.

A guest, Mr. Carter-Vaughn, was standing by, his ears cocked, silently scoffing that anything so dramatic could possibly take place at a country house party. He perked up when Everhart beckoned.

"You heard," said Everhart. The chap had eavesdropped. His lordship would not waste time pretending he need explain what needed no explanation. "Collect as many of the guests as you can find and direct them to the salon. If you'd be so kind," he added the trite politeness without thinking. "You'll understand that I must discover if anyone saw or heard anything that will help us."

Shaking his head that someone as sensible as Everhart would go to such extremes in order to soothe the obviously overly protective widow, Carter-Vaughn strolled off to poke his head into the various public rooms. It never occurred to him that he should send maids to check bedrooms and he certainly had no intention of going to the bother of finding those who were so foolish as to leave the nice warm house for the exceedingly chilly outdoors . . .

Everhart soon realized the inadequacy of Carter-Vaughn's efforts and, after hearing a report from his butler that none of the house servants had heard or seen anything, ordered *him* to see that the guests were collected in the salon.

Vincent, meanwhile, went with Penelope to the nursery where he assessed the same clues Penelope had noticed. "You have never known Matty to leave things undone, meaning to neaten everything later?"

"The missing cover," said Penelope pointing at the bed. "It is his special blanket and it is gone."

"You've looked everywhere?"

Penelope returned to the day nursery and went on to her own room. She returned to where Vincent was asking himself if there was anything else the maid would have taken.

"His toys . . . ?"

"Nothing seems missing," said Penelope, but she too looked around. Then she rushed to the shelf where Matty kept the serving pieces she used for feeding Tal. "His cup. His drinking cup!"

Vincent nodded. "I think you have finally found a clue that assures us that something happened, but that Matty is doing her best to make things as right as possible. She managed to convince whoever came for the boy that he has needs. She is with him," he said firmly and hoped it was true. "All we must do is retrieve the two—" He smiled his most lopsided smile. "—or should I say the three? We must not forget Ho."

Penelope tried to smile in return, but it wavered. Once again she walked into Vincent's arms and buried her head into his chest. "Will you," she asked, "forgive me if I admit that I sometimes think I hate my father?"

"My feelings for the man are very nearly as strong, my

dear, and I have held a grudge against the man far longer than you have."

She looked up, curious.

Vincent told her about the mantrap he'd discovered in the Tennytree woods, and, then, perhaps worse in one way, that he discovered Lord Tivington, his all-knowing, all-powerful grandfather, was *not*, that his lordship could not forbid the use of the things. It crossed his mind, but only briefly, that his despair a few years later that resulted in his running away might have been set in motion by that discovery . . .

"Mantraps? My father had mantraps set?" She looked horrified. "The man is a monster!"

"Yes. An unhappy monster," said Vincent and sighed. "Most monsters are. And, because *they* are unhappy, they cannot bear that *others* be happy. They do their best to see no one is happy. Perhaps it is the definition of monster-hood?" he asked, trying hard to lighten the burden of her fears.

It didn't work and he tightened his clasp, giving her of his strength as best as he could. The woman he loved was unhappy. And the child that he loved nearly as well was in trouble. Vincent vowed to right things as quickly as possible . . . and wondered if he should include his grandfather in his plans. Grandfather Tivington might not be all-powerful or all-knowing, but he *was* a power in the region and had more *nous* than most could claim.

"My darling," he said into Penelope's hair, "I would like to hold you for hours and hours, but if I am to rescue our son, then do you not think I'd better be doing something toward that end . . . ?"

Penelope, startled by his possessive phrasing, looked up at him.

He didn't pretend to misunderstand. "He will be my son, you know. As soon as we are wed. You do know I want that, do you not?"

Penelope felt herself relax. Vincent would rescue their son. He would. The boy would come home and be happy and lively and not have nightmares or . . .

As Penelope's thoughts raged, her body tightened. "Go," she ordered. She untangled herself from his embrace and backed away. "Bring our boy home."

As Penelope spoke, Georgi rushed into the nursery. "Penelope! How terrible. Vincent, you are wanted. In the library," she said in an aside. Her usual impetuosity propelled her across the room, moved her directly to Penelope. She took the taller woman into her arms. "Oh, my dear, we will get the boy back. The men are making plans now. They'll know just what to do."

"Will they?" Penelope stared at the door through which Vincent disappeared. "I hope you are right, my friend. I *pray* you are right . . ."

Vincent approached the bushes behind which one of Lord Everhart's most reliable grooms crouched. "Anything?" asked Vincent. "Anyone arrive or leave?"

The groom, turning on one heel so quickly he very nearly tumbled onto his fanny, stared up at Vincent. "How the devil . . . !"

Vincent's lips twisted. "Sorry. Something I learned when in the army and on patrol. One needed to be silent to get near enough to figure out what was going on among enemy troops."

"If you ever got this close you must have been insane," muttered the groom, beginning to relax.

Vincent knew he was not supposed to have heard that, but answered anyway. "Not insane. Young. Too young. Now, has anyone entered or left?"

"Two men left by the back. I assumed they were going to the stables, but they passed them by. Little bit later I heard a one horse rig move out along that back lane." He pointed.

Vincent nodded. "You're doing well. I'd have brought you an ale, but I want you to stay alert, so this is milky coffee. It'll keep you awake, so drink it even if you don't like it," he ordered.

The man tasted the brew cautiously. "Yuk," he said but then, manfully, downed the whole. Coffee was not a drink that had ever come his way and he wondered at the nobs liking such bitter stuff.

"This packet is bread with cheese and ham between the slices. You might want to hold on to it until later. Your relief will be here in about three hours."

The man sighed, but nodded, and pocketed the makeshift meal.

Vincent pursed his lips, frowning. "Snowed a trifle, did it not? Earlier? *Before* you saw those men leave? By chance?"

The chap grinned. "So it did. You just might be lucky, my lord."

"*Not* my lord."

"Right you are, lieutenant."

Vincent, about to object to that as well, noticed a twinkle in the groom's eyes and shook his head. Then with that gesture approaching a salute, he sauntered back to where he'd left Spot tied in a clump of young trees. Instead of mounting, he took the reins and walked in a rather roundabout way up behind the stables to where a lane led off toward the next village.

Once there he stared at the tracks. The only hoofprints led toward that village. His eyes narrowed, searching, as he walked on, not wanting to miss it if the rig turned off.

"Penelope will be glad to hear that Matty is still inside. And the pup, one assumes. Perhaps the boy will be all right . . ." Spot nudged him. "Very well. He won't. Nothing will make him forget that he was taken from his mother. A child does not forget. No matter how young . . ." Spot nudged him again. "You are not thinking of the boy? Of the men perhaps? You think they were from away, do you not? That they will keep going and not return?"

Spot stopped.

Vincent, tugged at the reins. When his mount didn't move, he turned. "Well?"

Spot shook his head.

"What has gotten into you?"

Spot stamped one foot and neighed softly. The sound was returned from not far away. One of Vincent's brows rose into a sharp arc. "Thank you, Spot." He spoke softly. "Do remind me you are to have extra rations tonight. You deserve every additional oat!"

He moved into the trees beside the lane and, again, tied Spot. Then, moving in a rough arc, he scouted out the men's camp. Creeping near, he saw one man near the horse while the other lay on a rough bed of evergreen boughs covered with a blanket.

"Oh, come back here. No one will come."

"I heard another horse. We don't want anyone poking around here out of curiosity."

"Anyone comes, they'll rue it," said the lounger.

"Don't make more trouble then we've got. You heard that maid. Her mistress isn't the sort of woman the old man said she was."

"What difference? He'll pay up and we'll be on our way."

"He'll pay? She seemed to think that unlikely, did she not?"

Vincent grinned. It appeared Matty had had plenty to say about Lord Tennytree—enough to raise discord between her captors.

"His lordship will return tomorrow," said the man with the harsher voice. "He'll pay."

"I'll believe it when I get my fambles on the rhino," said the man who stood near the horses. When the horse remained quiet and nothing more happened, he returned to the fire. "You shouldn't have made that so big," he said.

"The wood is dry. There's no smoke to speak of. No one will notice."

Vincent settled himself, hoping he'd hear more before he collected the two to take them to the local magistrate's lockup. When all he got was an argument about whose turn it was to collect more wood, he grew impatient. But then it occurred to him that one of them would, eventually, go for that wood.

Divide and conquer, he thought, a grim look tightening the skin around his eyes. *Good advice from whatever Roman said it . . .*

Much to Vincent's surprise the meaner-looking of the two men lost the argument and moved into the woods not far from where Vincent was hidden behind a thick fir. As soon as he dared, he followed. Once he was certain they'd not be heard, he crept close. The man had leaned down to pick up a fallen branch and, as he rose, Vincent's arm came around his throat, a knife held where the man could see.

"Not a sound," said Vincent, "and I won't have to kill you."

He felt the man swallow. The fellow dropped the wood he'd already collected and then, suddenly tensing, lifted one remaining branch high and attempted to turn in Vincent's hold.

Vincent was not a large man, but he was stronger, by far, than he looked and, rather easily, kept his burly prisoner facing away from him. He brought the knife nearer and pricked his prisoner under the ear. "Now behave. Drop that useless branch and not a word. I'll kill if I have to, but I would prefer to get answers. Corpses can't tell tales and I want a good one."

He sounded as if he meant every word, but, if he could possibly avoid it, Vincent had no intention of killing either man. On the other hand, he had to bring them to a magistrate, who could take down their evidence so they'd have it when confronting Tennytree,

The fellow gave him no more trouble—even when Vincent tied him up and then gagged him. "I'll not be long. You shouldn't get too cold," Vincent told him and then crept off to collect the other man.

An hour later the kidnappers stood before the local magistrate. Vincent was glad it was not his grandfather. Lord Tivington had been a magistrate at one time, but had, luckily, given up the position. Given Vincent's involvement as Penelope's intended and the boy's future father, his grandfather would have had to disqualify himself and they'd have had to waste time locating another, more distant man, perhaps someone who didn't know the mad Lord Tennytree.

Once the two prisoners were convinced that Matty, even though a mere female, was not easily intimidated and would not mind identifying them, in court, as the men who kidnapped Tal, they could not tell their story fast enough, the one contradicting the other as each attempted to put the major blame elsewhere.

"Silence," roared the magistrate, glaring. "One at a time. You first," he said, pointing to the one Vincent, standing behind the two, indicated. The milder of the two men sighed. "Ex-soldiers, sir," he said. "Can't find work."

That was an old story.

"Hungry, sir," he added, his voice apologetic. "When his lordship offered to pay us to collect his grandson from his whore of a daughter, we agreed. An innocent child, sir. The boy didn't deserve to be raised by a poor light-skirt, did he now? Not when he'd a wealthy grandfather who loved and wanted him." He shrugged. "So we went to get him and that wench—" He sighed. "—she insisted she come too. Don't go putting down there that we took her against her will, sir, because we'd have happily left her behind. Trussed up and gagged, of course, so she couldn't give the alarm, but she said the boy needed her." He laughed sourly. "Did too. You ever change a messy babe? I haven't. *Wouldn't,* for that matter. She didn't seem to find it a problem."

"So. You took them—"

"And the pup."

"—to Lord Tennytree. What pup?" asked the magistrate confused by the addition.

"The boy's pup. Wench said he'd be happier with the pup to play with."

"The boy's happiness was a concern of yours?" asked the magistrate skeptically.

The man straightened. "Yes," he said firmly—and Vincent believed him. "I'm not a criminal, sir. I wouldn't have had a thing to do with taking the boy if his lordship hadn't convinced me—" He cast a quick glance toward his scowling partner. "—*us* that his mother was worthless and unsuited to raising a tyke when the grandfather would do it so much better."

"I doubt very much the boy's nurse thought the mother unsuitable."

"No she didn't—but I was driving the rig and didn't hear her until we reached his lordship's and she lit into his lordship's butler."

"His butler . . ."

"You see, sir," said the man bitterly, "his lordship is not to home. We have to return tomorrow. To get our wages, you see."

"Or," muttered the other man, "we'd'a been long gone."

The magistrate's eyes narrowed. He nodded. "Now you," he said turning to the other man. That one told much the same story, but with less evidence that he'd any interest in anything but the money Tennytree owed him.

" . . . and now we'll never see it," he said, more bitter than the first. He pulled at his arms which the magistrate had had put in irons behind him. "Big man'll get his hands slapped and we'll find ourselves dancing in the picture frame with our hands tied behind our backs . . ."

The magistrate ordered the two taken out to his lockup. Almost as an afterthought he ordered them fed. Then once he and Vincent were alone, he turned back. "The lout's right about one thing," he said, his voice rather grim. "I can do nothing against Tennytree with what amounts to hearsay evidence. Tennytree will deny it and that will be that." The magistrate, who had had to deal with Tennytree far more often than he wished since his lordship had taken to the courts, added, "How I wish that just this once . . ." His wistful sounding voice trailed off.

"Maybe it *could* happen," said Vincent slowly. "I've an idea . . ."

CHAPTER 18

Penelope ran across the Everharts' salon, stopped from throwing herself against Vincent only because he grasped her arms and held her. She pressed her fists into his chest, staring up into his face. "You have been forever. And *you do not have my son!*"

"Hush, my love," he said softly. "Easy. Lord Tennytree is from home but returns tomorrow. Matty and Tally's Ho will see the boy is all right. We've a plan . . ."

Penelope searched his face the whole time he spoke and, gradually, she had relaxed. "I am behaving badly," she said.

"No. You are behaving like a mother," said Vincent, and grinned his lopsided grin. He turned her, put an arm around her shoulders, and, wishing he could take her away somewhere where they'd be alone, led her back to the group that were seated at the other end of the salon.

Lord Wakefield bristled, but his betrothed, noticing, lay her hand on her fiancé's arm and, with a sour glance in her direction, his lordship controlled himself. Perhaps he was not happy to find himself engaged to Miss Grimson, but it was a fact, and there was nothing he could do about it. His honor would not allow him to embarrass her by a public display of his jealousy of Vincent.

Miss Herning was not so reticent. The words she murmured into the ear of the dowager who sat beside her concerning forward widows and indulgent roués were absorbed with avid interest—not because the dowager would gossip about Penelope, but because she had a long-standing feud with Miss Herning's mama and was quick to find fault with the mama's daughter. Miss Herning would be the object of several paragraphs in her next round of letters. Forward widows were nothing. Not when compared to forward spinsters.

"What is the plan?" asked Penelope softly as they crossed the room.

"Later," murmured Vincent. "I'll explain it to you and Everhart after dinner which, I believe, is to be announced momentarily. You will stay down for it, will you not?" he asked, suddenly worried she might not. He squeezed her shoulders, encouragingly.

"I mean to. Georgi said I'd only stew if I remained alone up in the nursery and she is correct. Far better to be where the presence of others requires that I maintain some sort of equilibrium."

"Good—"

Dinner was announced.

"—not because you are forced to behave, but because I very much want your company."

He turned them and led them toward the door, going on to the dining room in an informal way that immediately set up the backs of two high sticklers who felt proper decorum and polite usage more important than anything. But Georgi, very like her cousin, also disliked strict formality and, given the excuse, urged everyone onward with no regard to status or proper precedence.

"You will have set the cat among the pigeons by such outré

behavior, my dear," said Everhart, offering his arm to his own wife rather than the most exalted woman present. His eyes twinkled.

"Vincent has no intention of letting Penelope away from his side the rest of the evening. It was no use at all attempting to separate them in order to form a proper procession into dinner."

"I agree. Still . . ."

Georgi sighed. "You think I should apologize?"

"Only to—"

He named three of their guests and Georgi promised to do so when they returned to the salon after dinner—the two ladies immediately and the lord when the gentlemen joined them.

When everyone was settled to cards later that evening, Vincent collected Everhart and Penelope and took them off to the library. "It is a simple plan and it may not work, but we must make the attempt."

Everhart's eyes gleamed. "A simple plan," he said.

"Nothing can be done against Tennytree if he does not confess to paying the men to kidnap Tal."

"True. And you've a plan to see he does so?" asked Everhart, his voice dry. "You've bats in the old belfry, my friend."

Vincent grinned. "No, it is quite simple. The two men have agreed to ask for what they've earned."

"Oh they have, have they?" Everhart's brows arched. "But not, I think, for no gain for themselves?"

"We have promised transport rather than hanging for the pair's cooperation."

"Ah."

"Besides the fact of saving their lives," said Vincent, looking at his nails as if they were the most interesting thing in the world, "the notion they might make a peer get what is coming to him—for once—makes them quite anxious to cooperate."

"What's coming to him . . . ?" asked Penelope, her heart suddenly cold.

"He should hang if there were any justice in the world." Vincent looked at her and noticed her distress. "He won't, of course. He is a peer so the House of Lords must try him. They are unlikely to hang him—the penalty any man of lesser rank would suffer. But he will suffer embarrassment and very likely ostracism. I think in the case of your father, Penelope, it will be sufficient punishment."

Penelope, relieved the ultimate penalty would not be asked, grew thoughtful, then nodded. "He cannot be allowed to think no one disapproves such behavior or he might try again. And again. I could not bear it, never knowing when he'd attempt to take Tal away, unable to allow the boy any freedom, watching him every moment—life would be intolerable—for my son as well as myself."

"If that is all, Vincent, I must return—" Everhart's brows arched again. "—but it is not," he finished.

"You, my lord, are part of the plan. As are Lord Tivington and two other peers, guests of other households in the area. Men who have had nothing to do with Lord Tennytree's idiotic inability to get along with his neighbors. We must have witnesses whose word cannot be disputed."

"Lord Tivington has suffered from Lord Tennytree's false accusations. You fear any decent magistrate would discount *his* testimony for that reason?"

"Yes. He is also my grandfather and I am Penelope's betrothed. He will not testify, but he will be present. Another set of ears Tennytree can never forget heard the argument between himself and our kidnappers."

"Argument?" asked Everhart sharply.

"Of course," said Vincent, surprised. "You do not think Tennytree will simply hand over what he has promised to pay, do you? I've made several suggestions as to how the men might gain what is rightfully theirs. One is that, if Tennytree will *not* pay what is owed them, they threaten to take the boy back to his mother."

"He would then insist he paid only to prevent his grandson's kidnapping from under his roof, would he not?"

"Perhaps, but there would still be the problem of having the boy under his roof, would there not? I'm hoping they need not go so far. They've been warned that if they truly want to do Tennytree all possible damage it must be their last resort."

Penelope felt sad. Why must her father be so impossible? Why could he not accept that she would like for her son to know his grandfather, like it if the two were friends as Vincent and his grandfather were friends. She sighed, aware it would never happen. Whatever it was that made her father the man he was, he was not going to change at this stage of his life . . .

"Nonsense," shouted Lord Tennytree. "I haven't a notion of what you speak."

The men hidden beyond the servant's door looked at each other. The plan was not, they feared, going to succeed. The harsher of the two kidnappers spoke again and then the other, Lord Tennytree responding that he knew nothing of any grandson . . .

"Here!" Lord Tennytree's voice held a note of fear. "Where do you think you're going?"

"Upstairs to get the boy."

"What boy?" Tennytree sounded honestly bewildered.

"The boy you ordered brought here. The boy you insist is your grandson. The boy you said would be ruined by his mother who is not pure enough to care for him . . ."

"She isn't. She can't have him! Come back here. Come back now," wailed Tennytree. "I'll pay. You come back here."

The witnesses heard steps coming down the stairs far more slowly than they'd been going up.

"Pay then," said the man.

"Here. Here . . ."

"That," said the other man's voice, "is not what you promised."

"Ten pounds. It is all I have by me. Now go away and leave me alone." There were more steps. "Here, you come back here! You cannot have him. He is mine, I tell you!"

"Who is yours?" asked the more intelligent villain's softer voice.

"The boy. My grandson. You cannot have him I tell you!"

"Then pay us what you promised if we brung him to you."

"I did. I just paid you."

"Not what you promised," said the softer voice. "You promised us fifty pounds. Fifty whole pounds."

"Nonsense. Never. I wouldn't." Again there was that note of panic. "No, no. You are right. I did. I'll pay it. I'll pay whatever you want. Just go away."

"You'll pay us what you swore to pay us if we brought you the boy?" asked the first voice.

"Yes, yes. The full fifty pounds. I'll pay you what I promised."

The witnesses looked from one to another. Was that sufficient, they wondered. Silently agreeing it was, they nodded. Vincent opened the door and the group of men trouped into the hall beyond.

Lord Tennytree swung around. He paled. He looked from his hired minions to the stern looking faces of the witnesses. "Go away," shouted Tennytree. "You are trespassing. I'll have you arrested for trespassing. I *will!* Go away!"

"Lord Tennytree," said the magistrate, "I arrest you in the name of the king for plotting and carrying through a plan to kidnap your grandson away from the boy's rightful guardian."

"No, no, you don't understand. Couldn't leave the boy with that—"

"Careful Tennytree. You'll be under arrest for slander, as well, if you are not careful," said Vincent.

"That . . . that . . ." Tennytree cast Vincent a look of hate. "You! You whoremonger!"

"I wonder," said Vincent musingly, "where the man ever got the notion I'm a panderer. Why would I be interested in supplying other men with willing women?"

One of the witnesses snorted, in his attempt to restrain a laugh.

"Go away," shouted Tennytree, wild-eyed. "Just go away and leave me alone." Tears ran down his face, much to the amazement of those watching.

Vincent sighed. Lord Tennytree was no longer his problem. Tal, Tally's Ho, and Matty were his problem. He headed for the stairs, taking them two at a time. On each floor he shouted. Only when he reached the top floor did he hear a faint response. He went down the long low hall trying doors until he found one that was locked, the key in it. He unlocked the door and looked in. And shivered.

"Matty? Dear Lord. Are you all right?"

"Cold," she said, her teeth chattering. "So very cold. I kept the boy as warm as I could. And Ho has snuggled in tight against him too . . ." Tears of relief ran down her pale cheeks. "Oh, I'm so glad you've come," she added.

Vincent was already picking up Tal and offering Matty a hand. "We'll get you warm in the kitchen before taking you back to the Everharts'," said Vincent, shaking his head, wondering if Tennytree knew how cold it was in the attic room. "Did he at least feed you properly?"

"A bit. Not much. He took the boy away to feed him, only Tal always came back crying, hungry, and sopping wet. I don't think he gave the boy proper food for such a young child and I'm nearly out of nappies, I am. Don't know what to do . . ."

Vincent sniffed. The cold had kept it down, but it was an unpleasant odor once noticed. He didn't bother worrying about dirtied nappies when Matty was stiff with the cold. He picked her up along with Tal and, calling to Ho to come along, headed back downstairs. He reached the hall where Tal put his head out of the covers and looked around.

Tal caught sight of Tennytree. "Bad man," he said, scowling. "Bad man cry?" he asked, looking confused.

"Bad man knows he's been bad," said Vincent. "He knows he'll be punished. He doesn't want to be punished."

"Poor bad man," said Tal, shaking his head. "Poor bad man cry." Then he looked farther around. "Mama?" He didn't see her and looked around more wildly. *"Want Mama,"* he said, his voice firm.

"Let me down, Mr. Beverly. Let me go to the kitchen and see if they know where Tal's drinking cup has got to . . ."

"You can ask, Matty, but you go straight to the fire and get warm before you come down with pneumonia. We can't have you sick. Not when Tal loves you so."

Tally's Ho stood half behind Vincent, growling. Tal's bad man had not treated the pup well and Tally's Ho knew it. He did not like the bad man at all. On the other hand, he'd been disciplined firmly when he'd put his little milk teeth into Tal's arm and hadn't liked that either. Instinct fought with training—instinct won.

The pup darted straight for Tennytree, grabbed a tassel hanging from a badly polished boot, and jerked. And ran back behind Vincent, his winnings hanging from his mouth. Once there he again peered around Vincent's legs.

Tal thought the pup's behavior funny and chortled, clapping his hands. Vincent frowned. "Ho, drop it."

The pup looked up, saw his boy's idol frowning at him, heard his most loved boy laughing, and looked confused.

"Drop it, Ho," repeated Vincent.

It was almost as if the pup sighed. He walked a few steps toward Tennytree, who was red faced with anger, shame, fear . . . and dropped the tassel. Then, when Tennytree shouted out threats against the dog's life, he scurried back behind Vincent, his ears laid tight against his head.

"I'm taking Tal back to his mother now," said Vincent to no one in particular. No one attempted to stop him. Some of the magistrate's men were taking the two prisoners away and two more stood, one to either side of Lord Tennytree, awaiting orders.

What to do with his lordship was not his problem. The thought made Vincent smile a rather hard smile. Tennytree should give thanks to Heaven that someone else had that responsibility—since what Vincent would like to do would *not* be comfortable for the man!

In the kitchen, he collected Matty who had borrowed a warm cloak for the journey home. She wrapped Tal back up in his blanket and Vincent reached for him.

"I'll take him," said Vincent. He'd tell no one how much he'd hurt when the boy was kidnapped, how worried he'd been . . . and how, now Tal was safe again, he didn't want to let the tyke from his sight.

They pulled up in front of the manor not too much later and Vincent hopped out, holding his hand to Matty who, once she was on the ground, reached in and got Tally's Ho.

"Have the footman walk the pup," said Vincent as the manor's front doors were flung open and Penelope rushed down the steps toward them, her arms out.

"Mama!"

Reluctantly, Vincent handed over the bundled up boy. And then, once kisses and hugs had been exchanged, took him back. "I'll carry him up to the nursery, Penelope. He's heavy and awkward, all wrapped up this way . . ."

Penelope, who was as reluctant as Vincent to let Tal even

so far away from her as into Vincent's arms, understood. She bit her lip, staring at Vincent—who also understood.

"He's safe, now, my love. Your father gave evidence of his villainy before witnesses. I haven't a notion what will happen to him, but you need not fear for Tal." He put one arm around Penelope's shoulders, settled Tal a trifle more comfortably in his other arm and, once into the house, headed directly for the stairs. Several people attempted to stop them, but Vincent's "later" had to be accepted—especially when it became clear he wasn't about to give into anyone's pleading that he instantly tell the story of what had happened at Lord Tennytree's.

"How," he asked when they were beyond the guest's ears, "did everyone discover what was happening this morning?"

"I have no notion," said Penelope, not much caring. Her fears, now her son was safe, returned to her father's fate. "Vincent, it is true my father won't hang, is it not?"

"He'll not hang." His cynical side appeared. "After all, the peers judging him will not wish to set a precedent that might affect any one of them, or one of their heirs, in future times, will they? Now if it were *murder* . . . that might be different."

Penelope choked on a laugh. "I see." The desire to laugh faded. "I wish there was something I could have done to have prevented my father's foolishness."

"His evil."

Penelope shook her head. "No. I don't think he understands another's feelings to the point he does evil. There has to be intent, surely, for an action to be evil."

She sighed and led the way into the nursery. Matty appeared almost immediately and released the pup. Tal looked around. For an instant he clung to Vincent's neck. When the pup came to stand before them and bark up at him, he grinned and leaned over, nearly falling from the blankets. Vincent scrabbled to hang onto blankets and boy, but, hurriedly, set the boy on the floor where he instantly chased Ho toward the other end of the long room.

"He'll do," he said.

"He will," agreed Penelope, "but I don't know how long before *I* recover. Matty, are you all right?" she asked, turning to the nursery maid. "I think I might have gone off in a fit of apoplexy if I had not known you were with Tal. I will never be able to thank you enough for your bravery," she finished sincerely.

Matty flushed. "Only did what seemed right. I'll admit I was scared when they bundled us into that coach. On the way out of the house, I thought maybe I'd see someone, that someone would rescue us before we got that far, but they chose the exact time when the servants had their dinner, so there was no one around."

It was a long speech for Matty. She didn't quite know where to look. Her gaze flew from Penelope to Vincent, back to Penelope and then toward Tal. "Couldn't let the boy be hurt," she added. "He's too precious."

"Precious indeed," said Vincent. "Matty, we would like you to know that Mrs. Garth and I are to wed."

The maid grinned, her eyes shining and her head bobbing. She dropped a curtsy.

"Does that mean you knew?" asked Vincent, his brow arching.

"Suspect everyone knows," said the maid. "We're all excited. A wedding!"

Penelope's smile faded and she looked toward Vincent. "I meant to keep it all very quiet," she said, worried.

"And I mean for it to be immediate. Penelope, if I acquire a license, will you wed me? At once, I mean?"

"No wedding breakfast? No dance?" Matty was ignored.

"At once, Vincent?"

"Just as quickly as it can be arranged. I want you and the boy safe. And with me. So that I know I've the right to do whatever is necessary. Not," he added quickly, "that I think anything more will happen, but . . ." He didn't quite know how to end that and rubbed the back of his neck, his eyes pleading for understanding.

Penelope drew in a deep breath. "I have written my father-in-law. He will not be happy that Tal is so far from where he lives, but I have promised to bring the boy for a visit each year—" She cast an embarrassed glance at Vincent and whooshed out a breath of fake relief when he nodded, and then grinned a quick grin. "—I also said that he is welcome to visit us whenever he wishes . . . ?" She arched a brow in query.

"Of course he is," said Vincent, realizing she was still worried she'd overstepped.

"You will like him, Vincent. He has a dry sense of humor that is very engaging. An intelligent and educated man. Well read."

"You need not convince me, my love. He'd be welcome if he were a bear or a goose, but it is nice to know he is a sensible man." Vincent stepped nearer and took her hands. He leaned to kiss her—glanced at Matty, released one of Penelope's hands to make circles with one finger and, when Matty, laughing, turned her back, kissed Penelope thoroughly. "I'll return as soon as I've bought the license," he said softly.

At the door he turned. "Matty, I very nearly forgot to ask. Will you come to the dower house and continue to be Tal's nursery maid?"

The girl blushed again, but this time with pleasure. "Oh yes. Yes. Please." Under her breath she added, "But I did hope for a real wedding and all the trimmings."

Later, when Lord Everhart returned to Minnow Manor, he went directly to the nursery after ascertaining that that was where Penelope was to be found. "I am very sorry, my dear," he said, "but I must inform you your father suffered an apoplexy soon after Vincent departed with your son. It happened when it finally became clear to him he was actually to be arrested for kidnapping the boy, that he would have to stand trial."

Her eyes widened. "He's . . . ?"

Everhart's hands tightened around hers. "No. No, I am sorry I did not make it clear. The doctor fears, however, that this time, unlike the last, he will not recover. It was much worse this time. He is likely to be bedridden for the rest of his life."

Penelope sighed. "Should I, do you think, go to him?"

Everhart shook his head. "No. The doctor has placed a nurse in charge of him. He must be kept quiet and . . ." He released one hand, brushed his fingers through his hair, and appeared to be searching for some acceptable ending to his sentence.

Penelope found it for him. ". . . you doubt very much that my presence would be soothing?"

He nodded. "Something of the sort. Once he is on the mend—or as much as he's likely to be—then you should visit, I think. Just not too soon."

She nodded. "Poor man. Does this mean he'll not be tried?"

"Not unless he recovers. Which, as I said, is unlikely." Everhart drew in a breath. "I should not be pleased this has happened, but it does mean you can cease worrying about his, er, *antics* with regard to Tal and I need not be concerned he will, somehow, harm Georgi, seeking revenge for perceived wrongs."

She nodded again. "I had forgotten that problem." She sighed. "I am sorry for him, but he brought it on himself." After a moment she added, "I think perhaps it is justice? Of a sort . . . ?"

Somewhat later, Vincent, packed for his journey to the seat of the nearest bishop, left the dower house into which he'd begun to move his things, and stopped by Minnow Manor for another good-bye—since it was on the way. Half an hour later, once Vincent tore himself from Penelope's side, he ran into Georgi as he left the house.

"I'm off," he said.

"Off where?"

Vincent looked all around and then lowered his voice. "Penelope has agreed to wed me at once. I must hope to find the bishop in residence from whom I will buy a license, but may have to travel elsewhere. I don't know how soon I'll be back." He gave his cousin a quick kiss on the forehead and completed his escape from the house.

Georgi stared blindly once he'd disappeared, and then, slowly, a grin appeared. She nodded once, and, in her usual brisk fashion, went off to do what had to be done . . . and done excessively quickly, too.

CHAPTER 19

Penelope gazed at the gown lying across the end of her bed. It was a very special gown indeed, with a pale brownish lace filling the décolletage. It was made of a heavy twilled silk in a dusty rose color she'd never before seen. Nestled into where the gathered edge of the flounce was sewn to the skirt were tiny bunches of silk roses.

Penelope whirled around. "Matty? From where did it come?"

"Lady Everhart, she brought it up," said the grinning maid who had just finished brushing Penelope's lovely long hair as they dried it before the nursery fire. "She crept in, her finger to her lips. I didn't dare say a word. A lovely surprise, is it not?"

"Very." Penelope glanced at the pale gray gown she'd meant to wear, the one in her wardrobe that looked least like mourning. She looked back at the beauty spread before her on the bed. "Kennet?" she asked, a breath of sound.

That wonderful warmth she'd felt once before flowed down through her and Penelope closed her eyes tightly, savoring it. Somehow she knew it was good-bye, that Kennet approved what she was about to do, that he wanted her and Tal to be happy.

She swallowed and silently promised, *I will, my Kennet. I will be happy and we will do our best to see that Tal has a happy life as well.* The loving warmth filled her once again and then faded. Kennet Garth was at peace . . .

After another moment, moving briskly, Penelope began to dress for her wedding to Vincent Beverly. He'd come for her and for Tal in less than an hour and they must be ready for him. He would drive them to the church where the minister had agreed to meet them.

And they would wed.

Color filled Penelope's cheeks. They'd be *married*. Tonight she would sleep at the dower house. Sleep in Vincent's bed . . . The color deepened.

"Oh, Mrs. Garth. You are so beautiful."

Forbidden thoughts of the coming night flew from Penelope's mind and she laughed. "Nonsense. The gown is beautiful, but I am the same old lady I was before I put it on."

Matty looked bewildered. "Old? You aren't old. Not at all old!"

"Nor," said Penelope, sighing, "am I young. I do hope Vincent knows what he is doing. I love him so. I would hate to disappoint him in any way."

"You won't," said Matty loyally. "Now don't you go a-sitting down and creasing your skirt. I'll just see to Tal . . ."

She rushed off and, not very long after, came back with Tal who, dressed in the new clothes Penelope and Matty had sewed for him, looked a proper young gentleman indeed.

"I'm going to take him on now," said Matty. "A groom will drive us in the gig. That way you and Mr. Beverly can have the drive to the church by yourselves." Matty's eyes twinkled and she turned to leave . . . but Tal, realizing something was happening, threw one of his rare tantrums, absolutely refusing to leave without Tally's Ho. In the end, all three left the nursery.

Penelope went to the high window and stared out toward the horizon. There was a bustle of noise in the yard below, but she paid it no attention. She was not tall enough to look over the high windowsills and down that near to the house and besides, she didn't care. Her thoughts were all for the man with whom she'd been lucky enough to find a new love. A second love. A man who not only loved her, but loved her son as well. It seemed a miracle to Penelope that it should be so, that she should have been so blessed twice in her life . . .

A rap sounded at the door. She turned and a smile blossomed, her cheeks coloring nicely and her eyes gleaming.

"Beautiful," breathed Vincent. "Lovely beyond my dreams," he added and, almost, stalked toward her.

"Don't muss me," she warned—but lifted her face for his kiss. His hands were warm on her shoulders and his lips still warmer against her own. "Oh, Vincent . . ." she breathed when he lifted his head and stared down at her hungrily.

He blinked, smiled his lopsided, self-deriding smile and then grinned widely. "I was thinking of tonight," he admitted.

"As was I. Earlier. Before you came."

"Tonight," he promised, and offered his arm. "I have been impatiently awaiting this day for what seems forever." A very slightly peevish note entered his tone when he added, "I do not understand why the vicar could not have married us more quickly. I have been in possession of the license for well over a week . . ." He ceased muttering and again grinned at her. "Ah well. Today has finally come. Are *you* ready, my dear?"

"Yes."

Vincent looked around and then frowned. "Where are Tal and Matty?"

"A groom is driving them to the church. Matty said we'd like the drive alone—and she was right. I am glad to have this time when it is just the two of us. It is hardly fair to you, Vincent, that I bring a child to this marriage." She frowned, vaguely worried by a new thought. "I wonder if you really understand how much *there* he will be . . . ?"

"There, yes," he interrupted, "but *with* us. Not *between* us."

They drove slowly along the lane to the village green and the church. The town seemed both crowded and deserted but neither was in the mood to wonder at it. Instead Vincent tied his pair to a ring in a post outside the churchyard and then came to take the rug from Penelope's lap. He helped her down from the carriage and offered his arm. Silently, they entered under the leafy arch in the well-clipped yew hedge and started up the path to the church.

"Music . . . ?" asked Penelope as they approached the door.

He frowned. "I didn't think to order it." He relaxed. "The vicar must have done so."

He held the outer door for his bride . . . and then the inner. And stopped.

Penelope, wide-eyed, looked over many heads and at others, standing along the sides. The church was packed. She looked up at Vincent.

"Georgi," he mouthed, half exasperated and half amused. "I fear, my dear," he said aloud, "that the quiet wedding you asked be arranged has become disarranged. Shall we go away and try another day?"

His voice, as he'd meant it to do, carried to the front of the church. Georgi bounced up in the Everhart box and started into the aisle, only to be pulled back and down. The couple heard a distressed, "But . . . ?"

Vincent nodded, his revenge complete. Trying very hard to restrain a smile, he quirked a brow questioningly and offered his arm. Penelope, rolling her eyes, put her fingers on it and, together, they walked firmly up the aisle to where the beaming vicar awaited them.

"Now," said the reverend, to them when they reached him, "you understand why I was unable to accommodate your wishes for an earlier ceremony. It was impossible to arrange everything so quickly." He beamed. Nodded once. And cleared his throat. Allowing his gaze to roam, he collected eyes, and silenced the murmuring voices.

"Dearly beloved, we are gathered together here in the sight of God and in the face of this congregation to join together this Man and this Woman . . ."

Penelope, the well-known words entering into her, filling her, forgot about the congregation. Forgot her son who, holding her skirts and Vincent's finger, had come to stand between them. Forgot the pup that, seeming to understand the solemnity of the occasion, sat beside his boy, his head cocked, and his ears pricked.

The vicar reached the part of the ceremony where he asked, "Wilt thou have this woman to thy wedded wife, to live together after God's ordinance in the holy estate of Matrimony? Wilt thou love her, honor her, and keep her in sickness and in health, and forsaking all others, keep thee only unto her, so long as ye both shall live?"

Vincent, his voice strong and firm, said, "I will."

And, impossible to ignore, the pup barked. Once.

Vincent frowned down at him, but it was Penelope's turn—and, once again, when she'd responded the pup yipped along with the woman's voice.

Vincent and Penelope looked at each other, then down at the dog that stared up at them, its big brown eyes shining. Vincent looked back at Penelope and shrugged ever so slightly. She smiled a small smile, and the ceremony continued, the pup remaining attentive throughout . . .

The service ended and Vincent leaned down to pick Tal up. "Hello, son," he said softly.

Tal looked at him. Looked at his mother. Looked back at Vincent. "Papa," he said clearly—and then ducked his head into Vincent's shoulder when those among the congregation who heard him chuckled.

Vincent looked questioningly at Penelope who shook her head, her eyes wide open. They turned, as one, to look at Matty who stood off to the side looking like a cat that had got into the cream. Penelope mouthed a thank you and the maid nodded and then came forward to take Tal into her arms. "Come scamp," she said. "We'll go take another ride in the gig, shall we?" Tal nodded, going to her without a murmur.

Vincent and Penelope moved to the back of the church where, as the guests departed, they received congratulations and best wishes. The last to come were Georgi and Everhart.

"You," said Penelope, "plotted plots, did you not?"

"Plots within plots," said Everhart. "Vincent, in case you thought to go directly to the dower house, you can't. Your grandfather and aunts have arranged for a wedding breakfast at the Place. The guests, even now, are headed that way."

Penelope sighed. "A quiet wedding. Just the two of us and Tal. And witnesses of course . . ."

"But there were witnesses, were there not?" asked Georgi, happy her plan had been so successful. "A whole church full of witnesses." Her smile faded and a frown flitted across her forehead. "This time your father will be unable to pretend you are not properly wedded." She nodded. Once. "Oh, do come, my love." She tugged on Everhart's arm. "We will be late if we do not hurry."

Penelope reminded herself she had yet to thank Georgi for the gown but, far more important, turned to her new husband.

Vincent, finally alone with his bride, stared down into her bemused face. "I love you," he said softly.

"I love you too, Vincent. I will do all I can to make you happy."

"We will all be happy, my dear," he said with such simple

faith Penelope finally managed to let go of her silly little fears and allowed herself to believe.

The day continued as all such days proceed. Vincent and Penelope were, almost at once, separated by the crowd of well-wishers and were unable to come together again until time for the toasts. These, too, were the usual toasts, some sober and solemn, some hilarious and rousing laughter, and some no more than quiet good wishes for the future.

Vincent came to his feet when he felt it had gone on long enough. Quiet settled over the guests crowded into the Place's dining room where the table had been extended to its fullest and then, sensing something, spread to those relegated by too little space to tables set in the hall beyond.

"I once believed I'd never wed," said Vincent, his voice carrying clearly to all. "I once scoffed at the idea I was capable of the love I believed a woman one asked to wed deserved. And then, in the midst of a storm, as I curst it up one side and down the other, it happened that I was in just the right place at just the right time. I believe I was led to that place at that time, to the one woman in all the world who could find the key to my heart and, having found it, was willing to turn it, to enter and warm the ice, melting it and me. I am blessed. May I never fail to keep my love safe, keep my love true and honest, and," he added, his voice taking on a dry note, "keep in mind that the beloved likes to hear of it now and again . . ."

A few women wiped tears away, even as the wry tone of those last words roused an unexpected giggle. Men cleared their throats against a tightening, the unexpected laughter helping. And Vincent, his gaze holding Penelope's, drank off the whole of his glass and then turned, throwing it into the fireplace where it shattered.

"Oh dear. The very best crystal!" said one of his aunts.

"Of course it was the best," said the other, sharply. "Vincent, you owe me a new goblet!"

"If I cannot find that pattern, my beloved aunts, I will buy you a whole new set. And now we are off. Thank you all. Every last one of you." As he spoke he half helped, half lifted Penelope from her seat. He hustled her into the hall where, again he told guests how pleased he was to have them share this happy day, but he never once paused, heading for the back of the house.

They reached the butler's pantry and he pulled Penelope into his arms, kissing her thoroughly. "There. I could not wait another moment for that," he said softly. "Now I wonder where they put your wraps . . . ?"

Twenty minutes later they reached the dower house. Turning the curricle over to a groom, Vincent swept Penelope up into his arms and trod through the door that a newly hired and watchful footman flung open. Vincent nodded his thanks, but didn't stop. He climbed the stairs . . . and then turned down the hall . . .

"Vincent!" said Penelope, embarrassed.

"Hush," he said, quickly reaching his bedroom. His valet opened that door for them and then, unobtrusively, closed it with himself on the outside.

"Vincent, they will all know . . . ?"

He touched her rosy cheek. "They would all know whatever way I managed to get you alone, my love. Oh . . . my dearest love!"

It was the last coherent thing uttered in that room for a very long time . . .

Epilogue

Penelope stood in the doorway, staring at the man lying so still in his bed. She sighed softly and then strode forward. "Father?"

One side of Tennytree's face had fallen slack but he could move his head. He tensed.

"If you would prefer I leave, I will," said Penelope softly. She turned Tal so he could look down upon his grandfather.

"Bad man," said Tal, solemnly.

"No, Tal."

Tears oozed from Tennytree's eyes.

"Sad, bad man," said Tal, and leaned forward in his mother's arms. When she released him onto the bed, Tal crawled closer until he could pat Lord Tennytree's hand. "Sad, sad man," he said.

Penelope smiled—a smile that had an equally sad note to it, but was a smile. She saw that her father attempted to locate a pad and pencil that lay near his good side. She moved around the bed, picked it up, and held the paper for him while he wrote.

She read the brief scrawl. "Why . . . ?" she read. She looked at him. "Why have I come?" she interpreted.

Tennytree nodded.

"You are my father. However much I have hated you I have also loved you." She saw her father's eyes widen. "Yes, of course I love you," she said, guessing at his meaning.

He tried to reach the pad and, again, she held it steady.

Picking it up, she tipped her head as she attempted to decipher it. "How? How can I still love you?" She caught his gaze. "Love does not depend upon behavior, Father. One may dislike behavior but still love the person. You are my father," she said, and shrugged.

Once again she held the pad for him. And then lifted it to read it. She chuckled. "Yes, of course you wanted the best for me. The trouble is, Father, you never once tried to discover what that might be. You merely *thought* you knew what it might be."

He scribbled and scribbled and Penelope wondered if she'd ever manage to make sense of whatever it was he wrote. His writing had not been all that good before, realizing he'd be forced to stand trial, he'd suffered his second apoplexy. She recalled that the doctors were now certain he'd never improve to the point he could be tried, so in a way, she decided, that was a blessing . . .

Penelope took the pad to the window where she could see better, leaving Tal sitting beside his grandfather. She managed, finally, to make sense of his words. "You didn't want me to follow the drum." She read more. "So far away." The last bit was harder to decipher. "So *miserable* . . . ?"

Tennytree, his weak hand trying to hold Tal's, nodded.

"I was not miserable," she said gently.

He looked stubborn.

"I know you think I *should* have been, but I enjoyed a great deal of my life with Kennet, following the drum. There was fear during actual battles. Fear," she added quickly, "for the men fighting, not for myself, but there were good times too."

He scribbled again.

"Yes. Occasionally we went hungry. As do many right here in England," she said, gently chiding.

"Not me?" she added after a moment, watching what he wrote. "And why not? Yes, I was *born* to luxury, but I am, despite that, merely human. I can suffer as can anyone. One does it bravely or one whines. Watching other army wives, I knew which sort of woman I wished to be," she said, and added, "I assure you, Father, I did not shame you."

Penelope took the pad and tore a sheet from it before handing it back. "You've begun crossing your lines," she said, smiling, and waited for him to finish another note. "You wanted me safe and warm and comfortable . . . and unloved, Father?"

He looked surprised.

"Kennet loved me quite as much as I loved him. Lord Wakefield merely loved my voice."

His surprise didn't lessen.

"Wakefield didn't know me," she mused. "Not as a person. Neither did you, for that matter." She sighed. "But Kennet and now Vincent love the woman I am. I have been blessed to find love twice in my lifetime. I know how unhappy you were when Mother died. I can remember from before, you see. Not a great deal, but enough I know you were a different man when she lived. I wish you, too, might have discovered a second love."

Penelope leaned down and kissed her father's damp cheek. "We must go now." When he looked horrified, she smiled that sad little smile. "We will return. Now Vincent and I are married and I live at the Beverly Place dower house, I am not so very far away. Tal and I will visit. Not every day," she warned, "but often."

Tal crawled up the bed and placed a sloppy kiss on his grandfather's cheek. The old sick man was crying when the two left. But somewhere deep inside he was almost happy again.

For the first time in decades, Lord Tennytree came near to being happy.

Dear Friends,

I remember when I wrote *The Family Matchmaker* (July 2003). I half fell in love with Vincent Beverly while working on Georgi's story and thought then that, someday, I should write his story. So I did and you just read it. I hope you enjoyed it.

My next book, *The Last of the Winter Roses*, will be released in December 2004. It was my very first book. I entered it, as an unpublished author, in the Romance Writers of America Golden Heart Contest. It was a finalist but didn't win the Regency category in which it was entered. However, one of the judges bought and published it, so I thought I'd won! It came out in hardcover in the early 1990s and I am happy to have it published for the first time in paperback.

A new series will begin in 2005. A peer, enamored of the theater, builds his own. When it is finished he holds a house party, inviting friends who are equally interested in drama and acting. He hires a professional actor and actress to direct several plays and, where appropriate, play a role in them. Each book will "star" another couple, each pair creating their own personal drama while playing in a staged one. I hope you enjoy them.

Cheerfully,

Jeanne Savery

P.S. I love to hear from my readers. I can be contacted via e-mail at jeannesavery@earthlink.net or by letter at P.O. Box 833, Greenacres, WA, 99016. Include a self-addressed stamped envelope with your letter if you wish a reply.

BOOK YOUR PLACE ON OUR WEBSITE AND MAKE THE READING CONNECTION!

We've created a customized website just for our very special readers, where you can get the inside scoop on everything that's going on with Zebra, Pinnacle and Kensington books.

When you come online, you'll have the exciting opportunity to:

- View covers of upcoming books
- Read sample chapters
- Learn about our future publishing schedule (listed by publication month *and author*)
- Find out when your favorite authors will be visiting a city near you
- Search for and order backlist books from our online catalog
- Check out author bios and background information
- Send e-mail to your favorite authors
- Meet the Kensington staff online
- Join us in weekly chats with authors, readers and other guests
- Get writing guidelines
- AND MUCH MORE!

**Visit our website at
http://www.kensingtonbooks.com**